LUSCIOUS

BITE

AN ENCHANTED MATES
ROMANCE

SARA OHLIN

The author acknowledges the use of trademarks for Band-Aid, Kleenex, and Tupperware.

Visit the author's website at www.saraohlin.com

Editing provided by Rebecca Baker

Ebook cover by Sara Ohlin

Print Book Cover by Sara Ohlin

Formatted in Atticus

ISBN 979-8-9903522-0-9 (print)

ISBN 979-8-9903522-1-6 (ebook)

LCCN 2024908438

ABOUT LUSCIOUS BITE

Dr. Nikolav Sarkozy has had centuries to perfect his arrogance, but his cold vampire soul is no match for the beautifully joyful ER doctor, Francesca Banetti.

Cursed never to drink blood or enjoy pleasure from a human again until he meets his mate, Niko has lived an extremely lonely vampire life. When he walks into Mercy General Hospital and meets Francesca, his penance crashes down around him.

Francesca is a healer, but with her haunted past, she keeps her witch status hidden. While she excels at saving lives, she flourishes when infusing her magic into food, doting on her niece and nephew, and teasing Niko, of course.

Niko is everything bleak and miserable. Francesca is laughter, light, and love. He craves her but denies the ancient instinct whispering she belongs to him. But when a sinister demon threatens her and her family, he steps up and vows to protect them. He had no idea she would tear down the chains around his soul.

Seven hundred years is an awfully long time to be alone. Perhaps the time has come to find his enchanted mate.

NOTE TO READER

This is a dark, emotional romance with adult themes including death, death of a child, grief, sex, and gruesome attacks by a demon. Please take care when reading if any of these issues bother you.

DEDICATION

for my beautiful friend Ani

CHAPTER ONE

D RINKING BLOOD ALONE IN his designer kitchen, as Nikolav Sarkozy did every evening, he took in the space he'd finished renovating a few months ago and scowled. Ten-foot-long island, with gleaming waterfall countertops, top-of-the-line appliances in a new shade of graphite, a temperature-controlled glass wine room, and the dining nook in the corner all breathed luxurious yet cozy. It was a space meant for sharing, meant for people, meant for more than one cursed vampire.

He tossed the empty bag into the hidden compost machine. Blood wasn't nearly as interesting to drink out of vacuum-sealed biodegradable bamboo containers as it was from humans. For one thing, it was cold, damn it. At least this was the first brand he'd found that didn't try to flavor it with fake fragrance or cinnamon. *The horror.*

Claws scraped at the expansive, glass patio doors. His hounds begging to be let in. Couldn't blame them. This wretched winter rain was a menace. His 110-pound bloodhound, Jupiter herded the female, Lollie, into the kitchen, barking at Niko in a rush.

"What's all this?" He frowned at his dogs.

Lollie limped to her bed in the corner by the fireplace and slumped down in a heap. Jupiter paced back and forth huffing and growling. Niko soothed Jupiter with a hand to his head and bent over to examine Lollie. A large thorn was wedged between the soft pads of her front paw. She pulled away and whined as soon as he touched the sore spot. "Decided you wanted to be my first patient of the evening, did you?" He grabbed his first aid kit from the cupboard.

Lollie licked his hand, looking up at him with those dark soulful eyes.

"You have to hold still, baby, so I can get it out. I know it hurts. Shh now." Niko tried to soothe her as he carefully extracted the thorn. Lollie's whines were soft but consistent with each breath she huffed out.

Sprawled next to them on his belly, Jupiter crept closer then backed away, like he wanted to be near but couldn't handle it. Niko knew who the bigger baby was, that was for sure. He got the thorn out, washed her paw, and bandaged it quickly to relieve both dogs' stress. Niko alerted his groundskeeper, Booth, about Lollie's paw before he left for work, thinking he'd much rather stay and hang out with a couple of bloodhounds. Pathetic that his life had come to this, but true all the same.

***

Under the cover of midnight, he strode toward the hospital en-trance. Charcoal clouds blocked out the sky and stars. A wicked, blustery wind pummeled his body. The rain, cold and relent-less, came in sharp dagger drops, one icy shard after the other. Even with the freezing wind tossing the rain around like knives, the stench, as he'd named it, greeted him like an abandoned refrigerator left to rot. Soiled garbage, bad eggs, and despair, all shrouded together.

So subtle that mere humans might not even detect it, it played at Niko's senses like an ugly taunt, slithering in and out, burning through his nostrils, and coating the back of his throat. If he'd had any food in his stomach, he'd be fighting a losing battle to keep it down.

Over the centuries he'd trained his sense of smell to be dor-mant at times. After all, death and battle held no pleasing odors. This heinousness before him now clawed past his defenses. Ini-tially, he attributed the decaying smell to the hospital grounds where too many people had been infested with disease, with chemicals to rid them of those diseases, with angry blood loss. Ahh the blood loss. So much had seeped into these hallowed grounds for hundreds of years while this place sat upon the land.

But there was something wrong with this smell. It was a puz-zle. Unsolvable thus far. Some nights he arrived, and the odor was far less powerful, or missing completely. Other instances it rained down upon him as surely as tonight's wet icy shards. At any rate, Niko considered the stench part of his punishment. It would be gone in the morning when his shift ended. It always was.

As usual, he didn't have the time to consider the obnoxious taunt. He had work to do. And here at Mercy General, like every hospital he'd worked at, his patients always survived. They were lucky they had him as a surgeon, that was all. He only did what he was ordered to do, no more no less. Luck wasn't part of his life. At least once he entered the hospital other scents took over and tamped down the vile centuries-old layers of the stench.

The doors flew closed behind him at the side entrance he'd ducked into. Fluorescent lights attempted to blind him as he bypassed the emergency department, skirted the nurses' station, and headed toward the locker room. He adjusted his vision to accommodate the brightness and kept his focus on work. He'd have to engage soon enough but for now, he had other secret desires.

He took a deep breath, and, with the precision of a scalpel in his hands, he scented his indoor environment. *She's here.* Despite the pervasive hospital odors of antiseptic, soap, life at its most brutal, worry—and yes, worry had a smell—and the familiar tinny odor of live blood pumping through humans, he could detect *her* scent within it all. Detect was the stupidest word on the planet.

Her essence *invaded* him.

This was his true curse. Since he'd met her last year when she'd walked into the ED in a flurry of laughter and effusive joy, he hadn't been able to dismiss her unique and powerful floral scent. What he'd admit to no one was that he never wanted to. Which was, in a sense, problematic. Locating her spirit caused his body to both calm and stir in anticipation. That was what he should be tamping down. But where she was, he wanted to be, however futile. He tossed his wet jacket and boots in his locker and donned his tennis shoes.

"You've brought the gloomy night in with you, Dr. Sarkozy."

She wasn't just anywhere in the hospital; she was right fucking here, overwhelming his space. Dr. Francesca Banetti stood in the doorway to the locker room. She took him in with those wide green eyes, that curious brilliant look of hers that said she could see inside him. See *everything*. Deceiving, it was. If she really had a line of sight inside him, she'd turn and run the other way.

She sighed like she was dealing with a child but was happy to do so. Grabbing a towel from the bin, she stepped up to him and brushed the rain off his shoulders. Niko braced. He commanded every part of his body into stillness. His eyelids grew heavy at her touch. Even through the layers of clothes and the towel, the shock of her caress seared into him. All foresight gone, he leaned into it. Never in his seven-hundred-year lifetime had he been so stunned by another's touch.

She affected him. That was putting it mildly.

He had to restrain himself from grasping her to him, leaning in and sniffing her neck, discovering if she rolled in flowers or fields or whatever gardens she used to dress her skin, licking her there, taking a bite to feed his desire, and never letting her go. It was her aura that did him in. Floral and musky, something soft and herbal, grass and roses, and sugared flowers. It drifted from her skin and soaked into his. *Who the fuck am I? Sugared flowers?* She was a drug, messing with his senses, his instincts, his cool unflappable demeanor. Whatever her essence was, it smashed all other foul scents away, until all he could smell was her. All he wanted was her.

"Or are you the gloom, huh?" She huffed out a soft laugh. "You really should let down the scowl a teeny tiny bit." Her laugh was as big as she was in stature, in beauty, in joy. And he drank it in. He could feed off it alone for the next hundred years.

Then she stepped away and her cheerfulness disappeared with her touch. "It promises to be a busy night with that kind of weather." She angled her head toward the window. Damn it, he hated it when anything diminished her exuberance. It caused a restless, dangerous ache inside him.

"Yes, well we certainly can't count on humans to be careful in this vile weather now can we, Dr. Banetti?" he said, vibrating with anger, with tension, with something animalistic. Roses and herbs, soft skin, that full-bodied voice, how her freckles paled with her worry. It wove around him and tried to work its way inside his bones. Turning away before he shoved her up against the wall and devoured her, he said, "Maybe for once they'll be reasonable and we won't have any emergencies." His scoff was harsher than he intended. Who was he kidding? She was already deep, deep under his bones. So deep he'd never be the same again. He'd already stayed at this one hospital longer than any others.

"Then we wouldn't get to witness you work your magic, now would we," she said, her face softening a touch. "The masterful surgeon come to do his shift in the lowly emergency department."

Teasing again, was she? He thought so but was there some hint of offense? Was he that much of an ass? Probably. It was the only way to keep them at bay, to keep *her* at bay. Why wouldn't she get the message? *That's hardly the message you wish she'd get.*

He craved her. That deliciously seductive voice of hers. It sang to him. But he could never have her. And never for a vampire was an extremely long time. He'd have to sustain himself with watching her brilliant mind and hands save lives during emergencies, as a colleague. One she put up with and teased and occasionally worked side by side with.

"You're wrong, Doctor," he said, punctuating his words with the slam of his locker. "There's nothing magical here." *Except you.*

Forcing himself not to track her every movement with his gaze, he peeked instead, watching as she sighed then stored her coat and belongings. Needing a moment, hell, a decade maybe, he sat down and rubbed the weariness off his face. The fact that he even dared hope for more than a professional relationship with her confused the living daylights out of him. After all, it was her kind that had cursed him into this infernal, pitiful life. And the only way to break that curse...it couldn't be. *She* couldn't be. His thoughts and emotions roiled inside him.

"Walk with me?" Her soft voice reached in and squeezed the breath from his lungs. "Coffee before shift starts sounds like just the thing."

What the hell? Coffee was one luxury he was still able to enjoy. He tossed aside his reasons for steering clear of her and went with her into the light. The silence settled between them as they walked toward the break room. He wished to obliterate it, but he was useless at making small talk with her.

"The Devil's on tonight." Voices reached them in the hallway.

Niko and Francesca paused outside the break room. Good God, did the staff have nothing better to do than gossip about him? That uninspired nickname they'd given him. If he possessed an ounce of humor, he would have laughed. They had no idea.

"At least we'll have some eye candy."

"You can give up the dream on that one, honey." The calm voice of Lanie Mitchell, a nurse practitioner he respected drifted across the room. He could detect all their voices.

"You're right. He doesn't notice anyone anyway unless they're bleeding profusely." A young male nurse named Thomas sighed. "Unless you count the way his eyes follow Frankie."

What in the hell? How had they noticed? Had Francesca? Niko moved silently so he was standing in the doorway. They didn't even see him.

"Wait, what? He has a thing for *that*? For Fatty? He'd get lost in all her, well...rolls." Dr. Madison's grating voice, first-year resident. Niko's blood threatened to boil over.

"Stop," Lanie admonished. "Don't be mean. She's gorgeous and lovely. You could use a bit of her lovely."

"No man wants a woman who matches him in size. Can you even imagine them in bed, him dark and hot, and her all thick legs and boobs? No stop, not Devil and Fatty. I can't."

Niko caught the sick look on Francesca's face before she closed her eyes and leaned back against the wall.

"Shut up," Lainy ordered.

"Whatever." Dr. Madison laughed. "He could have me in a second if he wanted, wouldn't have to exhaust himself."

Turning to fire at their insults, Niko's anger coiled like a snake waiting to strike. He was going to murder someone with his bare fucking hands tonight. It would be worth it to ruin his perfect record of saving lives. He stood in the doorway for a moment, trying not to burn the room down around him. And then he spoke. "You do not get paid for petty gossip." He let the heat consume him inside, while outwardly he pushed the sense of calm, cool, dangerous. They all startled at his appearance and fear blanched their expressions. *Serves them right.* Thomas put his head down and hurried out of the room.

"Dr. S. We were just grabbing a coffee," Dr. Madison purred. Her tone smelled like skunk.

"It's Dr. Sarkozy. And a piece of advice, speak that way again where I can hear you and I'll be filing reports on all of you. And just so you know, I can always hear you."

"I apologize, Dr. Sarkozy. You're right," Lainey said. She was friends with Francesca and at least she had defended her, called her beautiful. Francesca was far more than beautiful.

"It was a joke." Dr. Madison said.

"Making fun of someone's appearance isn't a joke," he said. "Doing it out of spite or jealousy is disgusting. Doing it to your superior is stupid. Could get you fired. Your shift started ten minutes ago."

They rushed out the door, careful not to invade his space. He took a few precious seconds to cool his temper before he had to use his focus and centuries-honed skill to put someone back together again when what he felt like doing was ripping someone apart. There were times, few and far between because no one missed the plague and lack of sanitation, when he missed the old days of slicing someone's throat open to silence their cruelty. Witnessing this disgusting behavior and doing nothing incensed him.

"No sense battling with ridiculousness," Francesca said quietly, sweeping into the room as soon as they'd all left.

He stared at her, trying to soak up her hurt and embarrassment at the petty gossip. Damn it, he'd do anything for her. He'd murder for her. It didn't matter that he'd been the one to insult her earlier. He did it to push her away. He had to. But witnessing someone tear her down like that enraged him. "What will you do?" He seethed. "Pat them on the back and feed them?" He allowed his anger to bleed out in his caustic tone.

She pulled two Tupperware containers from a bag and set them on the counter. When she opened them Niko took a step back at the essence that floated out of each one. "Well," Francesca began, "Dr. Madison is a bit constipated." She whispered the last word with a hint of mischief in her expression. It wiped out most of the hurt and made her eyes glow like stained glass with the sun pouring through it. Her brilliance blinded him. That, coupled with the magic she'd woven into the food items, nearly brought him to his knees. "And my groat nut bars are exactly what she needs."

"Groat—"

"They'll help her work through her issues." Francesca grinned, soft this time, intimate. "So, I don't simply feed people and pat them on the back, Dr. Sarkozy, I make things especially with them in mind. Now you, on the other hand, could use one of these." She nudged the second container toward him with a gentle push of her hand. Joy and delight leapt out from it in soft blue arcs of magic.

"What in the hell are those?" Had he taken a step closer? Were those sparkles glittering on the lollipop-like objects? A soft glow hovered around the items. *Impossible. Food doesn't glow.* It took every ounce of strength to force his gaze away. Only in doing so, he was caught in her intelligent stare where her green eyes reflected the gold sparkles, leaving him dazed and so fucking hard he couldn't stand it.

"Cake pops. My nephew's favorite."

There was fondness in her voice when she spoke of the boy. He latched onto that and battled his wild and feral lust back down, barely. Niko took in every nuance on her face, every change, every emotion. How would it feel to have her speak of him that way? He stepped back and took in the round frosted cake balls covered in...in sprinkles? They were filled with her power. He didn't know which was worse, to be lured by those, or snared in her gaze. It was imperative that he break whatever spell she'd cast or he'd take her right here, ruin her, ruin them both.

"Do tell, Dr. Banetti." The task was more difficult than he imagined. Being in her presence was enough of a struggle to stay in control, but when she brought in her creations, where she shared her true essence, whether she knew she'd done it or not, it was almost too much. The combination swirled around him. "What's in a cake pop that you think I require?" He forced a bored tone into his words, but it didn't sway her in the least.

She stepped into his space. He lost all thought. "A bit of fun, something sweet, some lightness to all this..." She twirled her hand around him. "All this darkness." And then she touched him again. Twice in one night.

A finger against his sternum. It was brief. Her eyes flickered into gems at the contact. All that glitter leaping and sparking. Was that desire he saw in them? Those witchy green beauties of hers. He'd wanted to know upon their first meeting, and again that day several months ago when she'd invited him to dinner and he'd refused, and every moment since. He was so desperate to know everything about her he couldn't breathe. His teeth ached in his gums, ached to lower and puncture the delicate skin around her neck.

And the truth of his curse came crashing down around him.

"I don't eat sweets." He tried to dismiss her, but she wouldn't fucking have it.

"I know," she volleyed back, but he'd caught the brief moment of hurt that clouded those magical eyes of hers again. "Well, as you said, our shift started minutes ago."

They walked to the emergency department together. He should have left her, but he couldn't bear the fact he'd put pain in her eyes any more than he could bear the ache in his soul when she was near.

The hallway drew in on him. It felt ten times smaller in the dim fake lighting and close walls. Those fucking roses wrapped around him again, musky, seductive. What did she do, bathe in them? He could almost reach out and hold her hand, touch the scent laced into her skin, drink it in. Simply because he could never have her was no reason to hurt her, not with petty words he'd carelessly tossed her way. Shoving her away with insults hadn't worked in twelve long months, when what he craved was to be so close to her he was inside her, fucking her while their bodies rolled together. Christ, every time in her presence it was getting more difficult to remain sane.

"Are groat nuts some new medical procedure I'm not familiar with?" The words were dry and dusty in his mouth, even as he offered them.

"Not exactly." The side of her mouth curved into a grin. "Buckwheat groats. They'll help her. Lots of fiber, if you will. Life's all about balance. Trust me." She pushed through the doors to the emergency department. And he watched her go, taking all the light with her. And when, before her, had he ever cared about the light?

Trust me.

He didn't want to trust her. He wanted to tie her to his bed and fuck her into next week, so she'd never leave him. But he couldn't touch her, because if he did, he'd kill her.

CHAPTER TWO

"**T**HESE ARE DIVINE, FRANCESCA! I don't know how you do it." Lainy took another bite of the sparkly blue cake pop and her eyes lit up as she savored it.

Francesca had finished writing notes on several new patients. One migraine, another had a broken finger, and the third was still waiting on tests to determine if they had ulcers, diverticulitis, or worse.

Her cake pops were amazing. Fabulous cake, mixed with rich frosting plus a few extra special touches, and viola! A sugary dream with sprinkles destined to make anyone smile, or almost anyone. *Struck out again.* She'd made enough for everyone on duty tonight, but her intended, Dr. Sarkozy, had looked at her like he should check her into the psych ward immediately.

Ahh, Niko. She sighed. That expression of his did give her a little chuckle to remember it. Was the word *fun* so difficult for him to comprehend? Honestly, she wasn't sure whether to laugh or cry for him. Perhaps some part of her had made the treats into cake pops simply to see his absurd reaction. It was delicious fun to poke at him, even though he was a fortress against her.

"One guess who you made these for," Lainy said and hip-bumped Francesca. Lainy was her best friend here at the hospital. Whip-smart, she had a joyful and take-no-nonsense bedside manner. Francesca adored her for her absolute love of life. Her sincere appreciation of Francesca's food creations didn't hurt either.

Francesca snuck a glance across the emergency room. Niko was already hard at work. He wasn't smiling, no none of that frivolity. However, he was very carefully checking the head wound of a teenager. A woman was hovering and asking a million questions. Calm as can be, Niko spoke softly.

"Mm-hmm." Francesca dragged her concentration back to the migraine patient. Chronic pain, been in twice in the last month, nothing was helping. Well, nothing was a big word to use in this situation. Many patients barely scratched the surface of treatments for migraines. Francesca might have a few tricks up her sleeve.

"Don't *mm-hmm* me, missy. That man, whew!" Lainy fanned her face with a folder. "I'm surprised the break room didn't incinerate into ashes with Dr. Sarkozy's anger. And it was all for you. I mean could a hot, sexy doctor burn things to the ground for me, just once in my life, that's all I ask."

Francesca chuckled. "Okay, Soap Opera Queen. Please, his anger was not for me, it was because people were wasting time. God forbid anyone flit away one single second here."

"Oh, Francesca, love, for being the smartest person I've ever me, and that's saying something because I'm pretty damn intelligent myself, you are acting like a big dummy!"

"You shouldn't use such enormous words on me. I might miss your meaning." Francesca batted her lashes.

"You're being deliberately obtuse."

Deliberately obtuse or protecting herself? Was there much of a difference? She knew there was a thread between her and Nikolav. She also knew he went out of his way to avoid it.

"That man is so damn hot for you he's going to melt all of us before he even gets the nerve to ask you out."

"Ha." Francesca barked out a laugh at that. "He is never going to ask me out." She leaned in and whispered, "And you know it. He won't even try my baked goods. He's had a year to ask me out. Although can you really see him doing something so mundane?" She lowered her voice. "Dr. Banetti, would you care to spend time with me outside these hallowed halls?" Heads together, she and Lainy both chuckled at that. So stiff, that man. More a robot than a...well, a...

"Dang, he is proving to be extremely slow. Wonder what's holding him back? Protecting your honor was pretty sexy. I mean, did you hear him lay into Dr. Madison?" Lainy grinned.

Mm. His defense of her had softened the insults. Francesca was used to people criticizing her size. At six feet, three inches tall, she towered over all the women here and most of the men too. She was large, she loved to eat and enjoy life and she was aware by many standards that she was overweight. She loved her body. That wasn't to say that insults, petty laughter, and Dr. Madison's shitty comments didn't hurt. They did. They always had. But Francesca had a million other things to occupy her mind. And living alone for the last few years had allowed her to exist however she chose, without one single person close enough to wound her.

Something lured her attention again and she found Dr. Unfun staring at her from across the room. His eyes locked onto hers. The heat of his gaze reached across the hospital and touched her, like a long slow caress. Confusing man. *What?* She wanted to yell. *What do you want?* It sounded silly to even think the question since he had given her no indication he was interested in anything other than a very serious very stiff work relationship, but it felt as though something had shifted tonight, or perhaps right in this very moment, some tiny spark finding its way out of his darkness, almost, *almost*.

"We're going to have words later, my friend." Lainy interrupted the fragile link between Francesca and Niko. "Since Dr. Sarkozy isn't going to eat his, I'm helping myself to seconds. I need to know what kind of magic you infused into these delicious pops. If nothing else, the sugar and pure delight will help me get through this dreary night of pouring rain and the promise of too many patients." Lainy's eyes got huge, and she covered her mouth. "Oops."

Francesca zapped her gaze to Lainy's. "You...you know...what I am?" Her words were barely a whisper. Shock filtered through her system.

"Sorry." Lainy waved her hand around. "I mean, yeah, I suspected. You're all...you sort of radiate with it. I don't think everyone can see it, or maybe they're just not paying attention. I had a friend once years ago who was a witch." Lainy whispered the words behind the folder she held. "I promise I won't say anything—"

Francesca grabbed her friend's hand and squeezed. "I know that. I trust you. You never mentioned it to me?" Her heart skittered but not for long. This was her friend, almost like a sister.

A touch of worry and hesitation hit Lainy's face. She lowered the folder and gave Francesca a small smile. "I thought it should be your thing to tell someone."

"I'm sorry I didn't... Well, my experiences haven't..."

Lainy took pity on her. "If you ever do want to talk about it, I'm here."

It was a shame they were right in the middle of a busy shift because Francesca wanted to take her up on that. "I'd like that, sometime."

"Good." Lainy grinned. "I better get to work. Can't let grumpy Dr. Sarkozy see me dillydallying." She winked at Francesca and headed over to a patient.

"Made it to work just in time tonight, eh? You really should let me give you a ride to work, Francesca."

Dr. Blythe. How had he snuck up on her? Usually, his cologne arrived before he did. She was thankful their friendship at work had survived him asking her out and her rejecting him. He was tall and good-looking in a generic sense, and his glasses gave him a layer of intelligence, but honestly, he was more needy and...floppy—like a dog who demanded her attention—than a man she wanted to, uh... Her face heated at thoughts of Niko. *Right, never mind.* However, she was also glad that's *all* their relationship was, work friends. Somehow Dr. Blythe's offers of assistance often came across as...egotistical and insulting.

She ignored his comment because it was better not to encourage him. Instead, she slid the small electronic device in his direction. "The patient in Bay 2 might be perfect for you, Dr. Blythe, with your expertise in digestive issues. He claims he has ulcers. I think it's more serious."

"How many times have I told you, it's Geoffrey to you, Francesca?" He took the screen and used his finger to scroll and read, a smug expression appearing on his face. "Indeed, something much more serious." He gave her one last glance, winked at her, and walked away.

Francesca sighed. Time to focus on her patients and healing. Closing her eyes, she found her small tin of soothing gel in her pocket. She rubbed a bit on both wrists. The rosemary would help wash away annoying interactions and the lavender would center her. The old-fashioned rose scent infused her with joy. She silently recited a soothing spell to herself. It was undetectable to anyone as far as she knew, but it boosted her composure.

"Dr. Banetti." Nurse Lennon quietly interrupted her thoughts. "Another assault victim similar to that...that pattern the police have told us to be aware of arrived earlier tonight. You asked me to let you know."

Shit. All sense of calm whisked away and was replaced by a different type of unease. "Same pattern?" Francesca asked.

Lennon nodded. "Multiple stab wounds, beaten and bloody, sexually assaulted, much of her hair ripped out. Some joggers found her by the lake. She died on the way here."

Shit. Shit, shit, shit. The same pattern as before. A shiver ran through Francesca. Were the mystery assault cases from last year back? Every victim had been brutalized and only one survived. Everyone had thought it was over, but suddenly the ground beneath them was unsteady again.

Chapter Three

THE NIGHT WAS ROUGHER than he'd anticipated. It was as if patients arrived at the emergency room with the frequency of the raindrops slashing against the windows. Too many to handle and chaos spilling out around them. One family almost drowned when their SUV was swept into the river. Mother and daughter were still alive, hypothermic, but they would live. Niko had performed surgery an hour ago on the father to remove part of the guardrail that had busted through the vehicle and perforated his kidney. The man was in critical condition. But he would live. Two women were out walking when one slipped and knocked herself unconscious. Grade II concussion, and lacerations up the side of one arm from the broken fence she fell into.

He'd walked back into the ED to observe Francesca dealing with a man who'd suffered a mild heart attack. The patient would probably only require a stent and be out of the hospital in a few hours. If he changed his diet and exercise plan and quit smoking, he might make it another thirty years.

An unnatural quiet settled over the department. It was as good an indication as any that things were about to blow up. The definitive calm before the storm. The low murmurs were there underneath his feet, rolling through the earth. In the eerie quiet, this fake calm of waiting, he could observe everyone closely, see each movement they made, hear each word and curse they uttered, scent each individual smell. Beneath it all, that awful stench lingered for a moment, perhaps brought in by the rain. For a moment, he tried to isolate it, see if he recognized it. A concern tugged faintly at the very back of his memories.

Francesca drew a smile out of her patient, bringing Niko's attention back to the present. Dr. Madison tugged off her gloves and wiped a sheen of sweat from her brow as she raced toward the restroom. A rare smile threatened Niko's lips. The poor woman had been spotted eating one of Francesca's groat bars. The gerontologist, Dr. Geoffrey Blythe, who wasn't scheduled to be on tonight, stood in the nurses' station laughing with them. *Slimy bastard.* He was always hovering around Francesca. He glanced up, caught Niko's glare, and stalked off down the hallway. Jesus Christ, this place was a soap opera. Could they fucking do their damned jobs?

A chill slithered through him. Straightening and facing the doors, Niko knew it was coming. Energy shifted in the air outside. The real storm was upon them. Stephanie, the Emergency Department head nurse, alerted them to a slew of ambulances

on the way, but Niko could already sense the oncoming nightmare. A bus accident with multiple fatalities and traumas. Several surgery patients. It was a bus full of children. The ambulance doors blew open, EMTs talking a mile a minute, and the
gurneys rolled in.

***

Niko had his hands in the open cavity of a ten-year-old's chest,
trying to find the source of the internal bleeding. *Come on. Come
on.* Each moment was vital and precious. The little boy was
covered in blood from the accident. They'd inserted the chest
tube and left the gas mask on his face to keep him unconscious.
And his tiny heart had stopped again. *Fuck. What did I miss?*
Niko had fixed the perforated lung, but shards of metal and glass
still protruded from the small limbs.

Motion surrounded him as the other patients were helped.
Yelling boomeranged, then slammed back into his consciousness. Orders for medicine and clamps, one patient sent to X-ray,
another to get casts put on both legs. Child legs that would heal
on a child that would someday run again.

Only seconds after he'd fixed the lung, the eerie quiet slithered through again and blood began filling the tiny body. There
was another tear somewhere. *Where the fucking hell is it?*

He closed his mind to the cacophony around him, located the
tepid pulse where the child was bleeding out, called out com-
mands to his surgical team, and put all his energy into healing.

But the life drifted away before he could save it, before he could ground it here for a future, no matter how skilled Niko was, no matter that he could almost always see the injury and trauma before he even inspected the patient. No matter that it had been hundreds of years since he'd lost a patient.

"Dr. Sarkozy, he's gone, sir."

Niko kept working, demanding tools and...and why in the hell had they waited to perform surgery? He could scent critical from miles away, and he'd missed this. But he hadn't. He'd had the boy under his hands in minutes, while simultaneously helping other patients and calling out orders. But...but...

"Dr. Sar—"

"Get away from me," he demanded. He felt his way through the open cavity, searching for the tear, searching for the source of all this blood. Fucking blood covered Niko's vision. It was all he could see. It whirled around him, darkened everything, even sound, even scent. Pouring out of a wound, it smelled differently from when it flowed through veins and arteries pumping life. This was...this was a white-hot light of fury. This was the freezing-cold blanch of fear. This was death.

Something lanced into his forearm, skin to skin. A touch so beautiful and warm and haunting it jolted him.

"Dr. Sarkozy."

Francesca's voice tunneled in through the din. Her hand on his shoulder. Touch, warmth, sparking life. He stopped the movement of his hands, slowly brought his head up, and took in his surroundings. Before him a body, no longer a boy. Two nurses stood watching him, waiting. Farther in his line of sight, the curtained barrier between them and other patients. The furious network of a busy emergency department flooded back into his ears. *I failed.*

"Nikolav."

Her soft voice hummed right against his head, saying his name. A salvation he didn't deserve. Nor did he deserve the graceful softness of her fingers soothing his back. He sucked in a ragged breath, let her beauty seep into his bones for one brief moment. Then he shrugged her hand off and stormed away.

CHAPTER FOUR

FRANCESCA DIDN'T FEEL THE cold on her way home, as the dawn painted the sky a cotton-candy pink. A crisp winter morning, clear now, barren and stark, and twenty-four degrees outside. Spring seemed eons away this vile February morning. It didn't matter that the sun was bright and shimmering on the winter landscape. The nightmare of work still shrouded her.

She should go to Crystal Park, do her walk around the lake that had never frozen over this winter. She missed the intricate design of ice shards spread out across the vast surface, the crisp splintered near-blue lines. But the place would be a crime scene again if that's where the most recent victim had been found.

She could go to the natatorium and swim, get all her despair out. But today she was too tired to do anything, to care. Her bones were weary. Grief sat heavy inside her. The rain from last night had stopped, and through the car's windows, the world looked shiny and new as if nothing horrible had happened in the night.

She didn't feel the cold in her garage as she climbed out of her old Toyota 4-Runner and shuffled inside. Didn't feel the empty bracing chill of her apartment whose old furnace always struggled to keep up with the freezing winters they experienced more and more, every year. She cranked up the temperature to seventy anyway because eventually the ache in her bones would be too much.

She didn't feel the chilly hardwoods on her bare feet as she kicked off her shoes and shrugged out of her socks, leaving everything where it landed strewn out on the floor behind her. She didn't feel the cold because she was already frozen, albeit a different kind of chill from a too-horrible shift at work. One where they'd lost more patients than they'd saved. One where children had died. Precious heartbeats there one moment, then snuffed out the next. As if the soul had never really been there in the first place. Some had arrived dead before she'd even had a chance to save them. She had no words. Sometimes nightmares came in real waking life too. She knew it, but it didn't make it any easier to swallow when it happened. Especially when it was her gift to heal.

She fingered the leaves of her Meyer lemon plant, sitting in the large kitchen window under its warming light. "You're looking lovely, my dear." So many blossoms ready to open. Their promised scent was heady. Leaving the rest of the lights off, she grabbed a large ice cube from her freezer and made her way to the small antique bar in her living room. Pretty bottles and vintage glasses she'd collected over the years, her little companions. Some witches had unique pendants and brooms. Francesca collected cocktail glasses and teacups, crystal decanters and old bottles, bitters and tinctures, and one very lonely lemon tree. All the nonsense one person needed.

Selecting a lowball art deco glass with cool ridges on the outside because she adored the way it felt in her hand, Francesca let the ice fall into it, then poured herself a bit of bourbon and two drops of her homemade grapefruit bitters. A little tonic for her weary body. This particular morning, she left out a splash of her soothing magic because there were moments when it was important to feel all the feels. To lean into the pain and grief lest it eat away at her soul. Curling up on her oversized couch, she dragged the badly knitted blanket her sister had made for her around her shoulders and processed the carnage.

It might only be seven-thirty in the morning, but a sip of bourbon would help her face the ghosts. Mother Earth had shifted and rumbled at the losses tonight. Francesca had sensed something else as well. A bitter acrid cloak of evil, a haunting presence she couldn't name had been with them in the emergency room, more than simply the regular trauma and death, as if a sheen of ugliness had coated them all. It was a scent she'd smelled before at Mercy General Hospital. And one she didn't fully understand.

Growing up, Francesca and her sister had had to teach themselves about their power, and that there were other unnatural beings out there. Perhaps they'd spent too much time trying to blend in and be normal, that they hadn't learned enough about those other beings. Ha! And who would have given them an in-depth education? The very first lesson they'd learned when orphaned and alone in foster care was to keep their talents hidden or risk death. It wasn't like she could ask random strangers about spirits and phantoms, demons and vampires and werewolves. It almost made her laugh to think of it, but it wasn't funny. It never had been.

The awful scent that had lingered near tonight while she'd worked to save lives seemed more unnatural and worrisome than anything she'd learned in her studies. It flitted in and out, almost making her question her sanity. It wasn't human. That was the only thing she could tell for sure.

She sipped her drink and focused on the honied sweetness of it, the hint of burn at the back of her throat. Perhaps she was being dramatic and the weight upon her was merely the reality of death. Having been in the ED for eight years now, she'd taught herself to compartmentalize her emotions, leave them at the hospital, mostly, and live her life outside without the trauma of each shift bearing down upon her. She didn't know many successful doctors who took it all home with them.

They simply couldn't hold on to it all and survive, at least not survive their careers, or their marriages. Either most likely. And she loved the ED, the pace of it, the uncertainty, being surrounded by people. It was where she thrived, where she was the least lonely.

And that is precisely why my marriage didn't survive. What a ruckus her job had caused. *No, dear, it had nothing to do with your job, but because your husband took advantage of your forty-eight-hour shifts to cheat on you.* Something she definitely didn't dwell on. Honestly, she'd been more disgusted than brokenhearted. And that, if nothing else, was a sign that she and Mr. Adulterer were never meant to be in the first place.

Ahh. She snuggled down into the cocoon and set her empty glass on the antique wooden coffee table. One lovely thing about living alone was that no one ever got to criticize her. For drinking bourbon after a hellish night shift like the one she'd just endured, for weighing too much, for being too tall, too redheaded, too freckled, too loud, too confident, too *everything*.

Nope. And no one could criticize her for believing in meant-to-bes and soulmates and happily-ever-afters. So her marriage hadn't worked out. If she'd paid better attention to her personal life, she would have avoided that catastrophe from the beginning. Anyway, she was stronger and smarter now. And she could warm herself up with all the dreams and hopes she desired. True love. Soulmates. Earth-shattering emotions. She would have it all someday.

Dr. Sarkozy's image flashed in her mind. To be fair, his image was a constant in the front of her mind, the back of her mind, the flutters in her stomach every time he was near, her heart, her libido, her dreams during sleep. Which was a warped kind of torture, since the man obviously loathed her. Although, he didn't like anyone. Dr. Nikolav Sarkozy had swept silently into her hospital last year during a night shift, an avenging angel. *And what would he think of being called an angel?*

Francesca closed her eyes and would have giggled at the thought if she had one single ounce of energy left. Dark hair, beautiful skin, eyes both mysterious and haunting, lips that spoke so confidently, arrogantly. She grinned. Could lips be arrogant? His certainly were. Lips she wanted to soothe and caress and taste. An expertly skilled surgeon, the likes of which she'd never met before. His record preceded him, both his arrogance and the fact that he'd saved one-hundred-percent of his patients.

Until tonight.

Francesca reclined down deeper into the couch, the pain in her chest acute. It was never easy to lose a patient. But a child? It wasn't fair. Nothing ever was. She'd been three beds away, heard his frantic yelling, but it was the anguish pouring out of him she'd felt swarm around her first. Quickly sewing up the lacerations on her patient's arm, she'd left the teenager with a nurse and rushed to Nikolav's side. It was as if an entire war had been waging right in front of him, and he aimed to win it singlehandedly. He'd pulsed with power, with intent, with rage.

Instead, the young boy, riddled by too many shards of metal and glass had bled out. There'd been nothing any of them could have done. For one brief moment, Nikolav's muscles had softened into her touch. Or maybe she'd imagined it, before he'd blown out a strangled curse and stormed away from them all. What she hadn't imagined was the thought snarling through his mind, *"I can't bear it."* Francesca had never read another's thoughts except her sister's.

She'd tried to find him later, but he'd pushed out of the locker room after a shower and disappeared into his ICU rounds, leaving the scent of soap and sorrow behind him. Francesca hoped he was all right. Stalking him and demanding he talk wasn't in her skill set. She had two days off and then it was back to work. She'd see him again as she'd be shadowing him on a spinal fusion surgery, something she'd yet to perform herself. She'd taken to learning from him as often as she could during the last year. Out of necessity for her career, and out of intrigue on a personal level.

Right before she dozed off, Francesca told herself it had nothing to do with her attraction to him, but rather his exceptional skill as a surgeon and a teacher. Even despite his brusque nature and those stupid comments he used to push her away, she liked him. Well, she somethinged him. *Like* was perhaps not the appropriate word to use for how she felt towards Dr. S.

She let thoughts of him follow her into sleep.

CHAPTER FIVE

S HE WAS GETTING HER walk in after all. Only she wasn't walking. She was floating or hovering. It was difficult to describe the sensation of dream walking.

This dream took her to one of her favorite places in the town of Mercy—Crystal Lake. A man-made lake in the middle of a gorgeous meandering park. The park was dotted with mature maple and birch trees and several gorgeous park benches. A smooth concrete path ran around the outside of the lake for walking or biking. In the summer, people kayaked and rowed, cutting across the glass-like water, and the north section was roped off for swimmers. It was her favorite place to swim outside, slicing through the water with the trees all around her. Once in a while, in winter, the lake froze completely, and people ice-skated on it.

Today the shiny blue water sat still as a mirror, even while the wind howled her lonely song and whipped through the trees' empty branches. Beyond the deciduous trees stood the forest of evergreens, mostly cedar and fir, and a few white pines boasting their frilly needles. Francesca's favorite, for their appearance and scent. Burning those branches on an open fire set that deep pine fragrance into the world. *Mm, I wish I had a firepit in the backyard. Huh, I wish I had a backyard.*

Francesca loved this park. It was a joyful place. She came to the lake when she craved the feel of the earth beneath and around her when she wanted to breathe deeply, when she sought her greatest connection with nature—water. But today, something stirred around her making her feel uneasy. Her smile disappeared as she studied the landscape. Everything was gray and shrouded, a fog moving in and out. Fine, dangerous finger-prints ghosted over the land. Here one moment, gone the next.

The path around the lake was empty, but she wasn't alone. A familiar ugly off-putting odor followed her at a distance. Something not of this world, something evil. It had a color too, that of smoke and tar. She saw it sneaking in and out of the fog around the trunks of the trees. Francesca walked closer to the lake and the scent drew back into the woods. She tested it, carefully walking away from the lake toward the forest and the obnoxious smell filled with glee, grew stronger, and surged up, an ugly bruise on an otherwise bleak winter landscape.

She sucked in air and hurried back toward the lake, its surface now rippling deep within. A warning. In a flash, rain came and she was in her car, hurtling around curves with no lights on, barely able to see through the water and the same thick murky fog. But the scent was there, following her, chasing her.

She woke on a scream.

Christ! What the hell? Chilly living room, an empty rocks glass on the coffee table. Francesca breathed deeply and tried to steady her racing pulse. Fear, thick and icy, slid around her heart and gripped it in its claws, leftover remnants of her dream. "Be gone evil being, be gone from this sacred space." Francesca chanted the words, listening to the spirit guide her. The fear and the odor vanished. All that lingered was the knowledge something awful had happened or was about to. She hadn't dreamed of something that scary in a long time. *Can't a girl have a calm day off?*

She pulled the blanket up and let her eyes adjust to the light slicing in through the break in the curtains. The only sound in the house now was the furnace chugging in overtime. "Come on, buddy, only a few more months until I'm going to replace you. I know you can do it." Sitting up, she squinted at the clock above the microwave. 4:30 pm. She'd slept deeply for hours. And still, she felt like someone had pummeled her in the boxing ring, one round too many. She rubbed the sleep away, folded the blanket, and picked up her mess, including her glass, and the clothes she'd left strewn on the floor. A hot shower was imminent. *It's been a while since I shored up my sacred incantations around home.* One more task to put on her list.

The scalding water helped to cleanse much of her melancholy. However, the dreams still lingered. *Dreams, right.* She'd been a young girl the last time she'd had a *mere* dream, as most people thought of them. Soft and floaty, odd and ethereal, or plain old weird.

Nope, not her. Once she'd turned fifteen, her sleeping mind had taken her on worldly, full-color adventures and provided her with movies of actual events, past and present. Once in a while, the future. She walked in her dreams, aware, alive, senses on full alert.

She and her sister called it dream walking. Sometimes she met people, carried on conversations, and helped solve problems. It was exhilarating and unique. The dream walk she'd just experienced had been different. It was layered with warnings, personal and immediate, with a horrible sense of foreboding.

Maybe it was the bourbon she mixed with her emotions last night. That would teach her. Although having lived with and honed her dream walking abilities for almost twenty years now, Francesca knew better. And she rarely ignored her experiences, happy or angry. And anger had definitely been the prevalent emotion surging through. *Why?* She'd been taught to ask, and the questions came automatically now. *And who? Or what?* The dream had all been shrouded with a thick fog of confusion. She'd walked through it nearly blind and that had never happened.

Grinding coffee beans centered her, the rich, smokey flavor tingling her nose with hints of a rich, warming cup to come. Or perhaps two large cups flush with heavy cream, her one indulgence. Who was she kidding? Francesca huffed out a laugh. She had many indulgences, and why should she be ashamed?

She paused, heightening her sense of hearing. The garage door. Only one other person had an opener for her garage and keys to her home, her sister, Gianna.

Checking her phone, Francesca realized she'd missed two calls and one text from Gia.

Gia: On our way!

The door opened and her niece and nephew flew through the hallway to her. Well, Ava flew. Danny walked sedately, doing an awesome impression of an eighty-year-old man at a funeral. Francesca knelt and gathered them in her arms. "My Boo and Monkey. I've missed you so," she said, hugging them and taking in a deep breath of their soft, clean skin.

"Danny says you can't call him Monkey anymore," Ava said. "He's too old and important." Ava threw herself down on the floor and tugged off her rain boots. Danny stood stiff by her side.

Francesca caught her sister's eyes in the doorway. "*Too old, huh?*" She and Gia had been able to speak to each other this way through their thoughts since childhood. It hadn't seemed odd to either of them until they realized not everyone possessed this special talent. It had saved Gia's life in foster care. One more thing to keep hidden.

"*New school. New kids. I think it's all getting to him.*" her sister shot back.

"*Ahh.*" Francesca was delighted her sister had packed up her home in Boston and brought the kids to live here on the edge of the Blue Ridge Mountains, but changing schools at age ten was difficult. Francesca and Gia knew all about that. They also knew what it was like, not only to be the new kid but to be different. Danny and Ava had the added burden of grief. It had been three years since their father, Douglas, had died. And one never really got over the death of a parent but rather learned to live with that absence.

Francesca and Gia had been babies when their father died, so they had no memories of him. And when their mom had been murdered, well that didn't bear thinking about. A shudder ran through her from that long-ago painful memory. History had an odd sense of humor, first, her and Gia's mom being murdered, then Danny and Ava's father. Were they cursed to have love ripped from them? Some days a curse was exactly what it felt like.

"This calls for breakfast for dinner," she said, forcing the past away. Ava had glommed onto her leg. Francesca scooped her up and tipped her upside down. The four-year-old's high-pitched laughter soothed her soul. Goodness, she was a tiny forest fairy. Francesca set Ava on one of the stools at the island and tried to brush her hands through her tangled brown locks.

"Owwww," Ava moaned.

"Sorry, Boo." Francesca kissed the girl's forehead and gave her sister another raised eyebrow. This time they had their conversation out loud. "Still struggling with tangled hair?"

"I swear." Gia rolled her eyes. "It's never-ending. Exactly like when you were a girl. Nothing works. Not conditioner, not special pillowcases. I swear she rolls around on the top of her head during sleep and mashes it into the worst tangled mess she can manage."

"Oh, Mommy. I do not," Ava said. "I fly in my sleep up to the clouds." She demonstrated with her hands.

"Do you now?" Francesca asked. "*I'll mix up some of my special shampoo later for her, see if that helps.*"

"*May the angels bless you if it works.*" Gia sighed and Francesca sensed the exhaustion under her sister's skin, all the way to her bones.

"Come on now, I need help making pancakes." Francesca gathered her ingredients and pulled on her apron. She mixed a bit of cocoa powder into the pancake batter and smiled at Gia as her sister set a cup of coffee with cream beside her. They'd been taking care of each other forever. Gia added a glug to her own coffee.

"I do fly, Auntie Frankie," Ava insisted. "And sometimes I take my dog with me."

"Your dog?" Gia sat next to her daughter. Danny came around the island to help Francesca. She handed him the batter to whisk and silently wove a spell of delight and joy and a touch of healing into the ingredients. She suspected most would think it frivolous, perhaps even a waste, but she enjoyed adding touches of spells to her cooking. When she'd finally started to get a handle on her magic, it was what brought her joy.

And she loved working beside her nephew. He was so serious, but he eased up a bit when he cooked with her. A smile even snuck onto his face. Right before Francesca flipped the pancakes, Danny added chocolate chips to them. She winked and was relieved to get a grin out of him. He'd hardly said one word since he'd been here, but she knew he was processing everything. Although Francesca was surprised that he'd made no outward disbelief at Ava's dog comment. "A dog, darling?"

"Yes." Ava used her hands again to tell the story and her eyes grew huge and shiny. "He's black and furry, very soft fur, not tangled at all like my fur." She shook out her hair and giggled. "And he's very quiet for how enormi he is."

"Enormi?" Gia poked her daughter in the side, eliciting another burst of laughter.

"Danny made it up. He makes up the bestest words ever."

"I've seen him too." Finally, her nephew uttered some words.

Francesca bumped his hip. "Oh really? In your dreams?" It wasn't uncommon for witch siblings to share dreams.

"Mm-hmm," Danny mumbled. Francesca wondered at her nephew's response. He was usually very precise and he insisted on clarifying facts to the minute detail. Maybe she hadn't gotten as much sleep as she'd thought. Maybe her own troubled dreams were messing with her perceptions.

Gia's eyes, wide and worried, met Francesca's again. "*Are they too young to be dream walking?*"

"*I don't know, but for how smart they are and how much energy they have, I wouldn't be surprised.*"

"*I...no way...*" Gia answered.

Francesca studied her sister, let her work through whatever was bothering her. Something larger was going on here. If Gia wanted to talk it through, she would, eventually.

Ava bounced on her seat. "Can we put chocolate chips in *all* the pancakes?"

"Good idea. Then we'll eat them." Francesca crossed her eyes at her niece and got another giggle. It was good. Laughter would help with whatever cloud was swirling around them. And Francesca had no doubt there was a cloud, possibly more than one.

***

"Are they asleep?" Francesca asked as Gia made her way downstairs to join her on the couch. Her sister climbed in next to Francesca, tugging the blanket over them.

"Ava is snoring away. Danny's still reading his science magazine."

"So serious that one?"

Gia rested her head on Francesca's shoulder. "Mm, more and more so, especially since the move. It's been months, but it hasn't gotten better. Did I do the right thing?" Gia whispered.

"Oh, honey. I think so, but what do I know? I love having you closer, but that could be purely selfish. You were drowning and lonely up in Boston. The kids weren't happy either."

"True, but at least it was an unhappy they recognized. Now it's new schools, new people, new house. Maybe it's all too much."

"I think it's going to take time. You know how he processes things. But they have you. And you all have me. And I think they enjoy coming to visit me as much as I enjoy having them."

"They love it. So do I. I wish I could stay."

Here it was, the truth of the matter. Francesca was a healer. Gia a mercenary. Sisters so different, and yet not really, both fighting a battle against evil. "I'm glad you can bring them to me easily now." A pause hovered between them. "Where are you going this time?" Francesca whispered as if that would keep them both safe from the dangers her sister fought. "Don't get me wrong, I love having them. And you know my neighbor Katie adores watching them on the days I have to work. I just worry."

"I'm not sure. I'm following the money trails. They're a tangled mess of vines or bomb wires. I have no idea which one will lead me nowhere or which one might be lethal. I'll leave you my encrypted contact information in our dreams tonight, but I'll be difficult to get a hold of. I'll be gone before the sun comes up."

"You don't have to do this," Francesca offered. She'd said it every time, anticipating her sister's response.

"I do. For Douglas's sake. I can't let his murder go unpunished. I won't." Her sister was nothing if not stubborn and loyal and desperately heartbroken at the death, nay brutal murder of her husband. "And you know I do it for Mom too," Gia whispered.

"We never talk about her," Francesca whispered back. It was true, they rarely spoke about their mother or the night she'd been murdered. When it happened and they were shuffled off to foster care, it was too scary even to remember. And they never knew who they could trust so they'd both locked the memories away so deep it was difficult to dredge them back up.

"I know." Gia was so quiet, Francesca barely heard her. "I miss her so much."

Francesca pulled the blanket tighter. "Me too." They sat like that in silence, still perhaps too afraid to speak their memories aloud.

"You're not disappointed in me, are you?"

Francesca's heart broke again at her sister's words. How long had it been since Gia had really been her little sister? She'd grown up too fast, endured more tragedy than one person should in a lifetime, and dedicated herself to taking down bad men and women. Francesca could only imagine how lonely she must be.

"Never, Gi."

"Hug them for me every day, will you?" Gia whispered before she dozed off to sleep.

"I will," Francesca promised. She closed her eyes and wove a spell of love and safety around her apartment, her sister and the kids, and her heart. Every heart needed a boost now and then.

CHAPTER SIX

H OME WASN'T ANY BETTER than the damn hospital. He'd been at his house for two days and it felt as if his skin was slowly being peeled from his body. The helplessness of the tragedy in the emergency room followed him like a wraith. Niko prowled through the hallway and out into the solarium. He'd added it last year when he'd moved here and started working at the hospital. Made of a special green glass he'd fashioned to allow the sunlight to nurture the plants but not affect him.

While the sun couldn't kill him—some vampire myths were exaggerated—and he was able to walk through daylight, sunlight did drain his strength. And even after centuries, there was still a level of uncomfortableness in being that exposed, that vulnerable. Simply because the sun wouldn't incinerate him on contact didn't mean it was healthy for him to spend hours in it.

This way he could tend his plants without the threat of exhaustion. He could work in the dirt, breathe in the plants' essence, and watch things thrive and grow under his own hands.

It was different than saving human lives, less risky for sure. It was safe to say, maybe until last night, he'd have cared more about his precious plants than any patient he'd ever had. Until last night he hadn't had to. Until last night they'd been maneuvers to perform, simple problems to solve.

Feelings riled him up. He'd remained stoic for centuries, taming his nature, creating routines, calming his heart. *Jesus fucking Christ*, his heart didn't even still beat. It had been stolen from him the same time his humanity had been. But ever since he'd walked into Mercy General Hospital and sensed Francesca's presence, scented her unusual cells, summer roses musky with humidity, growth, fertility, and the pure joy in her, some weird and foreign flutters took flight in his chest where his heart might have once beat. It had been over six hundred years since he'd been intrigued by another soul, human or not. It had also been six hundred years since he'd taken a person to bed.

Mine.

Fuck! He'd dismissed the thought as he always did. Because she couldn't be. It was impossible.

But after being close to her all these months, after watching her work, after the feel of her fingers on his arm, the searing beauty of it, the way she said his name...he wasn't sure anymore. His own personal siren singing to him. Was this some cruel twist of the curse? Were witches teasing him with her? A mate? The breath slammed out of him. He steadied himself on the worktable covered with small seed trays. His mate. It was one thing to dream of one, which he'd quit doing centuries ago. Mates were forever. Mates were precious.

For hundreds of years, he'd thought himself unable to find one, with everything that had happened. As a new vampire, he'd been overcome with rage and fucking and killing. For one dark century he'd lived that way. And then it had all been snuffed out of him and he'd been cursed, never to kill again, never to drink blood from a human or have sex until he found his mate.

Until he found his mate.

He hadn't believed the powerful witch back then. And now? Now it was almost funny. For a witch to be his mate.

Niko steadied his breath exactly as his old teacher had taught him and got busy grafting roses. It wouldn't take his mind off everything, but it promised to help.

***

They'd had two days of relentless rain, rain so heavy he could have stood outside and not gotten hit by one ray of sunshine. Normally Niko preferred this weather. It allowed him a calm he didn't always feel, allowed him to have more patience.

Currently, the rains had softened to a fine mist floating through the air and shrouding the sleepy mountain town in a thick fog. Fog was the worst. It was its own being, secretive and seductive, quiet and menacing. The muted sounds of cars crashing, people slipping and falling, or crime happening in fog didn't lessen the impact or horror. If anything, it made it worse, more macabre. The mist was one large invisible beast, slithering around, disappearing, and sneaking back in to haunt. And Niko felt it everywhere, surrounding him and from within his chest. It beat out a taunt. Even in the walls of the hospital. There was a muffled warning to every scent and sound, alerting him to...to...something being fucking wrong.

His shift didn't start for an hour, and she wasn't here yet. He could sense her absence. It was never a good idea for him to arrive early for work. The restlessness ate at him with nothing to do, but he'd had to come, had to be near her,.

"You're in an unusually piss-poor mood this morning?"

Niko paced along the wall inside the hospital's morgue, in the dark, cold basement. It didn't bother Niko. He found relief down here with the dead, with the acrid scent of formaldehyde, and the ancient scent of anonymous blood. The hospital housed the blood bank here in the morgue. It was Niko's respite, or punishment, depending on how much thought he put into it.

Dr. Augustus Clarke was the lead pathologist and medical examiner. The fact that he was a guardian demon was another reason Niko had always felt relaxed down here. Two lost souls who managed to eke out their days in Purgatory, they had much in common. Not to mention, Augustus was one of the smartest beings Niko had met. He retained every piece of knowledge he'd learned for the past ten centuries. Niko was a baby compared to Augustus.

Niko might consider him a friend—if he knew how to have friends.

"Have you had anything to drink?" Augustus asked, unlocking the glass-fronted refrigerator that housed the oldest blood supply. If it wasn't used soon, they'd have to dump it.

"I'm not thirsty." *Not for that.*

"Right, let me guess then, your Dr. Banetti not here today?"

Niko swore and continued his pacing. "She's not mine." *Liar.*

"You could try uh...asking her out, see what she says, put yourself out of misery." Augustus began to lay out his tools, hand-cleaning each one.

"And then what?" Niko snarled. He was coming undone. "Take her to the movies, maybe *Dracula*, how's that for a selection? Give her a hint before I expose all my secrets."

Augustus chuckled. "Hadn't thought of *Dracula*. Didn't know you had a sense of humor in there."

"I was kidding," Niko bit out. He shouldn't have come down here. It wasn't helping. Nothing was helping.

"Yep, got that. Still, it could do the trick."

"Christ, I'm not taking her to the movies. I'm not taking her out at all." The thought of sitting in a dark movie theater with her, holding her hand, while her wild and wicked scent surrounded him and he had to pay attention to the screen. It wasn't happening.

"Why not?"

"Have you lost your mind?"

"Uh yeah, a couple of centuries ago."

All the anger and frustration seeped out of Niko. *Shit.*

"It's taken me hundreds of years to crawl back from that madness. There has to be more for me, for both of us, than commiserating over dead people. At least you get to work with the living." Augustus smirked but it lacked the usual nod of humor.

Niko slumped into one of the metal chairs and rested his head against the wall. He was tired. So fucking tired. Augustus had lost more than Niko ever had and yet here he was with more hope and Niko was acting like an asshole. Again.

"I thought you preferred working with the dead?" Niko inquired.

"I appreciate the problem solving, the ability to figure out what went wrong, and if it happens, to help right wrongs, but it doesn't make for stunning conversation." Augustus joked, but the man's anguish pulsed underneath the layers of his skin. Where Niko's curse was damned upon him by others, Augustus' was self-imposed.

"Ask her out. Dr. Banetti's one of the good ones. And I think she likes you. You never know, Niko. Not in all my lifetimes did I imagine being friends with a vampire surgeon who saves lives and can't bite anyone. Stranger things and all that."

She is one of the good ones, the best. And Niko couldn't fucking get her out of his mind. He allowed his thoughts to travel to the thought of taking Francesca Banetti out on a date. He stood and brushed his hands on his scrubs. He certainly wasn't taking her to the fucking movies. Nothing so mundane as that. He'd trace her to an island paradise and give her the world if she'd let him. Against all rational thought, he wanted nothing more than to take Augustus' advice and ask the woman out. But want had been cursed from him centuries ago.

"Maybe she's the one to break your curse," Augustus suggested carefully.

"Really?" Niko scowled. "A witch my mate?" He'd barely allowed himself to contemplate the same thought. He couldn't have this conversation. Niko stormed out of the confines of the windowless, soulless basement. She'd probably laugh in his face if he did ask her out. No, he thought. The problem was, he had a feeling she'd say yes. And then what?

His torture today had hardly begun. He was going to see her and work next to her, something he both anticipated and dreaded. Who was he kidding? He looked forward to every interaction he had with her, even if it was painful. It was the sweetest kind of torture he'd ever endured. And the hardest.

And today's task would be even more difficult because he not only had to work beside her, he had to perform a spinal surgery while she stood in scrubs next to him, leaned in close, and...what the fuck had he been thinking, offering to teach his skills to her? *Good fucking question.* Nikolav Sarkozy had lost all rational thought a year ago when he'd stepped inside this hospital.

***

"Dr. Sarkozy, Dr. Banetti still isn't here. Shall we continue?" The words gathered in the forefront of his mind and forced his attention.

Where the hell is she? She was late for her lesson. Niko shrugged on his gown and tried to focus on his surgical nurses readying the room. *How the hell does she think she'll ever move into surgery if she can't handle showing up for class?* A gnawing worry tugged at the back of his mind. He was more on edge than usual.

"Pardon, Dr. Sarkozy?"

His thoughts were bleeding out into his words. "Nothing."

Something's wrong. Dr. Banetti was the ultimate professional. Additionally, she had a talent that was rare in most doctors he'd met, an absolute enjoyment of her job and the tasks and skills it demanded. Heck, she practically floated around the Emergency Department, bestowing her golden joy upon everyone she encountered.

Put her out of your mind. Niko let the room surround him, took in the layout, the patient, the nurses, the machines. The steady almost quiet hummed around him. Everyone waited for him. He took one last breath, commanded his surgical skills to the tips of his fingers, and got to work. But for the first time in his career as a surgeon, thoughts of a gorgeous redheaded woman and worry slept on the edge of his thoughts throughout the entire procedure.

And hours later when he stalked out of surgery, he allowed his worry over Francesca to manifest front and center. As if he had a choice. He shrugged off his cap and mask. The distinct prick of fear that something was horribly wrong clanged against his skull. It was time. It was time to find Francesca.

CHAPTER SEVEN

F RANCESCA DIDN'T KNOW WHETHER to slow the vehicle or speed up. The fog was a tricky bastard and, combined with the slick roads, could be lethal. *Slow down. Keep a steady hand.* This would be her normal mantra for driving on an afternoon like this, one masquerading as midnight as the strange haunting fog hovered around her. However, normal had flown out the window two miles ago when she realized she was being followed. Not followed, stalked, being chased. In a black fog. Along a steep and slippery mountain road. Her dream walk nightmare from a few mornings ago centered in her mind. *Shit-cakes.*

"I can't see anything, Auntie Frankie?" Ava's little voice came from the backseat.

"I know, Boo. It's foggy out."

"Goddess of the land, of earth and dirt and water, of fire and love, all the elements, please, I could use your help right now." Francesca used what concentration she could that wasn't

focused directly on the road in front of her and sought her connection through the asphalt and the soil beneath it to all the tangled web of roots holding the world together.

Getting into an accident was never a good idea but doing it with her niece and nephew in the back of the car was the most frightening thing Francesca could imagine. And her instincts told her that's where they were headed. The damn car or truck behind her wouldn't get off her bumper, its headlights blinding her like lighting through the murky air at every turn. Francesca tamped down her fear, gripped the wheel, and enlisted the help of all the ancients to get them safely down these mountains. A surge of power surrounded her car, worked its way into her chest, held her steady. Swirls of energy pulsed within her as she put her all into controlling her vehicle.

"I did like that place," Danny said.

Saturday was their day to do something fun. She'd taken them to a bird sanctuary up in the hills this morning. They were due back at her house in an hour for the babysitter to meet them before Francesca had to make it to work. She was supposed to work side by side, literally, with Niko tonight, calmly, on a patient's spine. Suddenly, though, nothing was as important as getting these kids to safety. *Focus on the road. Feel the ground beneath the wheels, the power underneath, the current of Mother Earth. Let it guide me.*

"But..."

"But what, honey?" Francesca tried to keep the worry out of her voice. *For fuck's sake.* The last turn was too quick, too slippery, no matter the grip of power the earth had on her. And the bastard's lights were still there, gaining purchase.

"But I think you're going too fast," Danny whispered.

Yes, she wanted to say but it was too late, the bonds holding and guiding her stretched to the breaking point. The Toyota slid across the slick road, slammed into the guardrail, crashed over it, and barreled like a tornado down the hillside into the trees and brush below, bumping and grinding, the sound nearly worse than the pain. "*Catch us gently.*" She willed with all her might.

It was too much too fast on her brain and body that casting a spell of safety was difficult. Instantly the car came to a crashing stop against the trunk of a gnarly old tree. Cedar, Francesca thought, as its wise old scent stole through her. She blinked through the shock and pain and the sudden blaring silence, pushing through the pain to speak to nature. "*Help, goddesses.*"

Suddenly the trees' roots rose out of the ground and began to form a cocoon of sorts around the car. The earth shattered and groaned and shifted around her. Magic, powerful, ancient magic. So much magnificent energy surrounded her, right before consciousness was snuffed out.

***

Something pawed at her side. Francesca tried to bat it away. Pain shot through her chest and her head. "What...what?"

"Shh, Aunt Frankie. The shadow might hear you." Danny's voice was so quiet she wondered if he even said the words out loud. "I'm finding your phone. I need to call an ambulance."

"I don't understand." She drifted in and out. Blinding white agony seared through her abdomen.

"Daughter." The goddesses were speaking back. *"Danger's coming. We can only hold you for so long. You must wake."*

"Danny?" she whispered. "Ava?"

"Shh, it's back, it's coming closer. Don't say anything, Auntie. Here it is..." Her nephew's silent plea reached inside her.

"Yes, please," Danny wasn't quiet now. His loud voice shocked her eyes back open. "Send an ambulance right away. My aunt is hurt. Someone bad was chasing us and it's trying to get us now! Hurry! Hurry!" He yelled into her phone. "He pushed us off the road by mile 9.1 on Old Mountain Highway in a big truck and now it's trying to get us! My aunt. And my sister is crying. Please hurry!"

"Honey," Francesca called, but her voice was weak. Her head throbbed and her hand shook as she touched a tender spot to find a piece of metal cutting into her temple. A black void threatened her consciousness as nausea roiled in her stomach.

"It's okay!" Danny yelled frantically. "The ambulance is coming. I told them where we were. Stay awake, Aunt Frankie."

"Okay." She pushed words toward him through the crippling torture in her head and arm, the very breath of her. *"I love you".* But she couldn't stay awake. A cloud silenced her mind and her voice.

CHAPTER EIGHT

"D R. SARKOZY, I DIDN'T know you were scheduled in the ED tonight?"

"I'm not. Dr. Banetti, is she—"

Stephanie held up her finger and answered the ambulance call. *Fuck!* The scent overwhelmed him. *Francesca, pain, ugliness.* The fear, the knowing swarmed around him like a dark veil of bats clamoring out of a cave. He turned and took off at a sprint. The doors opened, the ambulance pulled in, and the EMTs handled the gurney down. *Jesus Christ, blood.* She was covered in it.

"Thirty-five-year-old female. It's Dr. Banetti...she was—" The EMT coughed through his words, worry lacing them. "Car accident. Multiple injuries. Wounds to the head. We've stopped the bleeding here, and here. Compound fracture of the left radius."

Her pain screamed at him. *Get yourself together. She needs you.*

"Her arm is stabilized, and we've applied pressure to the bleeding while trying not to jar the bone. Most of her injuries were sustained on the left side. She's been in and out of consciousness since the accident scene."

More words zeroed into Niko's brain. He placed his hand on Francesca's uninjured arm to feel her pulse and send his energy into her. *"I've got you."*

He forced his mind to narrow and focus on the details the paramedics relayed to him and his team, as well as what her body told him. He took charge, assigning tasks while rushing with Francesca to surgery. They were wheeling her into the elevator when her eyes flickered, and she tried to shove the breathing mask off her face.

"Niko?"

Jesus Christ, his name on her lips and it was this serrated, hollow, barely there, confused ache.

"What happened?" Niko gently tried urging his thoughts onto her.

"Crashed the car."

He heard her words as clearly as if she'd spoken aloud. Tendrils of fire sparked between Niko and Francesca drawing them closer, growing a bond between them.

"I...I missed our surgery."

Jesus. That was what she was worried about. He didn't like her speaking aloud right now. He could tell how much it pained her.

"I'm...uhm..." She blinked. He ever so gently squeezed her free hand.

"I took care of it." His answer was harsh, unnecessary.

"Dr. Sarkozy?" A nurse inquired.

"Dr. Banetti, you've been in an accident." Niko calmed his rage and spoke gently. Had he caused the tears that seeped out of her eyes? "You're at the hospital. We've got you."

They wheeled her into the elevator. *"I've got you."* He pushed the words into her, brushing one tear away with his thumb.

"No." It was barely a whisper, but he heard it. "No accident."

"All right," he said. He gently placed the mask back over her nose and mouth and she closed her eyes. A thunder of rage threatened to drown him. He fought against it and, like a banshee, whipped away all sound and thought aside from one driving intention. *I must save her life.*

***

Niko stood in the corner of her room in the ICU and watched. They'd just brought her out of surgery. It was the most difficult surgery he'd ever performed, not for the severity of her injuries, but because it was Francesca on the operating table. *Mine.* Thank fuck he'd been in tune with her body.

He wanted to break things, destroy something, bleed his fury out. *Not an accident.* Her words haunted him. Niko hated to leave her, but a movement drew him into the hallway and toward the nurses' station. Rich, one of the regular EMTs, was filling out a form. He'd been with Francesca in the ambulance. Niko could see things more clearly now.

"How's she doing, Dr. Sarkozy?" Rich asked.

"She's going to be fine." She would be if he had anything to do about it, and he would have everything to do about it.

"That's great." Rich sighed and gave Niko's shoulder a squeeze. No one touched Niko unless he asked for it, but the man seemed not to notice the glare blazing in Niko's eyes. "Glad you were here tonight, Doc. She's special and no one takes as good of care of the patients as you do. And her, of course."

Niko swallowed through the words. He didn't need compliments, but this one burned through his chest for some strange reason.

"Glad those kids weren't hurt either. There must be some guardian angels in the world, that's for sure," Rich said.

"Kids?" *She has children?*

"Her niece and nephew," Nurse Lainy answered. "They were in the car with her when it happened. We can't get a hold of Francesca's sister, or anyone really. I don't...I'm not sure what she'd want me to say..."

"What is it?" Niko demanded then tried to use a less cranky tone. He stepped closer so only Rich and Lainy could hear him. "Francesca says it wasn't an accident. We need to do everything we can to keep her safe. That includes keeping those children safe." He pushed his intentions onto them, not above using his powers of persuasion to help them divulge the information he sought.

"Francesca doesn't have a lot of people in her life that she's close to," Lainy said. "I mean, she's got friends here at work. And then there's her sister and her sister's kids, Dr. Sarkozy. That's mostly it. She's very private."

Niko didn't know what to do with this information. At work she was gregarious, smiling, engaging, and friends with nearly everyone. Francesca was well-loved here. Because she treated people like they were special. But outside the hospital? Where was her family? Where was her community? She should have a waiting room full of people concerned for her.

"We patched up a few scratches and they're over there," Lainy nodded. "In the lounge with blankets and juice, watching a baking show. Rich was going to get them some fries and chicken fingers from the cafeteria."

"I'll be back in a few," Rich said. "I wanted to see how Dr. Banetti was doing."

A strange feeling came over Niko. It wasn't the first one of the day. "Thank you," he managed to get out. If Francesca had a niece and nephew, they were her family, which meant they were under his guard as well. As of this moment, they all belonged to him. "And thank you for the care you gave her in the ambulance. Well done." Niko nodded and made his way to the children.

"Hello," he said, the word like gravel scraping to get out. A young girl, maybe four or five, was curled up on her stomach asleep under a blanket. An older boy stood when Niko entered. Niko couldn't tell his age. His body was that of a ten or eleven-year-old, but his eyes held the wisdom of someone much older. They studied each other.

"Are you Dr. Sarkozy? The one they said was taking care of Aunt Frankie?"

Good, direct. Niko could deal with that. He nodded once. "I am. Nikolav Sarkozy." Niko held out his hand. The boy didn't blink or waver. He simply took his hand and gave it a strong grip.

"Daniel. Or Danny, if...if you want." It was the only indication the boy let slip that he was in fact a boy and not an established businessman with years of practice introducing himself.

"Danny." Niko went with his instinct, having extremely limited experience with children. "I prefer nicknames myself. You're welcome to call me Niko."

The boy smiled and suddenly Niko's life shifted into the brightness surrounding this young man. It made Niko extremely uncomfortable, but he didn't want to back away; instead, he wanted to bask in it.

"Did you fix Aunt Frankie? They told us she was out of surgery. She...she was bleeding a lot and not talking, and I think something was wrong with her lung because her breathing sounded very odd. I was scared because something awful was after us. A monster, but I tried to do a good job...I mean." Danny turned away and sat down with a large shudder. "It was hard to find her phone with all the broken glass, but the dark shadow was coming, and I had to call 911. I yelled so whatever it was would know what I was doing."

Niko braced, all his fear and rage tunneling together in his mind. *Dark shadow? For Christ's sake.*

"Did I...did I do the right thing?" Danny's whisper drew Niko back to the quiet room with the television on and someone on the show trying to balance a cake in the shape of an antique plane on top of another round cake.

Niko sat down beside the boy. "You did a great job. I suspect, Danny that you were put in that position at that exact moment to save the three of you." It might have been a dramatic thing to say to a child, but Niko gathered this special boy could handle the serious note, and praise would be good for him.

And Niko wasn't lying. Not many people on the planet could have scared a dark shadow away in much the same manner. Especially if it was what Niko suspected. Niko's thoughts turned inward and dark, searching his brain for what in the hell the child could be referring to. The possibilities were gruesome. Demons. Some demons were especially weakened by children. If this were the case, it had served Danny well at the accident, but it also meant the demon would be enraged.

"Thank you," Danny whispered and wiped his tears with the back of his hand.

That pain shoved itself back into Niko's chest. He wanted to wrap the child in a hug. Could use one as well. Niko hadn't hugged in hundreds of years. It had been so long he couldn't even remember what one felt like. The only thing that ghosted his memory was that hugs were a comfort, which also hadn't been part of Niko's life for eons. At least not the physical, intimate kind.

"Thank you for taking care of Aunt Frankie."

"You're welcome." Niko shoved away his memories, the haunted ones, and the empty ones. There was no place for them right now. "She's sleeping, but they're making sure her pain is managed, and I think after you eat, we should go see her."

"Yes, please. I'll try to...I'll try to stop crying before then." The boy was desperately swallowing back his tears.

Niko tagged the box of Kleenexes and handed them over. "I have a feeling your aunt doesn't mind tears."

Danny laughed through his emotions. "You're right. She says they have special magic in them, and that if we care for another's tears, that magic will fill us with love. It's...uhm...other people that don't always like them."

Love.

"Do you mind tears?"

It was Niko's turn to have trouble speaking. "Not in the least." *Special magic will fill us with love.*

Danny huffed. "That's a relief," he whispered in a small voice.

Rich appeared in the doorway with a tray of food, his girlfriend right behind him with a bag of stuffed animals and a smile on her face that said she had never endured a rough day in her life.

The little girl popped up to sitting and flipped her dark curls out of her face as if someone had loudly announced right in her sleeping ear that it was time for cake and ice cream. "I'm soooo hungry."

"You're always hungry, Ava," Danny said.

"I am." She faced Rich. "Did Aunt Frankie make that? I like everything she makes except her smoothies because she sneaks fresh herbs in them, and I don't eat herbs."

"It's pronounced herbs, without the h, Ava." Spoken with the annoyance only an older sibling could harbor.

"They pronounce the h in London, Danny," the sprite said.

It was the first time all day Niko smiled. He found he could sit for hours in this uncomfortable room as long as these two small humans were offering their opinions and delight to the world. Unfortunately, he had something extremely timely to do. He stood and took the tray from Rich and set it on the table for the children. "I'm afraid your aunt didn't make this, but Rich and his friend..."

"Kara," the woman said and entered the room.

"Yes, Rich and Kara brought you some treats. Kara, would you mind sitting with them while I speak with Rich for a moment?? When they pounced on the fries, Niko took a moment to pull Rich into the hallway. "Where exactly did the accident happen?"

"Right past mile nine on Old Mountain Highway, the last curve on the way down. Car went over the guardrail."

"I know that area. Could you do me a favor and stay with the children until I return? I won't be long, half an hour." *Something is very wrong. And I need to chase down a demon.*

"I don't want them to be alone." He couldn't very well admit his thoughts yet. It was one thing for Danny to speak of a dark shadow to Niko. After all, Niko was a seven-hundred-year-old vampire; magic, good or evil didn't surprise him in the least. But Niko had no idea how Rich might respond. That fact that Niko trusted almost no one in the world wasn't a path he could stick to. For now, he'd have to put his faith in Rich concerning these precious children. It was his only choice. He knew the nurses were keeping an eye on them as well.

"We planned on staying until they kick us out, me and Kara. Dr. Banetti saved Kara's life last May when...well when she was kidnapped and attacked... I mean you did too, Dr. Sarkozy."

Niko remembered the woman now. The last time he'd seen her she'd been beaten so black and blue she was unrecognizable. Blood had dried over one of her swollen-shut eyes and her hair had been partially shaved off. She was one of three women found to have been kidnapped and attacked by someone with the same pattern. And if Niko recalled correctly, the only one to have survived.

"But after...um...when Kara woke up. It took a while, and a lot of help from people, especially Dr. B, for Kara to heal. In her mind and emotions, you know."

Niko nodded. He couldn't find the right words. He'd been wrong many times this evening. This man and his girlfriend humbled him. It might have been forever since a human had done that.

He shook Rich's hand, retrieved his coat, and once again, surrounded by his cloak of darkness, Niko traced into the night.

It didn't take him long when he used his powers. He could focus his mind and be halfway around the world in a matter of seconds. He could have easily made it to the scene of the accident instantly, but he wanted to be very careful. He located himself half a mile from where Rich said, then slowed his movement so he could absorb his surroundings and make note of anything suspicious. Her scent drew him on. It lingered, present in the landscape. As Niko inched closer, he paused behind the trees, watching. The mangled SUV was still there, practically buried under an odd connection of branches. They'd had to fucking cut it open to get her out.

Breathe, he told himself. *It will do you no good to raze the land here and now, to take out your rage on the trees.* He was alone. Most likely the police would wait until morning to tow the car up the hill. Not safe now in the fog and damp cloaking the land. The rain was back as if it had never ceased in the first place, as if it came with Niko to cleanse the secrets.

Niko approached the car and touched it. Yes, her deep blossom scent was here, in the lining of the car, in the blood she'd shed at the scene, in the air around him. And although gone now, Danny had been correct, there had been a dark shadow present as well. Niko sniffed the air and did as much investigating as he could before he detected it more clearly. Fresh tar or acid, extremely strong and caustic, masking an underlying scent of something rotting. He narrowed his focus. Not human or made by humans. Altogether there was something familiar to it, but confusing. It reminded him of the stench layered around the hospital. Despair. Powerful. A hybrid demon made of...rage. At that realization, Niko swore and located back to the hospital. He was leaving nothing to chance.

CHAPTER NINE

I T WAS A SOUND she recognized, a quiet but steady beep. Francesca listened and allowed the familiar to wrap around her. Slowly images and memories pieced together so she could make out most of the puzzle in her mind, even if every second wasn't clear. Murky fog, pouring rain, gaps where the road rose up to meet her, and headlights assaulting from behind. Close, too close. Danny standing by her side and yelling, his words muffled by her tired brain. The smell of broken things and wet trees shaking off their auras around her, blood and...and...so much evil. Then nothing. She was dry now, all the rain and blood washed away while she'd slept.

Not sleeping, unconscious. Dry soap and plastic came to her then, the strongest scents she could make out. The soap she knew in an instant from scrubbing her hands a million times a day. She was in the hospital, but not for work, and her eyes were sealed shut with exhaustion. *You're safe. I've got you.* Steady words in a voice she loved came back to her. Fractured images.

Niko's face above her, telling her what was wrong in that infuriatingly dictatorial voice of his.

It hurt to breathe. *At least you're breathing. Good point. Am I though? Why is it so weird and painful?* It took a thousand pounds of effort, but she peeled her eyes open. It was too bright at first and it stung her eyes, but something urged her to keep trying. It was the most taxing thing she'd done in a long time. Blinking, heavy eyelids, weight pushing down on her. She pushed back, through the fatigue, through the pain.

What's wrong with my face? Francesca lifted her right arm and fingered a plastic tube. Her heart started to kick against her chest, the pain came roaring back, and with it the accident. The crashing sound, Danny...Ava!

"I'm here." A gentle hand against her cheek. Francesca took one exhausted blink and brought Dr. Sarkozy's face into focus. Dark eyes, lines on his forehead, fierce energy banked in the set of his brow, in his sharp jawline. But warmth from his touch soothed her broken body. "Can you hear me?"

Francesca blinked and tried to nod. She fumbled to put her hand on his, holding his steady warmth to her cheek. It did more to ease her pain and worry than any medicine dripping into her veins.

"You're in the hospital. You had surgery to set your broken left arm and repair a small tear in your left lung. We fixed it. You're going to heal nicely. You have two broken ribs, a head wound, and a concussion." His fingers brushed gently across her forehead. "We're going to take the tube out now, okay?"

She gave his hand a light squeeze. Two nurses were there, moving around, speaking quietly. She didn't know when they'd arrived...couldn't remember. She concentrated on the cadence of Niko's deep steady voice as it issued quiet orders. His hand rested on her shoulder, and he kept Francesca's gaze. He peeled the tape away. "I need you to take a deep breath. Ready?"

Holding onto his strength as her own, Francesca drew air in and began to count the seconds.

"Good, now exhale, cough it out for me, love."

Bitter slicing burning sensations laced her throat as she coughed and breathed on her own. *Fuck, that hurt.* Niko studied her, which might have been unnerving if she hadn't just been run over by a truck, literally. But with all her defenses down, it calmed her, centered her. It reached inside and grabbed ahold of something precious. Thoughts swished in and out of her head, one big blurry watercolor mess on paper, bashed around by the trauma. *Oh God.* "Kids..." The word was a thrashing of sharp pain against her throat. She squeezed Niko's hand harder.

"They're here." He nodded toward the corner and Francesca saw two sleeping bodies on the loveseats, bundled up under blankets. "They were unharmed except for a few cuts and scratches."

When she blinked this time, warm tears fell, blurring the room. "Niko..." How could she ever express the kind of gratitude it would take for watching over Danny and Ava? If anything happened to them, she'd...she'd...

"I've got you." His voice was harsh, commanding. "All three of you. You're safe now."

Francesca was confused, but she clung to his words and the way his hand wrapped around hers and she believed him. It was the only thing keeping her from shattering into a million pieces. Studying his face, that hollow, empty feeling she'd always tucked deep inside herself seemed to fill up with...wonder.

"Can you hear my thoughts?"

His voice was clear, a beautiful cadence to the current mess in her mind. Wonder blossomed into color and she nodded. *"Yes."*

"Do you remember what happened?" Gentle but firm, he asked her.

"Someone hit us...followed us, something evil, Niko."

Emotions whirled through him. They tangled with long-ago memories. Underneath all his rage, and anger, was a feeling he'd almost forgotten. Love.

"We can talk about everything later when you're feeling better." Her blood pressure began to escalate and that was the last thing she needed. He shouldn't have pushed, should have waited for her to recover. Niko gripped tightly to his calm voice lest his fury scare her. She'd had enough frightening experiences for one night. Trying to stop the shaking in his hand, Niko carefully wiped her tears away, memorizing the vulnerability in her eyes.

He knew her skin would be soft, softer than anything he'd touched in his seven-hundred-year lifetime, as man or vampire. Even her tears were beautiful, although he was an inferno of anger that she had to shed them, *love and magic* be damned. He wanted to bury his head in her neck, hug her to him, and demand every fucking detail of the accident. Who dared target her? But she needed the calm doctor, not the raging vampire. "The nurses are going to get you some water and raise you to sitting. Can do that for me?"

She nodded again, a stain of exhaustion and worry on her face that pierced his soul She'd been hurt—his entire world tilted—and...and thank Christ he'd been at the hospital when they'd brought her in.

"I need to know." Her voice was raw and thready. "How long...what day...Please, tell me."

"You were brought in this afternoon around five-thirty. Surgery went well. It's midnight now." Niko wasn't one for words or long soliloquies, but he'd talk to her forever if she'd set her beautiful eyes on him. And as tired as she was, her touch and the stark worry in her expression compelled him to do as she asked. He didn't mention the fact that she still held his hand. And he certainly wasn't going to be the one to pull away, not when for the first time in his existence, he felt true warmth. If she needed comfort, he'd give it to her. He'd give her everything. "Ava doesn't have a scratch on her. Unless you count the imaginary ones on her arms. The nurses pulled out the big guns, the unicorn Band-Aids."

Francesca's smile was lopsided and weak, but to Niko it was the most beautiful smile he'd seen. "Danny has a few cuts on his hands. Smart nephew you have there. He knew getting help was important. He found your phone and called 911. Very brave, if you ask me."

"He is." She went to wipe her tears with her casted arm and let out a curse. "Good Christ that hurts." She slumped her head back against the pillow. "I wonder how long it will take my brain to realize my arm is not only broken but weighted down with a cast from hell."

"It's time for more painkillers. We can finish talking later."

"Not yet, please." She shook her head again and swallowed. "More water." He filled her glass and helped her drink, anguish seeping out of her. A visible thing he could see and feel right to his bones. "Someone was following us. A large truck. It was dark blue or black. Hard to tell in the fog and rain. It shoved us off."

He wanted to tell her what he'd discovered, but explaining might be beyond the realm of what she could understand. The hollow feeling reemerged that they would never truly know each other.

"I have never been so scared in my life." She'd closed her eyes again, her voice drifting in and out. The dark circles around her eyes were stark against her pale skin. He could feel her pulse stronger at her wounds. "Who would want to hurt...I can't make sense of..."

"Shh." Niko placed his hand on her shoulder and silently pushed some of his intentions into her. *"It's time to sleep now."*

"Okay." She gently patted his hand before she slipped under. And Niko didn't know whether to be relieved she'd listened, or curious to the fact that they could read each other's thoughts.

And as far as who had calmed who with their touch, he couldn't tell. His hand burned like starlight where hers rested on it. Over the centuries, he'd taken to banishing his memories, especially the happy ones, because they were a lance to his soul. But this moment, right here, he was going to cherish forever.

CHAPTER TEN

"WHAT'S HAPPENING?" SHE'D BEEN in the hospital for just under a week and suddenly she was going home. Francesca had no control over the situation. In fact, she had no idea what the situation even was. This afternoon after she'd spoken to the police again about the accident, Niko had stalked into her hospital room, manhandled her chart, and signed Francesca out in all his pissed-off glory. No hospital scrubs for him tonight. Instead, he was dressed in all black. Midnight winter jacket over a black dress shirt, black jeans that fit his glorious thighs all the way down to black running shoes. *Dark avenging angel. See.*

The only hint of life came from his eyes, intensely focused on her, as they'd been every time he'd visited her hospital room. She couldn't remember him ever looking at her like that. *Whew!* She needed to fan the heat away lest his dark silver sparks light her on fire, literally. Fanning was a tad bit difficult to do with one arm in a cast and the other holding her sore ribs as she drew her legs to the side of the bed.

So she settled for interrogation. She liked interrogating him. It was one of her favorite things to do. "Why are you here? Why are you signing me out?" *Why are the kids gazing at you as if you hung the moon?* Not that Ava and Danny weren't great judges of character. Niko was a good man, even though he pretended at being that arrogant jackass. But how did Ava and Danny know? They had spoken about him an awful lot the last few days. "Dr. Niko is so smart." And "Dr. Niko knows everything. Dr Niko this and Dr. Niko that."

"I told you." He came to her side to help her into the wheel-chair. "You're all safe with me."

What did that even mean? Before she could ask, he'd summoned the kids to his side and begun wheeling her out. She did vehemently want to get out of the hospital, but was it too soon? The days were fuzzy. Any other patient with broken ribs and a punctured lung would still be in the hospital. Even though she healed much faster than regular people. Oh goodness, her mind was mush. She wanted her control back. She ached to get out, to breathe, to get her herbs, create something delicious in the kitchen. She was desperate to know what was going on.

The busy hospital buzzed around them.

"Oh shoot."

"What's wrong?" Niko's voice came to her silently.

"Incoming, Dr. Blythe."

"Aunt Frankie," Danny whispered.

"What?" She tilted her head to study Danny, but she was slow to do everything right now, including getting them out of this situation. And the cologne Dr. Blythe wore churned her empty stomach into a roiling wave. She caught Dr. Madison's glare from a few feet away as well.

"Ahh, Frances, it appears you're doing much better." Dr. Blythe issued that nickname he sometimes used. For some reason today it niggled under her skin. He stood towering over her now that she sat in a wheelchair. She made to stand, something in her needing her height, the extra inches she had on the fool. But Niko's hand pushed her back down. Warmth and calm flooded her system from Niko's touch, and she let him direct her, feeling sluggish after her ordeal and all the medicine she'd been on.

"Dr. Blythe, you're in our way," Niko said.

"Yes, you should get out of their way," Dr. Madison said in a nasty tone as she swept by them. "Look at how weak she is."

Francesca's head pounded. Was everyone determined to get on her last nerve? Dr. Madison's aura was caustic, and Francesca had no energy to try to urge balance into her life today. Could they just get out of here?

"Frances is going to be just fine," Dr. Blythe said. "She's our girl, isn't she?"

"She's Dr. Banetti to you. Don't ever call her Frances or for that matter, anything again without her permission. And she's not ever going to be your girl." Niko maneuvered the chair around the man and into the waiting elevator. Holding Ava's hand, Danny stood inside waiting for them, and at once the doors closed, leaving Dr. Blythe sputtering in the hallway.

"Wow," Francesca whispered. "I should be annoyed. He is my friend after all—"

"He's not your friend." Niko insisted. "He paws all over you like he owns you."

"I beg your pardon." The man sure knew how to ruffle her feathers. The way he glared down at her was fierce enough to have most people backing away. but that... *"Oh, you're jealous."*

"Hardly. The man's a disrespectful idiot."

"Hmm." She wasn't going to admit Niko was correct. She was enjoying this too much. And her banged-up body could use all the fun it could get right now.

"Careful, I might think you care, Dr. Sarkozy," she said quietly.

"Niko," he answered. "Call me Niko. All of you." It came out as an order, but underneath, Francesca read it for what it was, a plea. *"How interesting. How very, very interesting."*

"I'm not interesting."

"Ha. I'm going to have to watch my thoughts if you keep reading them."

"I'm sorry," he said out loud. "That was rude. I beg your forgiveness."

"We like calling you Niko. That wasn't rude," Ava said. "That was direct and to the point. Niko, are you taking us to Auntie Frankie's? Are you staying with us? She only has one guest room and that's where Danny and I sleep. And her place is very small. There's not even any backyard, but she bakes the bestest cookies."

"No," he said. *Brusque as ever. Arrogan*—Francesca reined in her thoughts. She had to admit, her soul sank a little at the thought that he wouldn't be staying with them, but her apartment was tiny. Too cramped for his aura, that was for sure.

"Now, I'm going to require your help to care for your aunt. She's going to be very tired and sore. We must do all we can to make things comfortable for her."

Around her, the children's voices mixed with Niko's as he led them all out of the hospital. Although she was healing quickly, she still felt fuzzy. As much energy as she could put into healing herself also depleted her. She was exhausted. Thoughts and questions warred in her mind, and she'd detected that awful scent again for a moment, the one full of evil. Then it was gone. Most likely a bit of remembered trauma.

A large deep-green Range Rover was parked at the entrance. Rich, her favorite EMT, was there opening her door for her. "Dr. B," he said and gave her a nod. Before she could even think how she was going to climb into the monster car, Niko was crouched down, leaning into her.

"I'm sorry for hurting you," he whispered so low she barely caught it, right before he lifted her and carefully set her in the passenger seat, softly dragging her seatbelt across her chest. The sharp stab of pain in her ribs stole her breath, but it was his words, his nearness, his care that had it whooshing back in. When he closed the door and stepped around to his side, she took the moment to steady her pulse, but the confines of the car forced the memory upon her, the night, the fog, the fear, the pain.

"My car..." The whisper escaped before she could strangle it back in. Her old car. It was the first purchase she'd made all on her own at the used car lot in Columbus all those years ago. It was big and ugly in that faded green that had become more of an overripe avocado over the years. But damn, she loved it because it was stupidly huge. She loved the bucket seats. She loved driving her niece and nephew in that thing. *Shit shit shit.*

"Hey." Niko's voice was there in her space. "What's going on?"

"I...I..." She flicked at the tears streaming down her face. She choked on the memories as they flooded her, crashing over the guardrail, diving down, the screeching, the blackness, the silence, Danny screaming into the phone. Her car. *My fucking car. Who gives a damn!* The kids. She'd almost gotten them killed.

"Breathe." He wrapped his hands around her face, cradling her gently but firmly, demanding eye contact. "Look at me. We're all safe now. You're safe. The kids are fine." That familiar warmth seeped in and swept away her fears. She focused on him. "I won't let anything happen to you."

"Aunt Frankie?" Danny's voice, so small, so concerned. He reached in from the back and put his hand on her shoulder.

"Everyone's okay now," Niko demanded again, and she almost laughed at the absurdity of him demanding that everyone *be okay*. But her hands shook, and her stomach churned so she held on and let Niko's fierce gray eyes steady her.

She gave Danny's hand a squeeze. "I'm good, a bit over-whelmed. I love you guys."

"Yeah," Danny said. "All right."

"I love us too!" Ava said, breaking the tension.

For a moment, Niko held Francesca with his hands, with his gaze, with this link between them she decided she wasn't going to question. She was just going to go with it.

"Okay?" He gently brushed the tears off her cheeks. A phantom feeling of déjà vu ... He'd done this before, sent his thoughts to her. Wanting desperately to believe, Francesca leaned into it.

"Yes, " she answered.

***

She was surprised to find she'd fallen asleep in the car. Apparently, a serious accident, followed by a panic attack, followed by Nikolav freaking Sarkozy holding her and communicating silently to her was enough to shove her into sleep. *Wow.* "What? Where?" She turned to face Niko as he unbuckled and got out of the car.

"We're at Niko's house, Aunt Frankie," Danny said. "We've been staying here." The rain had infused the setting with rich color. A wide green lawn rolled out to infinity toward a beautiful forest. In front of her, beside a curved gravel drive stood a massive gray stone house with small extensions stretching to each side. Behind the house and to the south stood a stalwart evergreen forest with a stream. She couldn't see the water, but its low soft trickle sang to her bones. A shingled charcoal slate roof covered the house, smoke spiraled from two of the many chimneys, and the word that hit Francesca's chest was cozy. They were safe here, and more. Only Francesca wasn't sure what the *more* was. Exhaustion and curiosity battled for control. So, this was what he'd meant when he'd simply answered *"No,"* that he wouldn't be coming to her home with them.

Ava quickly jumped out as soon as Niko unbuckled her car seat, but Danny sat still, waiting for Francesca, always cautious. "He wants to help us take care of you here at his house."

"We have everything you could need here. I had to get you all out of the hospital. Safer here."

"Sweet man."

"I'm not." Niko opened her door. *"I'm efficient. You require help. I can help you."*

"I have a staff," he said aloud. "Danny, there's Booth and Marie. I'll bet she has dinner waiting for us. Perhaps an episode of *British Baking* after? Hurry now so I can help your aunt get inside and out of the rain." Would it ever cease? This relentless wet winter, the dark gray clouds. She missed the sunshine so much it hurt. One more ache to add to her battle-worn body.

He stood there getting wet, waiting for her. "Go, I can get in by myself."

"You can barely walk. Just because you've been released does not mean you're capable of taking care of yourself and two children with your injuries."

"You have no idea what I'm capable of, Niko." Annoyance and exhaustion had her snapping. She glanced up in time to witness him let down that impenetrable guard he kept over his expression. For a split second his eyes were no longer calm. They were molten. He raised one eyebrow. Was that a challenge? And there was the smallest ghost of a smile. *Huh?* The air heated between them, his face a whisper from hers. How she ached to trace the lines of his cheekbones, his lush lips, sink her teeth into those lips. Eyes like flowing silver, hooded and desiring, flicked at her. *Oh my.*

He took a very deep breath, as if warring with himself, undid her seatbelt and placed his arms under her and around her to lift her again, all while she was drooling over the burning lust in his eyes. How could she be lit up from one glance? And in the condition she was in, bruised and battered? But there was no denying it. She desired him, wanted him to do whatever wicked things those silver flames promised.

Encouraged, inhibitions gone, Francesca moved her face closer to his. Caught by the way the rain smelled against his skin, fresh, mysterious... And then like a window slamming down, his smile turned serious, and he closed his expression away, every bit, even his eyes which had nearly branded her inside and out.

"I...*what?*" She reached out to touch his face, stoic and cold now.

"Don't," he warned and closed his eyes.

Mortification washed over her. He still held her, the warmth an empty taunt now and she felt like a floozy. He'd never be attracted to her. Carefully, with a slow, unsteady blink, she barred her mind. Practice had made her very proficient at this maneuver.

"I can walk. It's my arm, not my leg, that's broken." She tried to shove his hands away, but they tightened.

"Please." His tone was deep as he battled with himself to get the words out. "Let me do this." Penance was the word that slid through her then. Something wasn't right. And she would be no man's burden.

She gave a quick nod. Better to get this over with. Then she could get on with her embarrassment and confusion by herself. He didn't linger. He carefully gripped her to him, kicked the door shut, and carried her into the house as if she weighed a feather. Francesca did her damnedest not to study him.

"Don't hide yourself from me." He paused in the narrow entryway now shielded from the rain and the sky. Dark and quiet, her senses were heightened. His home smelled moody and delicious, the same as the man holding her. It was impossible to block it out.

She froze then as he leaned in and softly dragged his nose up her cheek. "What is happening?" she whispered. She let out a puff of air, wanted to sink her body into his. Talk about whiplash.

"Don't."

Don't what? He was as confusing as the rain was consistent. Before she could gain any sense of balance, he settled her on a large leather sofa in what she could only describe as a drawing room. *How silly.* Hysterical giggles threatened to burst forth. A drawing room? Where had that idea come from? They were in a very typical English home, one that reminded her of cottages in Devon. This one was warm and secure, unlike the drafty ones she'd visited on her tour. She was made even warmer with the wool throw Niko tucked around her, still wearing that heavy scowl on his face.

"Don't do that." He pushed his thoughts into her.

"What?" She opened to him, unable to keep things from him or utterly stupid, perhaps both.

"Hide from me." He glanced at her, giving her one instant of truth, the burning silver flickering into ages of pain deeper than anything she could fathom. And then he fled the room.

"Oh, hello, my lovies," Ava clapped her hands to her cheeks as two ridiculously large bloodhounds ran into the room followed by a man and a woman. The dogs sniffed at Ava, one slathering her face with kisses and turning her surprise into giggles.

They meandered over to Francesca and gave her approving sniffs before they returned to Ava's caresses.

"Aren't they handsome?" Danny said.

"Lollie and Jupiter, quite friendly dogs," an enormous older man with gray hair said. "They enjoy having children around. I'm Booth. Whatever you need, don't hesitate to ask. I'm at your

service. Come on now, Danny and Ava, time to feed the pups."
Booth led the children and dogs out of the room.

"Francesca...my dear...you're so much li...your...I beg your
pardon." The strange woman who looked as if she'd seen a ghost
cleared her throat and continued. "I'm Marie. I'm so glad you're
here. Young Danny and Ava have been a delight. I'll finish the
soup and we can eat. Soup and bread, how does that sound?
Warm chocolate pudding for dessert. Sounded like something
the children would like." The woman smiled at Francesca as
if she was absolutely giddy to meet her and had no idea how
ridiculously Francesca's life had been turned upside down.

Well, her life certainly had never been simple, that was for
sure. She lay back against the soft cushions, careful not to jar
her ribs, and breathed. An attack on her family, near death,
couldn't get ahold of her sister, swept away to Nikolav Sarkozy's
house—mansion, whatever it was—in his arms, confusing messages from said man and any strength she'd had left drained out
of her. *Perhaps we can go right to dessert.*

CHAPTER ELEVEN

F RANCESCA CARRIED THE SMALL bowl carefully down the hallway. Marie had called it chocolate pudding, but to Francesca it appeared more like an individual gooey cake, still warm from the oven. *I definitely need to learn how to make this.* Dinner had been nourishing if a bit too healthy maybe with the vegetable soup and the extremely robust multi-grain bread. Francesca had never seen so many whole grains in one piece of bread before. But dessert was right up her alley.

She'd itched for a walk after dinner, despite her pain and fatigue. It always calmed her to know the blueprint of a place she was in. Not to mention, her curiosity was piqued by this beautiful old structure, renovated with many lovely modern conveniences. Niko's presence grew stronger as if she'd specifically sought him out and been led his way. They needed to discuss what was going on eventually. Sooner was better than later in her mind.

She turned into an open doorway. A library. *How wonderful.* It was another cozy room, with dark wood floors, built-in bookcases that reached the ceiling, a low leather sofa, and another fireplace. All that was missing was a large soft area rug for one's bare feet. Of course, Niko probably never dared go barefoot. It was beneath him.

It was the perfect room to lounge in during these endless winter days. And...*roses?* How in the heck had Nikolav Sarkozy gotten a gorgeous bouquet of roses in February? She gently touched the petals and brought her fingers to her nose. *Lovely.* Maybe she could request a few things from her place if they were going to be here long. Her skin would be a hot mess if she went too long without her rose cream.

His back was to her, and she swore his muscles tensed as he became aware of her presence. *Mm, wonder what those fabulous muscles would feel like... Nope, not going there right now.* Not when he was so obviously avoiding her. Confusing man. He'd plopped her on the couch after insisting on carrying her, demanding she not hide from him, and...and that caress of his nose along her cheek. Whew, she'd nearly panted after him.

"You missed dinner." Which had been, if not decadent, at least nourishing. Tonight, despite the turmoil in her emotions and the frank confusion, and *everything*, she'd been starving. Francesca couldn't remember the last time someone had cooked for her. She could take a lesson or two from Marie, strange woman that she was, staring at Francesca the entire meal, or rather pretending she wasn't staring.

Niko faced her, wordless, shrouding his emotions. As afraid of his as she was certain of hers. There was a battle inside her. She didn't want to be anywhere she was detested, but ever since she'd set foot inside this house, something had eased inside her, settled warm in her soul. And at least for a few nights, she'd accept his kindness. The children were asleep, tucked into twin beds under soft blankets in an upstairs room with a lovely window seat and a soft nightlight. She did feel safer with Niko, after what had happened. She hated giving up control, but she trusted him. And her exhaustion weighed heavy in her bones.

"I don't want to stress you more, but we should talk about what happened. Whoever did this aimed to hurt you badly, Francesca. Do you know who it could be?"

So, straight to the point. Fine.

"I need every bit of information you have to solve this." He was so brusque.

"It isn't your problem to solve. I brought you one of Marie's puddings." Many difficult things could be eased with dessert.

He scowled at the offering. She had to bite back her laugh.

"Pudding doesn't answer my question, any of my questions."

"You have more than one?" She raised her eyebrow at him. He stood so far away in shadow by the tall, gorgeous window, clouds heavy in the sky behind him. She sat down slowly on the sofa, sucking in her wince of pain. Damn, her ribs hurt.

"Christ, Francesca. I'm sorry." He was at her side in an instant, gently fitting a pillow behind her back and another resting right behind her neck. She gave in and leaned her head back against the small soft one. Closing her eyes for a second, she took in the scent of this room. It was all Niko. She was surrounded by him. His deep lingering musky soap, all the earth elements, wood and stone, the leather, a hint of burning from the glowing fireplace, every single hint intoxicating.

When she opened her eyes, he was sitting on the coffee table in front of her, searching her face with that rare open expression on his. "You are healing. That is your goal right now. I will take care of everything else for you."

She ignored his orders. "If you're not going to eat it, I guess I'll take one for the team," she said, licking one more luscious bite of the warm dark chocolate off the spoon.

His eyes heated before her. "This isn't a game, Francesca." Snagging the pudding from her, he discarded it onto the table beside him.

Why did his scolding feel so horrible as it sliced across her skin?

"Someone tried to kill you. You're still in intense pain and you need rest."

Oh, oh. He's upset for me.

"Yes, I'm furious."

She let out her breath and with it any joy in chocolate puddings. And most likely with what she had to say, she was going to piss him off further. "They weren't after me." She spoke quietly, maintaining eye contact, watching for any hint of emotion other than anger that he might be willing to give her. "They were..." It hurt to speak this truth. "They were after the children." It came out in a strangled whisper. There was the real problem and why she'd let him bring them here at all. When it came to her niece and nephew, she absolutely was not playing games. Despite her stubborn habit of taking care of things on her own, she could use all the help she could get right now. That had been made clear when the car had careened down the side of a mountain.

"What?" He said. It was practically a hiss of rage. It matched her emotions. Only she'd had more time to process. Also, being exhausted and in pain dampened her temper a bit.

"Tell me what's going on so I can protect all of you. Why is someone after them? Where is your sister? Why haven't we been able to get ahold of her."

Protect? She and her sister had been the protectors since they were children, protecting each other, protecting Danny and Ava. Warmth bloomed inside her at knowing they had someone else on their side. Because the truth was difficult to swallow. That this time she'd been unable to keep those precious children safe.

"I don't know who it was," she admitted. "And my sister...well, she's working..." What exactly did she divulge to Niko?

"Working?" he scoffed. "Leaving her kids to nearly get killed, almost getting *you* killed."

Oh, this man. His pain seared deep and powerful. It bled through his eyes. Perhaps there was guilt buried too. She wanted to uncover all his secrets. No one held tightly to that much emotion for a person they didn't care about. And he was all kinds of pent-up.

"She's an..." *What do I tell him?*

"Everything. You tell me everything." He inched closer. She continued her study, calculating each tiny pinprick of emotion he allowed her to see.

He was all blustery insistence. Not that she didn't find some bit of pleasure in his tone. And perhaps that was a bit screwed up of her, but she couldn't help but wonder how demanding he'd be in bed. *Focus, girl.*

"Please, Francesca."

He could be kind too, even if it seemed to go against every fiber of his being. That made it even more lovely.

"It hurt you. Whatever it was could've hurt those children. I see how much you love them, and they you."

It hurt you. Yes, she'd also sensed it was an it rather than a who. That he thought the same only made her more certain to put her trust in him.

Francesca rested her head in her good hand. Her other one lay exhausted against her body. He was right and it scared the hell out of her. The only reason she'd been able to tamp down her fear in the hospital was because the kids were safe and fine right there with her and Niko. Niko. He was so many things. Safety hadn't been something she'd thought of with him, but since he'd held her hand when they'd rushed to the operating room, ease and warmth and protection had woven from him into her. More than that, a recognition of souls. Or perhaps that was simply her belief in dreams. There was magic inside him too. It was a connection that even now with confusion coiling around them, she sensed would never be broken.

"Three years ago, my sister's husband, Doug, was brutally murdered in their home. The kids and Gianna were visiting me. Before that..." God, how her sister had changed. A part of Francesca's heart was irrevocably broken, knowing what Doug's death had turned her sister into. After all she and her sister had already been through. Grief and anger throbbed in Francesca's gut. Grief upon grief. As if they were destined for it.

Niko was the kind of man who could take the truth and deal with it. "Before that, my sister was...well she'd finally found someone to love her. She had a family, stayed home, and baked bread, not very good bread, but she loved doing it. She took the kids to story time and taught them art. She'd found a real home. She'd dreamed of being a wife and mother and she finally had everything. Then someone, or some *thing*..." Her voice broke. "Something vicious took it all away."

"Jesus." He clasped her good hand in his, sending that delicious heat through her.

She wondered if he was even aware he'd touched her. "We don't know why. And so she...she's...you have to promise me you'll listen, please, and keep our secrets."

"Whatever you have to tell me is safe here, Francesca. You have my word."

He stroked his thumb carefully over her knuckles, a featherlight caress, and it burned through her. When she looked up, she saw the truth in his eyes. He would hold anything she told him. A small sigh escaped her. How long had she been keeping everything locked inside? Afraid to trust another?

"She's an assassin, a mercenary killer bent on revenge. Doug didn't leave her with much money. She stumbled upon something having to do with his murder and she became a killer for hire. She only takes jobs where the person she's hired to kill is extremely evil. She also uses her computer and math skills to find connections to those that killed her husband. Sometimes her in-laws watch the kids, and sometimes I do when she's gone. When she's on a job, it can be impossible to locate or contact her." *Oh shit.* Her brain really was foggy. "I do have a way that might work."

"I'm going with you." He stood up so abruptly she felt the loss of his touch like a wound.

"It's not..."

"Francesca." Her mind told her to be annoyed at his demands, but boy did her body respond to that gravelly caress of his.

"It's not what you think. I can... We, she and I can share dreams." Niko stared back at her with an expression she couldn't read. "I haven't dreamed since the accident. I think the anesthesia and pain meds affected my ability."

"Well, then you should try to sleep tonight so you can find her as quickly as possible."

Efficient as ever, she noticed. The sting that came with that command hurt, the way he dismissed her. He was so damn good at dismissal.

He'd put himself at the window again, far away from her, facing the sky, dismissing her with his body too, gravelly voice be damned. Well, fine. She didn't need someone ordering her around, especially not some infernal, exasperating domineering male. She stood, swiped up the small bowl of pudding, and swallowed another bite. The joy in it was gone now too. Double damn. But she wouldn't let him see it. She gave in to the pleasure and let out a small moan at the dark sinful chocolate. Niko placed his hands on the glass. Apparently, he couldn't wait to claw his way out of the room to escape her.

She made her way toward the door. Her frustration bubbled over. "Look, I know you don't want me here, interfering in your life." She tossed out the words with all the pride she could manage. "So—" In a flash, her back was up against the wall, Niko's hands pressing into either side of her head, his mouth so close to hers, the bowl of pudding thudding to the floor.

Whoa.

His intensity scared her, but not in the way that meant she was afraid of him, just how powerfully he controlled his tension. And how amazing that tension felt against her.

"I want you here," he whispered in a tortured voice.

"What's happening?" she whispered back. "I... Nikolav..." Her pulse beat everywhere. She sucked in a labored breath and with it his scent. It was like a drug to her, forbidden and mysterious.

"Christ, my name on your lips. Say it again." He rested his forehead gently against hers.

"Nikolav." Francesca wished to touch him.

"Don't ever say I don't want you. There isn't a word strong enough to describe how I feel about you. Ache for? Desire? I crave you so much it hurts. I've been burning for you since the first time I saw you." Niko dragged his nose across her cheek, down her neck, and back up. She'd blame it on exhaustion, but her head dipped to the side giving him more room. "My God, you're exquisite." No one had ever called Francesca such a precious word in her life. "Why do you always smell of roses? Do you bathe in them? I want every fucking *inch* of you."

The words were bold and dangerous, swirling around her, inside her. He moved into her, pressing his body slightly against hers and she felt every decadent hard inch of him.

"Then why..." Her words were a shaky mess. Words whispered in the dark, the two of them so close, his lips a breath away from her neck, her pulse fluttering toward him. "Why do you push me away?" She wasn't brave enough to say the rest out loud. "*When what I wish is for you to touch me everywhere. To have your hands, your mouth, your teeth worshiping me.*"

It was like she struck him with a lit flame how fast he shoved himself off. They stood feet apart, the air charged and heavy with lust, a storm about to ravage the land, thunder and lightning fighting a pulsing dance in the sky, a push and pull. Her skin was electrified with anticipation, her breasts heavy with need, her core desperate and aching where his hard length had throbbed against her. All that from a whisper-quick meeting of their bodies. How fabulous it would be to do this dance naked. And she had no doubt it would be a dance.

"Nikolav," she pleaded.

His eyes burned that glorious flowing silver combined with something else. As if he was being tortured, glimpses of trauma and regret flashed in his eyes. "I...I'm no man for you. I can't have you, Francesca. I can never have you."

Before she could blink, he was gone, disappeared in a flash of pain, leaving her standing alone in a dark library, her heart threatening to burst from her chest. *He's afraid.* The powerful, magnificent Nikolav Sarkozy was afraid, and she didn't have a clue why.

Chapter Twelve

THE HOSPITAL WAS AN annoying mess of gnats without Francesca there. Niko prowled through his surgeries and rounds, ignoring people or swatting them out of his way. As he had for the past four days. He'd only been home in the middle of the night each night to check on everyone and watch Francesca sleep. During the day he trusted Booth and Marie with her care, along with the protections he'd placed around his home and the additional ones around the children's school, which he'd strengthened the morning after Francesca had explained about them being in danger.

He stood in the waiting area of the emergency department. It was six in the evening; he'd been finished for an hour. *You're a fool.* He'd taken to visiting the ED all week, as if he could conjure Francesa up, magic her back to work where she belonged. She should never have been injured. The rage still burned beneath his skin. He couldn't bear to be in the same house as her, couldn't bear not to be. Today he had hours to waste before he should return home, but that only left more space for him to dream of her.

"Uh, Dr. Sarkozy?"

Rich's girlfriend, Kara, lingered in the sunlight in one of the ambulance bays. A crisp and cold day, the sun nipped at the winter melancholy. Taking a tentative step forward, a bag in her hand, she spoke. "I uh...I made this for Dr. Banetti, um, Francesca. She...asked me to call her that, if that's okay with you?"

Niko studied the young woman and nodded, trying to relax his stance. "Certainly. You and Francesca are friends."

She smiled and it was as if the sun came directly from her. For a moment a memory pulled at him of his three sisters, how they liked to dance in the mornings, especially after the rain. Rays bouncing off them, twirling with them as if the sun and his sisters were happiness and joy entwined. How they loved life, how they laughed. Until everything was snuffed out of them. All because of him.

Nico envied this young woman her sunlight, her warmth, and her belief in goodness, even after what had happened to her. Mostly he envied her something he hadn't believed in for centuries, her hope.

"Would you like to come into the hospital, out of the cold?"

Her smile fell and she shook her head. "I don't..." She glanced inside. A quick expression of fear or something awful passed over her face. "I don't...come in without Rich. I'm waiting for him. I'd rather stay right here where...um...in the sun." Whatever pain had sliced into her at the thought of coming in, she'd buried again and put that happy smile back on her face. Perhaps the hospital reminded her of when she was attacked and kidnapped. PTSD could be a powerful wound of its own.

"This is fine. You seem more comfortable here." Comfortable wasn't exactly the word he would use but something about this spot where they stood was enough to allow her the ability to talk to him, and he didn't want to upset her.

"You don't have to tell me if it's too intrusive," Kara began, "but is Francesca healing?"

"She's getting better every day." He could sense her strength returning rapidly. With a witch's powers to heal, there was no telling how quickly she'd be good as new, at least physically. No telling how long the emotional and psychological toll would last either. Kara would understand that. "I'm sure she'll be back to work soon." Was that what he wanted? He didn't know if that would be a good thing or a dangerous thing, to have her walking beside him again, working with him, smiling at him, teasing him.

Fuck! So much of his control around her had slipped since the accident, since he'd touched her, since she'd trusted him with herself and her family. No one had trusted Niko in a very long time. And the link stretching between them only grew stronger. He'd practically mauled her in the library the other night, intent on making her understand how much he did in fact want her. *Idiot.*

"Can you tell her I'm thinking about her? We all are." Kara peeked into the bag and handed it to him. "I thought she might enjoy a soft shawl to keep her warm and cozy. I made it for her. It's pink. She loves pink."

Damn. Every little morsel he learned about Francesca came from someone else. What he wouldn't give to have it come from her. Only, he had nothing left to sacrifice for her. The one who would have to sacrifice would be Francesca. And he would never allow that to happen.

"Thank you, Kara. I'll give it to her this evening." He tucked the present under his arms and turned away. It was time to get the hell out of the hospital. Sulking was doing him no good. A young woman with masses of trauma to live through had just taught him that.

After changing back into his regular clothes, Niko stored the gift in his passenger seat, climbed into his Range Rover, and stole through the streets to Francesca's home, anxious to get there. He could move faster by tracing, but he needed his SUV. After parking in her driveway, he stood outside scenting the neighborhood. It was a crystal-clear night full of stars. Pine and wet dirt infused the air from all the rain they'd had. As he moved closer to her apartment, he froze, detecting that same hideous scent of rage and madness he'd sensed at her accident. But there was something else here too, a raw elemental being. *Canine.* Niko followed the scent. It seemed to be keeping the evil scent at bay. Powerful, large canine. *Werewolf. What the fuck?*

A thick film of jealousy covered his vision. He had to drag his mind back merely to keep from burning his own scent into the ground. Except, unlike demon and werewolf, he had no mark to leave, not on land at least. As he moved into her apartment, it was her scent everywhere again, that deep aroma of roses and herbs. It swamped him with lust, but he preferred that kind of torture to jealousy and rage. No sense of evil or canine inside. Thank fuck.

It was a mediocre home, with a few unique pieces of furniture and antiques, plush rugs everywhere, and a minuscule but tidy kitchen with two plants in the window and a miniature lemon tree in the light of the balcony. Niko inspected everything carefully. Opening the door to the tiny balcony, he found an even tinier counter with pots and garden tools. *She must be waiting for spring.*

The place was clean and comfortable, but small. Too fucking small and boring for Francesca Banetti. Why the hell was she living here in a plain beige box of an apartment with no yard, hardly a kitchen at all for all the cooking and baking she did? And why the hell was she living alone? Where were her people, her friends, her lover?

He dragged his hands through his hair. He couldn't handle the thought of her having lovers. He wanted her all for himself for eternity. But his job was to keep her safe and protected until he solved the mystery of her attack. Danny had left him a note, sneaky child, suggesting his aunt might feel more comfortable with more of her things. Nico had had Booth grab a few things from her place last week, as well as the kids' bags, but he hadn't been thinking clearly of anything besides getting her well enough to leave the hospital.

Ridiculous that Niko had required a child's instructions, but the boy was correct. Niko found a suitcase in her bedroom closet and, tuning out all thoughts of Francesca in bed, he filled the suitcase with items he thought she'd like. He was struck dumb in her bathroom. It was old and could have been boring, but she'd hung a gauzy light pink shower curtain and another soft fluffy rug that would probably feel nice on one's feet. Nico rubbed his eyes. Since when did he give a fuck about comfort?

A small counter surrounded the sink, littered with glass bottles in all shapes and sizes. He lifted the top off one to find a thick rich lotion inside, and desire overwhelmed him. It was her, garden roses and musk, sensual and lovely. Niko fingered the jar. There was no label. *She makes it herself.* He found a small bag and gathered all her bathroom essentials. *She may have made this place comfortable for herself, but she is never coming back here. Not if I can help it.* He didn't spare a second questioning his delusions.

After he'd packed her clothes into the car, he returned inside. There was a small, delicate hand-painted blue cabinet in the living room with crystal glasses of all shapes and sizes. This woman was a mystery. Special antiques in a plain beige living space. Everywhere she could, she'd filled her home with beauty, with meaning, with intimate stories. He fingered the antique coupe glasses in a pale shade of dusty rose. He carefully packed them in a box with some towels so they wouldn't break, grabbed her lemon tree and the pretty glasses, and set them in the back of his car with her clothes.

Fuck it! Tracing back inside, he packed up the rest of her delicate bottles and glasses and took them and the cabinet with him as well. He'd come back for anything else she requested later. It was earlier than the other nights, and he risked encountering her awake, but Niko threw caution to the wind. His blood ached for her. Besides, he needed to know why in the hell there was a fucking werewolf marking her home.

CHAPTER THIRTEEN

A FTER WATCHING THE CHILDREN drift off to sleep, Francesca made her way downstairs to the kitchen for an evening cup of tea. Each morning, since she'd been at Niko's she'd discovered sunlight streaming in through the large windows of this gorgeous corner room. A dream kitchen. A kitchen that he never used, as far as she could tell.

Her body was healing, not even a twinge of pain around her ribs anymore, which she knew was remarkable. In a normal human, that pain could take months to disappear. She'd spent hours sleeping, albeit, alone in his enormous, fabulous bed wishing he was in it with her. But it was more sleep than she could remember getting in the past ten years, at peace with the knowledge that the children were being taken care of and protected by Niko, Booth, and Marie. And the dogs, of course. That thought made her smile.

Each day after Booth brought the kids home from school, she sat in a lovely cushioned chair outside and watched Ava and

Danny frolic with the playful hounds. It was difficult to say who was happier, Francesca surrounded by nature and the almost hint of spring bursting up through the ground, or the children who loved dogs. Before dinner, they would take a slow walk toward the woods. It was invigorating to get a bit of exercise. And every second she spent in nature helped heal her.

Francesca should be ecstatic, grateful, at ease. But it had been four days since she'd seen Niko. He'd thrown those potent words at her in the library, then disappeared, leaving her alone and cranky. Well, not completely alone.

The past two nights she'd finally dreamed, hoping to locate her sister, but it was Niko who haunted her sleeping world, following her like a wraith, but never fully showing himself to her. She wasn't the least bit surprised to discover he could insert himself in her dreams too. The first night she'd tried to speak to him, but he'd vanished in the click of a heartbeat. The second evening, she allowed him to linger and watch her as she walked through a shimmering green forest under a blue sky dotted with white puffy clouds. She strolled along the edges of his land, recognizing it even though she hadn't yet covered it all in her waking life. His dogs followed too, keeping watch. But she was growing quickly tired of him avoiding her in the daylight.

"Did you get them to quiet down?" Marie was cleaning up the dinner dishes. Tonight, Francesca had cooked. And it had been lovely. Marie's meals had been a gift, but Francesca suspected the woman had never seen a pat of butter or cup of cream in her life. Francesca had gone with an old familiar recipe, her creamy tomato pasta with salad and garlic bread. She'd only had the strength to add a touch of extra, although she could feel her magic restoring alongside her health. Marie had only had to help her a bit. *I can't wait to get this damn cast off.* No matter how fast she healed, until this cast was removed, she wouldn't be one-hundred-percent.

One thing was certain, she drooled over Niko's kitchen. An enormous six-burner range sat against the back wall with a gorgeous emerald tile backsplash. White quartzite countertops stretched the length and flowed down the sides of an enormous island she couldn't wait to use for baking. The handmade cabinets were black, and the floor was the same rich hardwoods as the rest of the house. It might have been too dark of a kitchen if not for the acres of floor-to-ceiling corner windows letting the sunlight stream in.

"Yes, they were exhausted and happy. Such a good combination. I...I wish I could locate my sister. I'm getting worried, Marie."

"Sit and have some tea."

Francesca didn't need telling twice. "I feel like my healing has something to do with this tea you're making me."

"I wondered if you'd sense that," Marie said. She wiped her hands on her towel and turned the dishwasher on.

"I can taste the chamomile and echinacea, but there's something else I'm unfamiliar with."

"Mm," Marie said. "I'm happy to show you?"

"That would be lovely." *Are you like me?* Francesca was so close to asking, but admitting she was a witch to the wrong person had hurt her in the past. She was especially wary now with her and the children recently being attacked.

"I knew your mother. Bianca."

Francesca whipped her gaze up. "What?"

"She was from this area, up in the hills. Her family lived here for generations until they were driven out. Many of us were driven out. People are often afraid of those that are different."

Francesca nodded, shell-shocked by the revelation that this woman knew her family, knew *what* her family was. Years after her mother had been killed, Francesca had searched for any information she could regarding her ancestors. It was how she'd ended up working at Mercy Hospital. Even without much information, this land had a feeling about it. A good feeling, a right feeling. And Francesca had learned to listen closely to her instincts over the years. Sometimes they were all she had.

"She was born in that hospital. So was I, on the very same day." Marie smiled and fingered the leaves of a lemon balm plant she'd been trimming. Each snip sent a glorious citrus puff into the air. "We went to the same school and became fast friends, probably because we kept getting into trouble. Your mother was a powerful witch."

Francesca sucked in a breath. No one had spoken to her of such things since she was sixteen. Her mother was the last one to shortly before she was killed. That night came back to Francesca in a rush of feelings. Waking up to the screaming, feeling the weight of the world crushing down on their house, she and Gia running downstairs to find their mother dead, a man escaping through the broken front window like a ghost whisking away on the wind. The aching finality of it all, even though it was so difficult to believe, to accept. It was something Francesca worked hard never to relive. The slicing pain of old wounds punched her gut.

"She was brilliant," Marie's soft voice cut into her pain. "Even as a child, clairvoyant. She could read people's minds, no matter how they tried to block themselves, and most people don't have a clue how to block. I had a knack for seeing things happen before they actually happened. Neither one of us knew as girls how to control our powers or what to do with them, but let me tell you, we learned quickly."

"You...you're a witch?" Voicing the words out loud felt almost sinful, dangerous to Francesca.

"I am. As are you." Marie studied her.

"I...I haven't met very many." *Any besides my mom and Gia.*

"I suspect after what happened to Bianca that you and Gianna have kept everything to yourselves."

"How do you know so much about us?" Anger seeped in amid the pure shock. She and Gia had been worse than alone. And this woman, this kindred spirit had simply left them to it.

"I had a premonition the day your mother was killed. She'd moved away to Ohio, and we lost touch for a while. She didn't want to be a witch. It can be a heavy burden. By the time I made it to her, she was already dead and you'd been whisked away to foster care. I searched for months, started expanding my search to other states, but could never find you."

"We hid our powers," Francesca began. "We didn't know who to trust." As far as she was concerned, not much good had come from being a witch, let alone talking about it. Except for her ability to heal the human body, her fun experimenting with oils and lotions, and her insight into how food could heal and care for a person. But even those skills she had to dim or hide behind traditional jobs like becoming a doctor. She had limited knowledge when it came to plants, but she suspected she might have skill there as well. *My poor lemon tree is probably all twigs by now.* She'd have to ask Niko to get some things for her. She'd have to corner him and demand he talk to her first.

"It wasn't until Niko found me that I rediscovered you."

"We got sent to so many homes over the next two years before we ran away," Francesca whispered. "The last one wasn't good. None of them were. I got an old car, and we lived in it and finished high school. When I got accepted to college, I took Gia with me. We lived in a tiny cold apartment. Slowly things got easier. Gia met Doug. I started my residency. We put the past behind us. It was too painful to remember." Truths she'd never admitted to another soul. Being a witch didn't necessarily mean being able to wave a magic wand and instantly fix every-thing, especially for young, inexperienced, *alone* witches. And Gia hadn't even realized all of her powers yet before she tried to ignore them altogether for a while.

"I'm so sorry," Marie said.

Francesca allowed the warm mug to calm her as she rested it against her cheek. The realization that Marie may have used magic in her tea warmed her as much as the heat. Maybe Francesca wasn't alone in the world. So much had changed in a week. "Wait, what do you mean Niko found you? How? Why? What does that have to do with me, with Gianna?"

"As it happens, I wasn't only your mother's friend. I was her cousin. Which means—"

"We're family." Francesca smiled for the first time in weeks. Her instincts were fired up now. Everything was awake; she *was* healing, no more foggy brain. "And you..." She gestured to the tea. "You...I'm like you."

Marie smiled and nodded. "I suspect you're a powerful kitchen witch. My best strength is as a garden witch. Most of us have several abilities. Nikolav found me right after you were hurt. I was in California. After he told me what had happened, I packed my things and came here to Georgia. I waited to tell you until you were feeling a bit better, dear. I knew it might come as a shock."

"I..." Francesca didn't know what to say, let alone how to feel. She had a cousin, a witch no less, whom Niko had tracked down across the country, for her. "Why would he... It doesn't make any sense?" Her thoughts were on overdrive, trying to connect all the dots. Something else tickled at her senses. Powerful, flowing silver. Strength like the sun, but hidden, banked into a coil of tension, Blood and life and anger. Niko was close. *Good. I have a few things to talk to him about.*

Chapter Fourteen

E VERY BONE INSIDE HIM ached for her. Niko held himself
back from storming into the kitchen, wrapping her up
in his arms and tracing her away forever. How could he truly
protect her from this mortal life she led? Their mother had been
murdered. They'd escaped rotten foster homes and lived in a car,
in the winters of Ohio. How? How in the hell of all the demons
and angels had she and her sister survived?

"Well…" She turned on her stool to see him watching in the
doorway. "If it isn't the sneaky devil himself, actually showing
his face this evening."

Devil. She had no idea. And that saucy tone of hers made
him feel exactly that, sinful, on fire, like he'd burn in hell for
all eternity for one taste of her. Powerful, resilient, gorgeous
woman. He wanted to devour her as much as he wanted to
protect her. Hell, he should have stayed at the hospital. *I should
have gone farther than that. There is nowhere far enough.* He
never had a chance.

"You missed a delicious meal. Again. Come to think of it, you haven't eaten one single meal with us since we've been here."

The slight hint of hurt in her tone sobered him. Of course she would take offense at him not eating with her. She fed people as an act of love and much more than that, healing and caring for people with her food and tinctures.

"I apologize." If he kept everything formal, he could get in, say what he had to say, give her her stuff, and get out again.

"You apologize?" One of her eyebrows curved in that beautiful arch. He imagined tracing it with his fingers, his tongue. "For what exactly, Nikolav?"

Fucking hell, when she used his name in that raspy, fiery tone of hers, it made him come undone. "Marie, would you excuse us, please?" Niko said.

"While I'd love to stay and watch you two circle around each other, I'm afraid the sparks might singe me." Marie laughed. "Francesca, I'll be in my cottage if you want to chat later." She ducked out the back door. There was silence with a life of its own now, stretching and clawing and wrapping itself around them, a tightly wound band.

"You lost both your parents? I overheard." He could do this, small talk. Wasn't that what they called it?

"They both died a long time ago." Her voice was so soft, laced with the grief that comes with haunting old memories."

"That must have been very difficult, uh, lonely. Maybe sometime you'll tell me about that."

Her eyes narrowed. Her normal joyful spark was gone, or muffled. He was too slow to comprehend the situation, the state of her emotions. Keeping his own in check took every bit of energy he had.

"Why do you care?"

"What?" He was confused. Was he doing it wrong, communicating? She had him turned upside down in a million different directions.

"All this time, all these months working together, and I thought you didn't like me."

"Francesca." Her name was silk on his lips. There was a frayed thread, wearing thinner every moment between his base desires and keeping her safe.

"Acting all high and mighty, barely speaking to me, pretending you don't care, that you don't like me—"

"I don't *like* you." It was the truth. Like was too mundane a word for his feelings, but seeing her flinch pierced his cold heart and tumbled his emotions into a tailspin.

"Yes, your disappearing act this week made that clear. And yet..." she continued, trying to mask the shake in her voice. "You saved me and the children, found a relative on my mother's side, brought her here to help me. You're offering sympathy about my dead parents. So, you can't stand me, but you want to protect me? Or is it crave? You tossed that word out the other night in the library."

Niko paced the room's perimeter, keeping his distance behind the dinner table. It didn't matter. She was all he could see, all he could smell. He might as well have been a caged animal, feral to get to her. Afraid to speak, Niko answered with a nod, not even certain which of her questions he was answering.

"You gave up your bedroom for me, so you could what, sleep alone in a cold guest room? You entered my dreams." She gripped the back of the chair and tossed those words at him in challenge. "What is going on? Why are you doing this to me? I don't need some asshole with a savior complex who ignores me most of the time, then swoops in when he thinks he can save the day. I'm worth way more than that."

She absolutely fucking was. "Did you not hear me the other night in the library?" His words were practically a hiss. Her eyes flamed in question. Even now, when he might have hurt her with his words or his lack of, she still didn't back down. *Stunning woman.*

"Oh, I heard you all right, and I've heard the silence of your absence for the past few days. And now you come strolling in telling me you *don't like me*. What the hell is your problem? Why would you want me here?" She was a goddess when she was angry. "Which is it, you crave me, you want to protect me, or you don't like me?"

"All of them!" he yelled, tossing a chair aside. "Everything. I want everything with you. *Like*," he seethed. "Another pithy word, Francesca. It is worlds away from how I feel about you. How I've felt since..." Christ he was saying too much. Claws scampered down the hallway and his hounds burst into the room.

"Babies," Francesca cooed to them, and the dogs slid to a stop right at her feet, plopped their butts down, and waited for her touch like a benediction. Something violent surged up inside him at the memory of the scent surrounding her apartment.

"And I can't keep you safe if I don't know the truth, Francesca." Was he torturing himself by saying her name when he could never have her? Absolutely.

"What the hell is that supposed to mean, Nikolav?" A million times more potent hearing her name whispered between her sweet lips. "You're confusing, to say the least. For months you avoid me as much as possible at work, then you care for me more precious than a piece of gold. You want me but you can't have me. You track down my family, a witch no less, and bring her here to help me, a woman I didn't even know existed, but you did. You read my mind, but somehow *I'm* hiding something from *you*."

"The animal, specifically the canine who's marking around your home. Who is it?" he demanded, ignoring all her inquiries. No good could come from answering any of them.

"What?" she said, shock apparent in her eyes.

He stepped closer, drawn by the fire in her eyes, the flush on her cheeks, the way she dragged her fingers through his dogs' fur. "Jupiter, Lollie, come," he commanded. He couldn't think straight. The dogs ignored him. Jupiter tossed a look over his shoulder that might as well have said, "Are you kidding, jerk? We're staying right here by this wonderful creature."

"I was at your place, tonight. The same evil that surrounded your car accident was there on the ground, but a canine mark was there as well, inside the circle of evil, protecting you, your home. Who. Is. It?"

"I have no idea, Niko. With either scent. The last time I was home, neither of those were present, I can assure you." Confusion and fear splashed across her expression. "Had they...were they..." The fight drained out of her, and she sat on the stool, both dogs bending in to lean against her legs. "Inside? Had they gotten in?"

"No." Niko calmed his voice. Damn it, the last thing he intended to do was worry her more. "Whatever protection you'd placed held strong."

"Good." She sighed and rested her head in her hands. "Half the time I don't know what I'm doing." Her muffled words were so quiet he might not have heard them, except his heightened sense of hearing never failed him.

"Yes, you do."

"How do you know?"

"I can recognize a powerful spell. Extremely powerful."

When she raised her head and penetrated him with that gaze of hers, the one that threatened to break down all his walls, all his reasons for not touching her, it nearly shattered something inside him.

"You don't seem surprised by the fact that I'm someone who can cast spells."

"I'm not."

"Are we going to talk about that, or shove it into the ignore category with the rest of what's burning around us? You know what, never mind."

He wanted her to trust him completely, but perhaps he hadn't given her good enough reason, and that plagued him like a festering wound that refused to heal. She waited for his answer. Then before his eyes, she began shuttering her thoughts, and he nearly demanded she quit doing that again. He couldn't bear to be shut out.

"What were you doing at my place?" She sent a glare his way that should have incinerated him. "Is this what you've been up to while staying away from your own home, trying to solve my problem without informing me or asking me for my input? Christ!"

She stood abruptly and shoved her hands onto her hips, drawing his eyes there. Those should be his hands right there tugging her into him. "Why do men always think they know more?" She stalked toward him. His blood thrummed under his skin. The closer she got, the more it muddled his mind. All he could do was ache for her. All he wanted, all he ever wished was for her to make her way close enough to touch, even if it would damn them both.

"Are you going to answer me? Why were you at my home?"

He swallowed and motioned toward the open kitchen doorway. "I...uh..." He cleared his throat. "I brought some of your stuff. Most of it, I put in your room. That is from Kara."

"What?" she whispered. She was too close and not close enough in the narrow space between them. He had to grip his hands into fists to keep from reaching out and snagging her into his lair and never letting her go.

"Niko." The fight went out of her, but not the energy. It surged between them.

"I thought you might want more of your things." He rambled on, desperate to put the light back in her eyes. "It was Danny's idea. He left me a note this morning. And Kara was in the ED today. She ah...mentioned your comfort. I should have thought of your comfort. Forgive me. I'm sorry. I'm not very good at any of this."

Silence was something he was comfortable with, even preferred. But now a sense of vulnerability swamped him as she stayed quiet.

"This?" she finally whispered gesturing between them, giving him an opening.

How much weight a word could take on merely by the situation and the person whispering it. And all the unsaid things between them. He couldn't speak. His throat was tight, probably because his heart was stuck in it.

"Niko, please say something."

"I can't." The answer was ripped from his insides.

"Right." She shuttered her mind and eased toward the doorway. "This is all just temporary anyway, whatever it is. I won't bother you with nonsense anymore. And you, stay the hell out of my dreams."

CHAPTER FIFTEEN

WELL, DAMN HER FIERY temper. Francesca came to a halt in the library doorway. There, sitting diagonally in a corner by the window, looking as if it had belonged in this old home forever, was her small blue cabinet with the curved sides. The pale pink and yellow flowers painted across the doors glowed in the firelight. Atop sat her bottles, decanters, and some of her precious cocktail glasses.

She'd put her clothes away, cried a bit at the luscious, soft, knitted shawl Kara had made, then came back downstairs to apologize to Niko. He had his reasons, whatever the heck they were, why he couldn't have her, as he'd said. Keep her distance and make sure her emotions stayed hidden, or be patient—not her strong suit—and try to figure the man out. Those were her options. He had saved her...*their* lives. He was protecting them in his own home, which was apparently much safer than hers. She should be grateful. And she couldn't help it. Something deep inside her was drawn to him. Never on this Lady's Earth had she been drawn to another person in this way. She wanted to be surrounded by his power and feel hers grow with it.

She was either a masochist or an idiot or both to even try to figure him out. She hadn't lost her temper in her entire life, aside from that one time in foster care when the husband had his hands on Gia. *That* had been the worst and the last time. As a rule, she kept her negative reactions to at least below a boil.

Now, in this moment, warm and protected in his domain, the emotions that threatened to spill over were joy, a bit of gratitude, and downright confusion. It was the confusion she wasn't familiar with. She made her way to the window. The room was empty, and no Niko to be found. Sighing, Francesca ran her fingers across the smooth wood of the cabinet and fingered her dusty-rose coupe glasses. Along with her clothes and toiletries and her soft pink bathroom rug, he'd brought her cabinet here, her ridiculous but precious belongings.

How had he known how important it was to her? It was nothing imperative, nothing life or death, or even as essential as her face cream, but it was special to her. Very special. After her divorce and move to the small town of Mercy in the Blue Ridge Mountains, she'd been lucky to find her apartment, and the cabinet was the first piece of furniture she'd bought for herself, at a little antique store while out exploring one day. Slowly she'd treated herself to unique old glasses, some bottles, and a few gnarly but beautiful bowls. She found she enjoyed collecting pretty things, something she'd never done before. Each moment of discovery was marked as a special step of beauty in her life. Her very own belonging.

He'd put it in the library, set it up for her. And she'd tossed those words in his face. *"This is all just temporary anyway."*

He'd given her no reason to think it *wasn't* temporary. Worse, there simply was no *it* or *this*. He'd made it clear there couldn't be. Months ago, it might have soothed her ego to know that he desired her. But now, knowing that and watching how severely he put himself at a distance, all it did was make her cranky, and stir up her red-hot emotions until she pricked at him with any little scratches she could, like there was a pent-up hissing feline inside her. What a good look that must be on her. Mostly she hurt herself in the process too.

She flung herself on his wonderfully comfortable leather sofa and swore at her arm. Inside the cast, her skin itched under the elbow, a spot she couldn't reach, even with the aid of a long flat butter knife she'd managed to work in between her skin and the cast. *Niko, Niko, Niko.* He wasn't in the library with her, but he was still in the house. Unlike other nights when she'd been unable to detect him.

Had her words hurt him? Was he capable of hurt? The emotions raging in his eyes told her he was extremely capable but perhaps uneasy, and she should be ashamed for trying to inflict pain on another, especially the emotional kind. Those kinds of wounds could stay raw for an eternity. God, she needed to find her sister and get out of here. Rewrite their lives back to before all this. Whatever *this* was...wasn't good for any of them.

It was time for bed.

On her way to the stairs, she sensed him. Perhaps she should try one last time to apologize for being testy after he'd taken care of her and the children, providing everything. *Well, not everything.* Her smirk lacked feeling. Oh to be serviced by Niko Sarkozy. That was a dream she'd have to bury.

Following his scent, she found herself at an unassuming wooden door. One she hadn't noticed before, or perhaps hadn't bothered with in her explorations. Francesca closed her eyes and leaned her cheek against the surface. Scents flooded her at once, dirt, growth, plants, humidity...Niko. Opening her eyes, she studied the door again, differently this time. *What secrets are you keeping?* She knocked, but there was no answer.

Carefully Francesca pushed it open and what lay behind it was both shocking and delightful. Secrets indeed. She'd been woefully wrong. An enormous solarium or greenhouse, made of the palest green glass and black iron, with a pitched roof that allowed the above starlight to shimmer and spread out over her. The size of a four-car garage easily. And it was bursting with life, namely, roses.

"What are you doing here?" She turned at his voice, low and thrumming with accusation, or something she couldn't quite put her finger on. He was extremely efficient at cloaking his emotions from her. Covering his shirt was a denim apron. His hair was a mess, and his cheeks, *oh, he's blushing.*

She turned slowly back toward the interior, took a few steps in, and breathed deeply. "What...you..." Francesca fingered the perfectly healthy green leaves of an old English climbing rose and leaned in to sniff the white flowers. Musky, earthy. *Delightful.* It wasn't very mature yet and hadn't managed to grip the wire trellis behind it, but it was lovely. Next to it were two roses with peach blossoms on them. Rubbing her fingers softly over the petals, the scent hit her nose. Goodness, lemons. A rose that smelled like lemons, how perfect.

Feeling Niko's eyes on her, she ignored him and tried to make sense of what she was seeing. *Why do you always smell of roses?* His whispered words came back to her. A few feet in another lush plant to her right had enormous pink blooms on it. A garden rose, messy and beautiful. There was a clear slate path for her feet to follow laid in a perfect line down the center, with paths cutting off to the sides. The flowers grew at all angles and heights, stretching up against the windows, and blossoming over the path in a riot of color. The vast place smelled overwhelmingly of roses and humidity and...lust.

"Please...you need to go. I...I..."

He wouldn't meet her gaze now. Hands in his hair, he faced the solarium, trying to hide that same tension he'd vibrated with the other night in the library when he'd had his body pressed up against hers, warm and hard and...

"Niko." She took a step toward him. "You grow roses? It's beautiful. Did you build this...is this for—"

"Please," he begged. He was in pain. Something was hurting him, and she stumbled back, desperate to not be the thing or person causing it. God, she was in a mess deeper than she comprehended.

Giving herself one more second to study him and one last longing glance at the greenhouse, she said, "I'm sorry." Then she slipped out and raced up the stairs. It was more imperative than ever that she find her sister quickly and get out of this house. Her heart was involved, racing like a sprinter to the finish line, and she could see only ruin if she stayed much longer. Niko had demons to slay, but she couldn't do it for him, especially if he wouldn't let her in. She certainly wasn't giving her heart to someone who couldn't man up and be honest, who was going to punish her by withholding his true feelings.

***

Ignoring her shaking fingers, Francesca got ready for bed, soothed her skin with her cold rose cream, and gave a defeated sigh. Roses. Her beloved scent. He knew that. That solarium was so beautiful it was hard to think about, yet she'd never forget it, or the look on his face when she'd barged in.

Climbing under the covers, she realized how tired she was. It was easy, when she was healthy, to slip into dreams. Not quite as effortless to slip into someone else's, but she and her sister had been practicing for two decades and their bond was powerful. A bit more difficult while she was healing, but thank goodness tonight, when Francesca dreamed, she'd been strong enough to venture past the acres surrounding Niko's land.

Her strength was nearly back to where it had been pre-accident, thanks to her ability to heal quickly and to Marie's medicinal herbs. The hours of rest hadn't hurt either. When had she ever simply let herself rest? When had anyone made it possible for her to? Niko was always there, making sure she had everything she needed, except himself.

Her surge in energy certainly had something to do with Niko. Infuriating man. Confusing man. Sexy, kind, powerful, infuriating man. Infuriating begged to be said more than once. Taking deep breaths and calling on the powers deep within the earth, the wind and fire, the air around her, and her true heart, the water that gave them all life, Francesca roamed across the land, high into the midnight sky full of stars. The blue-black sky was brilliant, refreshing, and simple yet beautiful with its twinkling lights.

She took a deep breath and set her intentions.

Francesca listened to the air, closed her mind to the echo of the world's voices, and calmed her way into a meditative state to pinpoint Gia. Saturated colors bloomed in her mind. Deep greens of forests and nurturing soil beneath. Gray-white ash after a fire. The buttery low winter sun. Even the royal peaches and pinks of Niko's roses came to her.

"Gianna Violetta Banetti Reily, sister mine, where in Mother Nature are you? Lady, Mother, Goddess, your help in finding my sister would not go unappreciated."

It was unlike Gia to be completely out of touch for so long, especially in their dream world. It had been their secret hiding place of communication for so long.

Having soared her body out over the land, Francesca found herself lured to a series of foreign places. Across a vast ocean, wild and dangerous with surging waves calling the storm on, Francesca rode its power. A busy city she didn't recognize was covered in smog so thick she could hardly see her way through. And now she stopped at an old factory outside of this foreign city. Her heartbeat centered and glowed from within, but something was wrong. *"You're here, Gia. Why do you feel so out of my reach?"*

"Frankie?"

"Gia, what's wrong? Where are you?" Noiseless and light-less, the dilapidated building appeared abandoned. The surrounding area was dark and eerie. No lights shone on the inside. Francesca entered and moved carefully through each room following her sister's aura. She sensed pain, blood, danger.

"I'm a little stuck at the moment." Gia's thoughts nudged her. *"And I should be asking you what's wrong, I can feel...your heart...beating...I mean...damn it, I'm struggling to..."*

There were bad people here. Francesca could smell them, like beings without souls, dank, putrid, the worst of the world's creatures. Fear licked at the back of her neck, causing goose-bumps to shiver across her arms. Where was Niko now? Too bad she'd kicked him out of her dreams. Another scent assaulted her senses, someone else, some*thing* else. It prowled the perimeter of the building then leapt to the roof. Powerful. Canine.

Gia needed help. Her soul was distorted. It was one thing for Gia to cloak herself from Frankie in dreams if Gia thought her sister at risk or if Gia's mission required the element of secrecy, but now, Francesca could feel her sister's desire to be found, only something vile kept them apart.

"Gia, why can't I see you? You're there but you're not."

"I'mmm okay, or I'm gonna be. This partic...particular job is proving to be more...difficult than I... Are...are kids okay?"

Gia slurred her words as if she was drunk. Her blood ran with an unnatural energy.

"Listen to me, Gianna, I know your work is important, but something happened. I need you to come home. Everyone's fine, but we were in a car accident. I think...someone was after the children."

"What?" Francesca could feel her sister's pulse speed up in panic. *"Danny, Av—"*

"Gianna!" An earth-shattering growl yelled her sister's name. The sound boomed around Francesca, sending shockwaves of anger, possession, and fear. Anguish overwhelmed Francesca at the roar of that one word. In an instant, a blinding flash of light and a rumbling explosion threw Francesca backward in a spiral. She crouched in on herself and rolled with the force of it. Shrill alarms pierced her eardrums. Gia yelled. It was too far in the distance. Breaking bones and snarling echoed over the land as Francesca tried to claw her way back to her sister. As desperately as she tried, she was powerless to hang on to the vision. She woke scrambling up, clawing at the threat, a scream bursting out of her body.

Chapter Sixteen

U NABLE TO FIND PEACE in the stillness of his rooms, Niko paced the length of the empty hallway. Even his solarium sanctuary did little but antagonize him tonight, especially after she'd set foot inside. Through the glass, the crystal-clear sky taunted him. It mirrored the night all those years ago when he'd been turned into a vampire. Beautiful, ominous, haunting all at the same time. In the end completely devastating. *Francesca.* Now she was all he could think about. He would never be able to separate the solarium from her again. Who was he fucking kidding? He'd built the damn thing for her.

Niko wrestled with himself, desperate to go to her, but instead respecting her wishes to stay away. Unlike the other nights, however, he didn't disappear. His form of self-torture. For a moment, as he forced himself to remember the words of his curse, the silence of the house stole over him. Until the dogs both began a low growl and crept into the hallway before him, hackles raised. "Francesca," he called as her scream reached him.

Niko burst through the bedroom door and was by her side in an instant. Kneeling in the middle of the bed, covers askew, she grabbed at her throat, frantically, pure horror marking her face. One hand reached for him. "Niko," she said on a strangled cry. The dogs were there beside the bed, whining their concern.

He cradled her onto his lap and wrapped his arms around her.

"I've got you." Always. *I will always fucking have you.* "What happened? Are you hurt? Breathe."

She clawed at his shirt and buried her face in his neck. "My sister. Something has her. An explosion. I don't..."

"Shh. Tell me again. I'm here. You were dreaming?"

"Yes." She gulped in air, clinging to him. "I found her. I mean I could sense her and hear her, but Niko, something is desperately wrong."

"Tell me everything you remember."

"Shit," she swore and pounded his chest. "This never happens to me."

"Take some deep breaths. You can do it." Niko drew calming circles on her back, willed his magic into her, and matched his breath with hers until she settled. Once she did, the dogs calmed too and curled up beside the bed.

"She's worlds away, across the Atlantic. I couldn't get to her. She was blocked from me and her blood was altered. I think she'd been drugged. I..." Francesca pulled away and looked up at him. "I sensed..."

"What?" She was irresistible even like this, all fired up for someone she loved, her emotions whirling out of her. He cupped the side of her head and traced the bones of her cheek, soft, freckled skin, all flushed with her blood rising to the surface, with love for her sister. It took every ounce of strength he had to hold her and steady his hand, to focus on her words, her needs right now, and not feed his own body with hers.

"You mentioned the scent of a canine around my apartment. A canine was there too, where Gia was, prowling...searching for her. Its cries sounded as if it would die without her, the sadness of a century bottled up in its feelings for her. Niko, I could feel it ripping open my heart. Before I could do anything, there was a massive explosion and the dream shattered."

Fuck. Even Niko knew there was nothing good when it came to a severed dream. "What do you want to do?"

She put her hand over the one he cupped her cheek with. "I need to try again. See if she's...if she's..."

"Listen to me." Niko gripped her head with both hands, tangled his fingers in her wild hair, and brought her gaze to his. "We're going to find her. You would know if she was gone, wouldn't you?"

Francesca nodded. Niko carefully wiped her tears with a soft caress of his thumbs. There would never be enough time in the world to study her beautiful face like this, completely open and full of emotion. He would look his fill now, while he could.

"Will you stay with me? Please, I know you don't want to, Niko, but I—"

"I'll stay," he said, assuring her and damning himself in the same instant. "Here." *Fuck. In for a penny, in for a pound. Of torture.* Niko stretched out and nearly drowned in the scent of her. He tugged her down next to him and wrapped his arms around her. She was still shaking, and he would warm her, soothe her, be her rock while she needed him. He would allow himself this moment of perfection, her lush body pressed up against his, her arm wrapped around him like she craved him as much as he craved her. "What else can I do?" Niko took advantage and nuzzled into her, whispering in her ear.

"This is perfect. Thank you for being here when I need you," she whispered back.

"Always."

"Stay."

"I'll be right here."

"I know."

Christ, her trust did him in. The night wrapped around them, and Niko watched her as she closed her eyes and eased into sleep. Memorizing each second, he reveled in the feel of her soft warmth snuggled into him. Her vulnerability, the faith she put in him. How? Why? He didn't understand her, yet he longed for the opportunity. To have such goodness in his life every day, to capture each of her smiles, to tuck away her tears for safekeeping, to blush under her teasing, witness her emotions rise to the surface, have her wrapped around him, it was enough of a fantasy to have him aching.

CHAPTER SEVENTEEN

"**W**HATEVER IT WAS WASN'T after me. I've told you, Niko, that night of the accident, they were after my...my—" Francesca spoke in hurried whispers. They'd already had this conversation and she absolutely wouldn't repeat it in front of her niece and nephew, tiny but incredibly perceptive little boogers that they were. She, the kids, and Niko were rushing out of the hospital, *again*.

"You need rest and I'm still uncertain of your safety here." The efficient, infuriating asshole was back. Gone was the warm, compassionate man of last night who'd held her and comforted her in her dreams, and almost had her believing maybe they'd turned a corner. A good corner.

The hospital hall was empty as they made their way. The hum of routine continued around them, only she wasn't part of it. She was on the other side, a patient, and she hated it. In addition to that weird feeling, an uncomfortable one stole under her bones and had her more worried than she already was. It had started as soon as they'd entered the hospital today and she detested it. Her hospital was her second home, her sanctuary. She wanted nothing to mar it.

"I *need* to work," she said. *I need to find my sister.* Last night sat heavy in her mind, confusion layered on top of fear, murky and dark. She'd dreamt again with Niko's hard body wrapped around hers, keeping her safe and turning her on at the same time. He hadn't relaxed for one moment. The man stayed awake all night to make sure nothing happened to her. And although she'd sensed her sister was out of danger, she hadn't been able to locate her again. She'd woken midafternoon to find Niko no longer in bed with her. Instead, he stood in the corner, piercing her with those intense feral eyes of his.

As soon as she'd told him what she'd found, he'd said nothing, offered nothing. And although she could see the wheels of his brilliant mind working, she didn't know what anything meant. Niko Sarkozy was pricking at her like blackberry thorns, annoying as hell and a bit painful, but with the promise of delight. Well, she had to laugh. No problem she'd encountered had turned her on so fiercely even while it also stoked the flames of her annoyance and frustration.

After her shower, he'd hustled her into the car. They'd picked up the children from school and driven to the hospital for her checkup without even asking her if she in fact wanted a checkup.

"Infuriating man! You're being pushy and impossible." She was cranky. Her entire being, body, mind, and emotions hurt.

"Aunt Frankie, it isn't nice to criticize people," her nephew admonished while holding tightly to her good hand. She held her injured arm to her chest as if that would soothe away some of her worry. The fracture had healed rapidly, and, as of ten minutes ago, the cast was gone, which was great, but her arm felt weak. Pale and weird, it resembled a dead shriveled animal. Not to mention how awful her skin smelled.

Oops, she'd said the infuriating part out loud. She expelled an enormous sigh. "Oh, you're right, monkey. I apologize to all of you. I'm the one who's cranky. I'm tired and worried and I want my arm to be back to normal. How are you, dear?"

"I'm worried too. And I'm hungry," Danny said.

They'd been at the hospital for two hours, mostly waiting, and Francesca hadn't even remembered to bring snacks for them.

"Wouldn't it be nice to get burgers and milkshakes?"

"And French fries?" Boo chimed in. She skipped along beside Francesca. Niko brought up the rear.

It was an ongoing special date she and the children had, going out to dinner for cheeseburgers and milkshakes on the weekend when they stayed with her. Some meals were made of magic all by their very nature and the traditions wrapped around them. "It would indeed. Perhaps we can go to the grocery store before we go home. Otherwise, I'm afraid it's leftovers for us tonight. Sorry, loves. We can eat in front of a movie if you like." Wouldn't it be nice to go out to eat, to be normal, to not have to hide away? To not be afraid. She'd smashed through her fear so many years ago when she and her sister had escaped their last foster home. To be stuck in it again grated at her.

All the way through the parking lot, Niko acted as her bodyguard, scanning their surroundings, his muscles tensed and alert. She could feel it even though the only part of him touching her was his hand at her back. He scooped Ava up in his arms and secured her in her car seat while Danny climbed in. Then he held Francesca's door, offering his arm. She ignored it. Touching him, skin to skin, would make her crankier, because she wanted to touch him in other ways, to rub her naked body all over his, take out all her frustrations on his muscles, discover all his secret spots, and tease him until he lost control. Just like she was on the edge of around him every second. It was whiplashy trying to understand him, especially when he worked so so hard to keep her out.

No, she didn't take his hand, but it didn't matter. His gaze penetrated her thoughts, nonetheless. He might as well have reached inside her chest and caressed her heart. Thankfully he closed the door without incident. Good thing too. They were likely to incinerate each other.

It wasn't long before she realized he'd driven a different way, along a curving road surrounded on both sides by enormous old flowering dogwoods, craggy and tired with their bare branches and scaly trunks in winter. She imagined how gorgeous they'd be in spring covered in white blossoms, a brilliant flower tunnel over the road.

Niko drove out of the barren branches and into a forest of white pine so beautiful. The rhythm of the drive cocooned and lulled her into a sense of wonder. It truly was beautiful here. They pulled up in front of a small collection of connected buildings. Old, built out of stone, off a small road in the forest, glittering through the mist. Somewhere she hadn't seen before, and not too far from Niko's estate.

"What is this place?"

Francesca didn't seem angry anymore, but exhaustion still laced her voice. More than hear it, Niko could feel it seeping from her pores. All night and well into the morning he'd stayed with her while her dreams had been fraught and, in the end mostly empty of information. It had been hours of dream walking for her, frustrating and taxing on her already compromised body. He'd intended to wrap her back up and order her to stay in bed for the day, but she'd needed a checkup first.

"A pub."

"I thought we couldn't go out." Fuck, even her pouting turned him on.

"A friend of mine owns it. It's safe, and it'll give everyone a nice break, a treat if you will. I thought maybe you'd enjoy that."

She stared at him, her face neither a smile nor a frown, but intensely focused. He couldn't handle the intensity. "And," he said to the children, breaking the tension, "the best burgers and fries in the world."

The kids scrambled out of the car as fast as they could. Francesca was slower but still slid him a tiny smile before she turned toward the pub. He'd take it, desperate man that he was. He'd take anything from her.

"If it isn't the devil himself. Good to see you, Nikolav," the man standing in the entryway said. "And who are these lovely patrons you've brought with you?"

"Callum." Niko gripped the man's hand. "This is—"

"I'm Ava and I'm hungry and I would very very much like French fries, please."

Niko smirked at the young girl's bravery. Callum stood over six and a half feet and was close to two hundred and fifty pounds of pure muscle. Black vine tattoos snaked up his arm and stretched around his neck. His unruly, curly hair was the only hint of softness about the man.

"And I'm Danny. This is Aunt Frankie. She's taking care of us while our mother is dealing with a very bad man."

The quiet settled between them. Yep, her nephew was sharp as a tack, that one, didn't miss a thing. Also extremely polite, which was, in Niko's mind, a positive quality of course. But he worried for the young man. Danny had skipped childhood and gone right to the polite, restricted confines of being a very careful, watchful adult. The boy should be playing and laughing, not worrying over his aunt and his sister.

"Well, young man, I suppose you're doing a good job taking care of them then, is that it?" Leave it to Callum to come to the same quick assessment.

Danny swallowed and shook his head. "I tried my best, but we were in an accident. Aunt Frankie got hurt." Francesca sucked in a breath and Niko immediately put his hand on Danny's shoulder, giving it a quick squeeze.

"I'm certain that wasn't your fault. You'd better come with me and see the pinball machine." Callum lifted Ava up and offered Danny his hand. "We can start with sodas and get some food ordered for you. Best milkshakes in the world for dessert too." Callum winked and drew a smile from Danny, who carefully placed his hand in the man's and let him lead them inside.

Niko gestured toward a booth in the back and Francesca, after giving him another one of those studying glances, allowed herself to be guided. She sat down and scooted in. It only took him a fraction of a second to throw caution to the wind. He slid in beside her.

"What are you doing?"

"Sitting next to you. Shielding you in case someone I don't like comes in."

"So, basically anyone who walks through the door."

"Correct." He didn't like anyone. She *was* correct. So there, perfect response. He might not be able to have her, but he'd decided to take advantage of every moment he could be near her. If he had to tell himself lies to do it, so be it. He hardly considered himself a good man. That part of him had been ripped away and shredded before he was seventeen. The long centuries since then had only buried those remnants deeper.

"This place is lovely. I've never seen it before." She sounded put out. And he suspected her annoyance was aimed more at him directly than at a pub she'd never been to.

"Mm," he answered.

"Mm." She mocked him, nearly drawing a grin out of him. She took in the space around them with her wide insightful gaze. "It's almost magical. Appearing out of the mist. Somewhere you'd allow us to visit other than your estate, that is."

"There's a lot of magic happening around here," he challenged.

"Mm." She mocked again, luring him with that sexy voice of hers that was one part annoyed and one part curious and so many parts tantalizing. He was certainly under her spell. There was no denying it. Sitting here, close to her, in this cozy dark space while the familiar warmth and delicious scents wrapped around him, he only got pulled in deeper. And it was becoming more difficult to know why he had to stay away, why he couldn't have exactly what he wanted, her in his bed, captive, naked, aching for him, while he fulfilled every single one of his fantasies. What were *her* fantasies? He was rock-hard imagining. Every need of hers consumed him.

"Niko?" Her soft voice swirled around him.

"Hmm?"

"You're touching me," she whispered.

Niko trained his mind away from the image of her tangled in his bed sheets. He held her injured hand in his, lightly brushing his fingers over hers, as if they were the most precious things he'd ever touched. Magical, powerful, beautiful. How he longed to be under her spell, fully. When he pulled away, the ache was painful, as if his ribs were crushing the organs beneath. "Concerned, that's all." Swallowing back the pain of separation, he willed himself to communicate. "How does your arm feel?"

The way she stared at him, sending those silent messages of her desires. How he wanted to echo them. He might as well have been flayed open for her to discover everything about him. Holding his breath, he waited and was surprised when her features softened and she gave him one of her almost smiles, like she knew. Like she *knew* how much he'd suffered his entire life. She didn't prod, didn't try to demand he talk.

"My arm." She nodded as if signaling her agreement that they'd remain on shore, where things were simple, rather than dive to the whirling depths of truth.

"Yes. It healed rather quickly. Dr. Raj was amazed. Your cast is gone, but you're still favoring it."

"Well, have you ever had a cast, Dr. Sarkozy?"

Dr. Sarkozy. He shook his head. Was she teasing him now with the Dr. title, or stepping back behind her walls?

"In addition to feeling weak, it's..." She scrunched up her face as she ran her fingers over the pale skin where the cast had been. "Weird, tacky, soggy."

Niko chuckled at her response. The tension defused until he met her gaze once again and watched her eyes shimmer and her smile turn to pure stunning beauty, wide and open. Part of his dark soul broke open in wonder. She'd reached in with that smile and touched him, healed that small part. And hope, the thing he'd left in the bloody battlefield of revenge the day he'd watched his family murdered and for months after, unfurled low in his belly, a mere flicker of it.

"I knew you had it in you." Her smile turned flirtatious then. She lured him in with her voice and her scent. A stronger man wouldn't have leaned closer, desperate to understand her.

"What?" He didn't mean to sound harsh. He wanted that flirt under his lips. He wanted to taste that smile and every other one she had.

"Laughter, Niko. Joy."

Somewhere along the way, she'd begun crumbling his defenses as if a fortress of centuries-old anger and a curse were nothing to her. Like she truly did believe in him, that he was more than an angry old vampire without a hint of love or comfort in his life hell-bent on revenge who could no longer access that revenge. It was as if she saw a different path for him, one he'd never thought possible, one she desired to be a part of.

"Aunt Frankie, I won!" Danny said, full of excitement and disbelief, smashing the moment to smithereens.

Both children were there, scrambling into the booth. Ava climbed over Niko's lap and situated herself between Niko and Francesca. Danny climbed in beside Niko in the circular booth. Surrounded by their warmth and touch, he braced for the pain. How long had it been since he'd had the physical touch of someone merely for the sake of being near him? Afraid to move, Niko waited, his pulse kicking up.

"What did you win, lovey?" Francesca gave Danny her attention while hugging her niece to her side. She sent Niko one hint of a smile before leaning into Danny's response. The vise around Niko's chest eased. Without any thought at all, she made him feel as though he belonged right here with them.

"Pinball. Mr. Callum says I'm a quick learner, that I concentrate very well."

Joy bloomed on her face and Niko took in every nuance.

"I'm sure you're amazing. Concentrating is something you excel at. Was it fun too?"

"So much fun!" Danny's eyes were wide and happy. How serious the boy had been since Niko had met him. It warmed him inside to witness the change.

"Here we go." Their waitress arrived, arms full of baskets of food. "The best cheeseburgers and fries you'll ever eat. Milkshakes and chocolate cake for dessert." She winked at Ava before she left, and the little girl giggled. Niko was instantly glad he'd brought them here. They weren't used to being cooped up in the dark like him.

Callum set a mug of coffee in front of him. "All good?"

"Mm, it's delicious," Francesca said, wiping her mouth. "Is there magic in these fries?" She was teasing, but Niko wanted her teasing reserved only for him.

Callum quirked his brow and sent her a sneaky smile. "Perhaps." Suddenly Niko was filled with a black rage. Callum barked out a laugh and gave his shoulder a shove. "Easy, old man," he said and walked away as if hadn't just flirted with

Francesca, trying to get a rise out of him. Jesus Christ, Niko was losing it.

"Thank you for bringing us here," she said.

"You're...you're welcome." He cleared his throat and sipped his coffee, welcoming the burn to his throat. Physical pain he could handle. Physical pain meant nothing to him. It was the emotions churning underneath centuries of rubble he was unequipped to handle. This simple dinner shouldn't require thanks. She deserved so much more. He was suddenly embarrassed.

She sighed and leaned back against the booth. "The only thing that would make it even better would be some bourbon."

He drew his brows together and snuffed out all his emotions. Back on guard, where he needed to remain. "You're still on antibiotics."

She pouted but gave him a soft laugh. "I guess we can't always get what we want. Isn't that how the song goes?"

CHAPTER EIGHTEEN

N O, THEY ABSOLUTELY COULDN'T always get what they wanted. He'd gone straight to his solarium after they'd returned from dinner. But what used to be an escape clawed at him like torture tonight. Surrounded by humidity and roses while he ached for her, knowing she was right above him, a thin ceiling barely separating his dark twisted soul from her gorgeous bright one, right here in his home. *Where she belongs. Christ!* Niko threw the pruners across the room, not nearly satisfied enough with the crashing sound they made as they skittered across the floor and into a terra cotta pot.

He stalked up the stairs two at a time. They hadn't had any more time at dinner to discuss serious things with the children present. And there was so much to discuss. He thrust his hands into his hair, he didn't want to fucking talk.

"Francesca," he demanded, trying to keep his voice below a bellow so as not to wake the children.

"Niko?"

He burst into the bedroom. *She isn't here. Where the fuck is she?*

"Oh shit," she swore.

She's hurt. He followed the lure of her voice and rammed the bathroom door open, ready to save her and... *Fuck me.* Francesca lay before him, soaking in the large, silver, free-standing tub that he swore at the time he hadn't had made specifically for her, even though it was all lush curves and a gorgeous piece of art, even though it was big enough for two. She was soaking in clear water that had a subtle greenish-blue shimmer to it with a few petals floating on the surface. Nothing more. And yet it was all her, beauty, mystery, allure, and desire tantalizing him.

"Niko?" There was censure in her voice, but he couldn't bring himself to move away. If he'd still had a beating heart, it would have stopped here and now. And he would have welcomed this kind of beautiful death.

"Where are your bubbles?" he demanded, fueled by swarms of lust he didn't know what to do with. Didn't women use bubbles, for Christ's sake? For pampering, for scent, to hide themselves. He, he...

"Excuse me?" Drawing her words out in a reprimand, she flicked a droplet of water at him. "What are you doing in here?" She didn't move to cover herself, simply stayed there in the water, eyebrow raised, red curls coiled in a loose bun on top of her head, neck waiting for him to lick and kiss and bite, cheeks more flushed than he'd ever seen them and the rest of her...an abundance...luscious...exposed...

"Fuck, I'm sorry." Swiftly he turned around and closed his eyes as if that would make what he'd done appropriate, as if that would hide her from him. But he saw her there in his mind as clear as crystal, naked, under the water, fitting the lush curves of the tub. Pale skin, rosy nipples...and...her neck. That graceful gorgeous neck wasn't under water.

Mercy. No, there was no mercy for him. Francesca's pulse flickered beneath the perfect column of skin, taunting him. *Get a fucking hold of yourself.* "I thought... I thought..." His soul ached. His mind was foggy, his body an inferno. "I heard you swear, I thought you were hurt."

"I have no idea what I thought. I just needed to get to you."

"Oh really?"

Christ, he'd forgotten, or maybe that wasn't quite true. Maybe it was so natural, so seamless, so right. She could read his mind as easily as he could hers. It both surprised him and drove him wild for her. Right now her thoughts were tantalizing and everything a man could want. A man, not a beast.

"I'm fine, Niko." Her voice softened, taking pity on him. No one had ever had to pity him. "The water was a bit hotter than I realized when I sank in," she said. "It's fabulous, this tub is...*something.*" That dreamy low voice of hers wrapped around him like the steam in the room, leaving its mark on every inch of skin it touched. The way she drew out the word *something* as if it were a gorgeous indescribable gift for her pleasure. How he wanted to be her pleasure. Jealous of a bathtub. That was a new low. "It was a good swear, Niko, honest."

"Fine." He wasn't fucking fine. Nothing was fine. What an idiotic word if he'd ever heard one. All these fucking ridiculous words that suddenly didn't mean what they had in the past. As if he could ever go back to the past, any sort of *before her*. Before. There was another word that had lost all meaning.

"Would you like to join me?" She teased, soft, seduction.

She fucking dared. She had no idea how close he was to breaking, to imploding to...

"Fine, Niko..." She blew out an exasperated breath. "Please, I can feel you vibrating anger or something fierce into the atmosphere."

There it was, that *something* said to poke and prod at him, a new meaning in its depths again.

"But I'm trying to relax and you're not helping. What is it you wanted when you stormed upstairs searching for me?"

Could she feel the pull as strongly as he could? *I wanted*... No, he dared not think it. "I apologize. I know you're worried about your sister, about everything that's going on. Do you ...shall we...talk? Is there anything you'd like me to do? I can help you find her. I can help you..."

"Oh, Niko."

There she was tossing out emotions again in just a few words, emotions he couldn't name. Was that what he'd been reduced to? Did he care?

"Thank you. I'm going to try to find her again tonight in my dreams, thus the bath, to rejuvenate me a bit." She flicked the water again. Even that sound mocked him. "Bathing with the right oils and candles is wonderful for restoration. If I can't find her, I will ask you for help. I promise."

He wanted her promises all right. "Certainly...I'll go. I apologize again." Niko stumbled out of the room, barely able to stay upright, making his way to the bedroom next to hers that he'd taken so she could have his larger bedroom, so he could imagine her sleeping in his bed, and in the bath... He should have built a separate wing for her.

Something...bathing...restoration. He raged. The house shuddered as he slammed his door. Stripping his clothes, he stalked into the shower, right into the punishing cold spray. But even that wasn't enough to calm his raging desire, to flush her words from his mind, to rid him of every image and scent of her. The fucking taste of her blood he could already imagine. Nothing worked to rid her.

He flipped all the sprays to as hot as he could stand. If he was going to burn in hell for all eternity, he might as well *burn*. And he would fucking enjoy it. He was hard. Each muscle strained toward her, toward the image of her in that water, bared and calling to him, that fucking tilt of her neck as if she knowingly taunted him with that precious skin, so soft and open. An offering. His cock throbbed at the memory now seared into his mind, the sensual wet curves of her, how in tune she was with her body, how comfortable. That was a sight in itself. He'd watched her walk and move and perform surgery with confidence and even joy most days, but in that tub, under that magicked, shimmering water, not one bit ashamed of being naked in front of him, almost...almost reveling in it.

Now the steam that surrounded him was by choice, the pain by choice, the action by choice. He took his cock in hand, bracing himself against the wall with the other. There was nothing calm or subtle as he stroked himself from root to tip, punished himself. He let need and desire take over and fuel him with only one intention, to purge this lust from his body, once and for all.

Gripping himself hard, he tugged, racing toward a climax that was going to break him. He pictured her breasts, slipping and rising above the surface of the water, those fucking rose petals teasing him as they slipped over her hard nipples, the dips and curves of her hips, her belly, her fucking invitation to join. God, to rut her right there in the water like animals with no finesse, to take her, water splashing around them, her gripping the sides of that tub while he grabbed her hips and thrust into her over and over again until neither one of them doubted who they belonged to.

That was it, the tipping point. He failed to stay silent when it roared through him, yelling out the one name that would be his salvation and his ending. "Francesca! Fuck! Fuck!" He panted and tried to catch his breath. Niko sank to the floor of the shower, spent, and not one bit saved, instead more damned than he'd ever been.

CHAPTER NINETEEN

"**G**UESS WHAT, LOVES? I talked to your mom and she's coming home soon."

"Why oh why didn't you let us talk to her?" Ava asked, twirling around the kitchen with the spatula.

"Yes, Aunt Frankie?" Danny had gone serious again. Her little worrier.

Francesca put her hand on his shoulder. He was carefully scooping out cookie batter and placing it on the parchment. She urged a bit of relaxation into him. "Because it was late, while you were sleeping." It hadn't been a call, but rather in her dreams last night. Thank goodness. After discovering her sister was okay and coming home, Francesca had slept like the dead. It was glorious. *A busy night will do that to a woman.* Especially one where she gave her body pleasure in the bath after Niko stormed out, after he...whew...after he nearly made her come from his gaze alone, then denied himself, denied them both.

Damn it. Remembering it frustrated her all over again. It was clear the man wanted her. He'd said as much, pierced her with a gaze so hot she thought he might light the bath on fire. He vibrated with it if she was reading all the signals correctly. And she, Francesca Rosmarino Banetti, was no idiot. Roses. She sighed. All those roses he tended to under a glass ceiling, under starlight. Poor man had it bad. Now she had to figure out how to make him lose control and give in to his *craving*. She'd never been any man's craving.

She wiped her brow. Just imagining it made her hot everywhere. Craving indeed. These cookies were going to be extra special today with all her pent-up frustration. These were her signature chocolate chip cookies with dark and milk chocolate, that secret browned butter, and a special touch of magic. A cookie to make you love it, to make you want to eat it again and again. Now they were infused with craving too. Hmm, couldn't be a bad thing, not when it came to her cookies. Not bad at all.

"Look at the sun!" Ava had her nose pressed up against the massive sliding doors to the backyard. It was a beautiful almost spring morning, bright blue sky, the grass glittering with overnight rain. Wonder and frustration both bubbled up inside her. She snagged a cookie off the tray and bit into it. *Wow.* Perhaps her best batch ever. But even its dark chocolaty goodness couldn't ease her annoyance at the blasted man. He had her in an unyielding state of arousal that was making her extremely cranky. And she didn't get cranky. It was supremely annoying that even her mouth-watering warm chocolate chip cookies couldn't get her out of her funk.

"What are you doing?" His voice came at her like a low growl right before an animal let loose. Niko prowled into the kitchen, long black sweatpants the only thing covering his body, his miraculous, gorgeous, fantastic, massive chest on full display for her. His black hair was a tangled mess. His eyes blazed with fury, with desire, with her.

Holy Hell! Francesca took a step back from the force of his beauty.

"We're making cookies for breakfast! You have to try one. Aunt Frankie makes the bestest chocolate cookies on the planet because she uses huge dark chunks so they melt in your mouth."

Francesca watched as he took in the scene, sparing her niece, who had more chocolate on her face than in her mouth, a glance. A glance that seemed to calm him only slightly. Tension rolled off him. The electricity cut thick in the room, that simmering, approaching rainstorm on a summer's night, heady, humid, sexy all rolled into one, thunder sparring with the lightning that hovered around their emotions, the earth vibrating its anticipation for the battle. *Oh yes, please.*

"Let's take some to Marie," Danny said. And then the children were gone in a blur out the door to the sunshine.

"You are testing my patience, Francesca." Each word, all hard edges of desire, carved into her deepest places, caressed her there where no one had touched her before. No one had bothered reaching. "The aromas, the sugar, *you*. I can smell it all inside my sleep," he accused. He rounded the counter, sleek, panther-like, each muscle...efficient. "And still, I can smell *you* underneath it all."

Oh, how efficient was he now, hmm?

Slowly, Francesca took another bite of cookie. *Let him come.*

"You taunt me with it? With your creations, your scents, with your body, luring me closer. Do you have any idea what you do to me?"

Swallowing the last bite, Francesca leaned her back against the counter as he met her there, barely brushing up against her and yet she could still feel how needy he was. *Thank the goddesses.* She sighed.

"What is this?" The whisper of his words teased the skin of her cheek as he fingered the soft sash of her wrap, his knuckles brushing against her belly. She only had to tilt her head up slightly to meet his gaze and each breath she let out brought her body against his.

"A sweater."

"Mm." Niko hummed. "Barely covering your shoulder," He tossed his frustration right at her.

She was ready. Bring it.

"Might as well not be wearing one at all." He drifted his nose to her neck, over her exposed collarbone. It was like he spoke to himself, lost in her.

Goody.

"Taunting woman. Making bad decisions."

"Mm."

"If you only knew."

Even his thoughts were carved and harsh. And she wanted it all. *"I know more than you think..."*

He slid his other hand up her bare thigh. And she let out a heavy breath.

"And these? This tiny, ridiculous piece of cloth?" He was a master at distraction.

"Pajama shorts," she whispered, tilting her head farther to the side, giving him all the access to her neck. If he wouldn't let her tell him, she would show him, give herself to him. She wanted him there as well as what his other hand promised, toying with the skin under her pajama bottoms, setting her on fire for him.

"Francesca."

Pinned against the counter she was completely at his mercy. But she didn't want his mercy. She wanted him uncontrolled and wild, feral for her.

A tortured expression moved across his face as he closed his eyes and slowly parted the sash tying her sweater closed. He ran silky fingers over her bare stomach, causing a shiver to run through her. When he opened his eyes again, their gazes met, scorching.

"There's chocolate here," he said, fingering the side of her mouth. "I was dreaming of chocolate. Not a dream, though...you...here...how can I crave you so much?" Francesca sucked in as he carefully licked the chocolate off the edge of her lip.

Yes, please. She sighed as he breathed her in, leaned in even closer, if that was possible, crushing their bodies together.

Francesca reached up and touched him, finally, slowly running her hand up his cheek, tracing the bones of his jaw. Niko growled out a deep moan at her touch and it fueled her on. "I thought...I thought you didn't like my cooking." She brushed her thumb across his lips. He accused her of taunting? Then she would excel at it.

"I never said that." He leaned in again, brushing his nose up the column of her neck.

"You, you..." She panted, arched her head to the side to open fully to him, and put her hands on his naked chest. *Good glorious lord.* "You hated it when I brought food to the hospital, didn't eat..."

He dragged his lips back up and over hers.

"Please kiss me already," she whispered.

But he denied her. It seemed they were both playing a dirty game. Roaming down her neck again, stopping at her pulse, he placed his open mouth there on her, where every cell in her body now beat from.

"God, yes, right there, Niko."

Gently he sucked, and Francesca felt the pull everywhere.

"Sugar. Dark chocolate, something beneath it all...I knew it," he said, all deep accusations. He used his other hand to grip her thigh. Then he took his gaze from hers to watch his thumb run along the edge of her shorts, till he slipped his touch underneath and teased the soft skin of her inner thigh. "That if I ate your food, I couldn't control myself."

"Oh." She moaned as his thumb traced higher, inching its way closer and closer up her body to her core.

"That I'd want you more than I already did."

"There, oh, yes."

Finally, he touched his thumb to her aching core. "This pussy's wet for me."

"Uh-huh." His touch against her throbbing skin nearly set her off. He stilled.

"No, no, please don't stop."

She dropped her head to his shoulder and rubbed closer so their bodies razed against one another with each dragged breath either one of them took. He began to circle his thumb against her and with every pass, he was closer and closer to making her scream. It was too much, this luscious torture. And not enough, not ever enough.

"Turns out, all I have to do is smell you. You reach me even in my dreams, Francesca. Do you know what power you wield?"

He lifted her sweater and gripped her breast.

Teasing her nipple that was perfectly hard and waiting for him. She arched into his palm. Finally, he rolled his other thumb right over her wet core, pressing harder in little efficient circles until he slipped his finger into her wetness. Assaulting her everywhere. Thoughts and feelings boiled inside her while he took his pleasure. Francesca moaned and nipped at his shoulder.

That was it. Her nip shattered the careful moment. His control snapped right in front of her, as if the few moments before were him pretending carefully, as if every single second leading up to this had been controlled. But it was simply the calm before the storm. Gripping her neck with his free hand, Niko licked and sucked, bucking into her.

"So wet and needy, this pussy and this special clit of yours, how it swells for me." He pressed naughty circles against her, and finally, finally, let down his fangs and pierced her neck with his bite.

"Niko," she cried, instantly awash in dazzling, colorful waves of pleasure that began to swirl around her in brilliant turquoise, but he ripped his mouth away and stumbled back abruptly separating them, a shield of blackness covering every part that had just been open to her, his breathing harsh and so, so angry.

"No," he swore and vanished from the kitchen faster than she could blink.

A pounding silence surrounded her, while inside Francesca pulsed everywhere, with arousal, with goddammed frustration. What in the hell was that? *He...he...all of that and then...he left.* Her skin vibrated as she plummeted from the high. The kitchen returned to focus. She turned and faced the sink, gripping the countertop to steady herself, and tried to catch her breath. Carefully, she touched the spot on her neck where he'd barely left a scratch. *Niko.*

Marie was outside with the children. They laughed and chased the dogs. Sunshine had smoothed all the clouds away.

While inside Francesca had been ripped into pieces from one existence to another and back again, then left to bleed out all on her own. With more calm than she felt, Francesca opened the window and called, "Marie, would you mind watching the children for a bit longer? I'm...I'm going to...uh...shower."

"Not a worry, dear," Marie called.

Francesca wasn't letting this go. She deserved an explanation. She hoped she'd get a lot more than that. Because for one spectacular second in her life, she'd been whole. And then he'd ripped it all away.

CHAPTER TWENTY

N IKO GRIPPED HIS HEAD and paced around the cold, boring bedroom. *Fuck!* He could never go back to before. He'd tasted her. The curtains were drawn. One tiny, slivered sunray snuck through the gap. Darkness all around him, except the taste of her had lit his entire body up. Finally, the most beautiful lightning strike, forbidden and deadly all the same. What had he done? His blood boiled. His insides raged for her. His cock stood stiff and rigid at attention, all for her.

If he closed his eyes, he could still see her, standing there barely dressed in his kitchen. She was always right fucking there in the front of his mind. He'd never be able to rid himself of today's image. Those tiny fucking shorts, the soft gray sweater hanging off her shoulder. The sunlight bathing her neck for him.

"What the hell was that, Niko?"

He turned and she was there, slamming the door shut like an angry beautiful dragon woken from her long boring slumber.

Her life would never be boring with him. Right or not, the thought thundered through his mind. *"You're so fucking beautiful."* He took a step toward her, the taste of her still lingering on his tongue luring him on. Never boring.

"Don't communicate unless it's to explain why you did all that downstairs and then slammed away like I'd poisoned you. Why you keep shoving me away."

"Not you, me!" He roared. *"You are perfect."*

"I don't understand, Niko. We desire each other. I know what you—"

"I can't protect you!"

"From what?" she yelled back. "You've done nothing *but* protect me, care for me. Are you...do you have any diseases?" She scoffed at him. "Is that what this is? You're being awfully dramatic. I'm disease free and it's been a very long time since I've had sex, Niko. Embarrassingly long." The last came out on a whisper. Her cheeks flushed deep red.

She dared tease him with the knowledge no man had been inside her in a long while. Every defense he had shattered one by one.

"I can assure you it's been longer than you can imagine for me. And I can't carry diseases. I'm perfectly healthy," he said.

She laughed and shook her head, making light of this, this inferno or turmoil he was in. "Then what else could there be? What could you possibly need to protect me from right here between us?"

"Me! I'm a monster," he bellowed, hoping to scare her back, scare her away for good. That was his last defense.

"No." She thrust her hands on her hips, all fire and anger, standing up to him. It was the sexiest thing he'd seen. "Listen to me," she demanded, and he was putty in her hands. Her words sang to him. The scent of her arousal, still cloaked around her, beckoned him. "For once, please listen to me." Flushed and angry, wild and gorgeous beckoning him in his dark bedroom. He'd listen, he'd listen to anything she had to say. "I know what you are. You know what I am. You are a protector, Niko. You're my—"

It was over. He was done walking away. He stalked her back against his door. *"I must touch you."* He was desperate. She hadn't even bothered to tie the sash of her sweater and he wanted to tear it off her. Fierce, brave beauty of his. He lifted her slightly, so his cock nestled right against her warm pussy, and held her there against the door, her feet not touching the ground. *Mine.*

He could barely stand to be apart from her for a second now. His blood recognized hers and soared with the contact. She was his.

"It's all true," he whispered against the spot of her neck where he'd barely broken the skin in the kitchen, healed over already, but he knew where he'd tasted her. It was a brand on his soul as much as one on her skin.

Francesca gripped his head there. "What's all true, Nikolav?" Her words, a whisper, a breath, sultry, needy.

"I want you so much it hurts." He thrust against her. She lifted her legs and wrapped them around him. Was he holding her or she him? He would drown if she let go.

"I'm here. Can't you feel me humming for you? Every time you're near. Please, Niko. The rest can wait. Let me, let us have this now." Her hand was on the bare skin of his back, soothing and tantalizing all the same. Her touch was nothing he could have dreamed. She kissed his temple, whispered sweet words into his ear. He'd have to explain everything, but maybe he could have her this once. His body ached for her. There had to be a cure, a way he wouldn't destroy her life if he had her, one small taste.

Her skin smelled of musky roses and sugar now, and lust pouring out of her. And her blood held all of that and more. There was spice and excitement inside her, all her light and love. He could taste the remnants on his tongue. God how he wanted it for himself. Craved it before he'd ever sampled her. Now? Now he was forever changed.

"If I have you, it's all over. You will be mine."

"Why do you say that like it's a bad thing?" She panted out her words, sexy woman, as she stroked the skin of his back. Her desire was its own aphrodisiac.

"You don't know me, Francesca." He licked her neck, right where he'd nipped her, had to do it. "My past. How demanding I'll be."

"I know you, Nikolav Alexander Sarkozy."

She wiggled and brushed the sweater off her shoulders, let it fall to her waist, caught between them until he ripped it away and tossed it over his shoulder. Before him, an offering, her gorgeous, rounded breasts, rosy nipples hard and aching, the blood pooling there for him. All the eons he'd gone without the taste of blood. It was all worth it to wait for this.

"My gifted, generous, mysterious, talented, surgeon," she whispered. "I know you. And I want you."

Then she rested her head back against the door and drew him to her. A beautiful invitation. He couldn't refuse her now. Wouldn't. They'd have to deal with the consequences later.

"And moody." A teasing grin softened her face. Her hand dragged down his chest.

"I'm not moody." He could barely get the words out as she toyed with the band of his sweatpants. She slipped her fingers inside, eyes widening as she brushed against the tip of his cock, hard and aching for her. She was miraculous. Watching her explore and take and offer and enjoy. He'd been a fucking idiot, pushing her away. It was easy to believe that now with her scent swirling around him, her blood humming for him, as she'd said, all for him.

She arched, bringing those rosy nipples even closer, begging with her body. "What do you call all this hot and cold, then?"

His woman was a vixen, a delicious tease, a feast. With one hand, he held her close, while he used his other to ghost across those nipples, lost in the exquisite touch for the first time. How often he'd imagined her this way, naked for him. She moaned and writhed against him. Fuck, her noises were going to be the end of him.

"Never cold, my love." He offered his own truth. "I burn for you." Lifting her breast to his mouth, he sucked the tip in, watched her eyes flame. Her legs gripped him tighter.

"Oh, yes, please. That feels divine."

He sucked and licked while brushing his thumb along the luscious soft skin, and she moaned and danced against him. Fuck, he was lost in her. He lavished attention on the other breast, licking the skin between them as he switched, drinking in and tasting every part of her she offered.

"Niko, please. No more begging—"

Finally, he dragged his mouth away to seal his lips over hers. Soft against his, warm, and sensual. He slowed his thoughts. He was going to memorize every single second. How her lips felt drinking him in, the hint of chocolate still there, stirring him up again, need pounding through him. With one lap of his tongue, she opened, and he plundered, tasted, and poured his soul into this kiss. And she gave back, gripping his head and tangling his tongue with hers, sucking and nipping at his lip. That fucking nipping of hers was going to get her in trouble. *Fuck!* Her kiss was everything.

"Oh my God."

Their thoughts twirled together as they devoured each other, as she rubbed her breasts against the bare skin of his chest, as the warmth of her pussy lured him on, even through the thin barrier of clothing.

"I've never kissed while being able to share the other person's thoughts before, Niko."

"Me neither." To be fully one with another, with her, was Niko's secret dream.

"It's luscious and wonderful and...and...I can't think of the words."

"Stop thinking." He was going to come right here and now if she kept being so fucking amazing and honest. How long was he expected to hold back after centuries of waiting? Good Christ, and her warm and willing against him. *"May I?"* He gripped the soft sleep shorts she was wearing.

"Yes, please...naked."

He tore his mouth from hers and ripped her shorts down.

"Oh, fuck, Niko. You too." She wigged her hands between them and tried to drag his pants down. He brushed her hands away and tugged them off himself, never letting her go. Holding her bound with one arm, he gripped his shaft and dragged it over her pussy.

"So ready for me, Francesca."

"Yes," she whimpered, her gaze drawn to where their bodies were almost connected. "I need you. I'm on the Pill. Please, please come inside me now."

"Do you ache, the way I do?" Niko sucked her nipple into his mouth again, grazed his teeth against it, watched her thrust toward him.

"So badly, Nikolav."

"Say it again," he demanded, leaving her breasts to hold her head steady, so he could watch her eyes when he entered her.

"Say...say what?"

Now he was the one teasing her, parting her wet folds with his cock. Her lips and chest all flushed and brutally, beautifully used. He'd stay here forever to see her like this, fucking beautiful indeed. He tried to make it last, but the edges of his control slipped all around him. She'd done that, stripped him of everything. And he was as certain as he'd ever been of anything that she would put him back together again. If he didn't destroy her first.

"My name. Say my name." He stilled his cock at her entrance.

"Nikolav."

And he was gone. He thrust into her. Sheathing himself with her was the most exquisite torture while she pulsed around him.

"Nikolav," she moaned, and her core gripped him as if she was made for him, as if she'd never let him go. No more teasing, no more hot and cold, only the inferno of them beating together.

"My Nikolav."

"Yes, fucking yours. And you, Francesca. Mine." He thrust again and again, trying to get deeper, trying to make them one from the inside out. Pounding them against the door, careful to protect her head.

"Feels like nothing I've ever—" He stole her words with his lips, sealed them together. Niko gripped her lush ass and lost himself to her.

She ripped her mouth away, and threw her head back, baring her neck to him again. "Yes, harder, like you don't want to stop, Niko."

"You have no idea."

"I do. I oh...the way you rub against me with each thrust, Niko. Do it again."

He complied and with each movement he grew harder for her, coiling like a predator. One lick against her neck, the way she held him to her as if she too craved it, the last dregs of his sanity. He could hold back, just that, for now.

"No, don't hold back on me. Nikolav."

It was there barreling down on him. *"I need you to come, Francesca, now".*

"I can't. I..."

Niko smoothed his hand between their bodies and used his thumb to rub against their connection, finding her clit. *"You're all swollen for me. Now, show me what you're made of. Show me how good it all feels, this, us, finally connected. How we were meant to be."*

"Niko."

She exploded around him, dragging him closer still until he couldn't hold back, and he was pummeling into her, spilling everything he was inside of her. "Francesca," he yelled as it all hit him at once—a mate, connection, belonging.

Their heavy breathing brought him back to Earth. Her slow caresses up and down his back, the sweat across her brow, and shimmering eyes. Her smile was natural and lopsided. Exactly how he felt, lopsided. The door dug into the hand of his that cradled her head. A shiver ran through her. "Christ, I took you against the door, like an animal. Francesca, I am s—"

Her lips were on his. "Don't you apologize for one single second of what just happened, Nikolav. That was…" She kissed him again and this time when she smiled it was against his lips, a thing of pure beauty. "Incredible."

He settled into her, wrapped his arms around her, and swept her to the bed. Then he settled into kissing her, really kissing her, exploring every soft swollen bit of her lips. One day he'd spend hours simply learning her lips, watching the gold flecks in her eyes heat up while he kissed her, drugged her with his touch the way she drugged him. He was nearly lost in his explorations, the little sighs she kept gifting him with, when something stole over his instincts, and he pulled up abruptly.

"Niko?" Her expression changed to one of concern, then awareness. It was amazing to watch her from this vantage point, close and vulnerable and completely *with* him. He would never take another one of her expressions for granted again.

"Someone's here," he whispered. They stilled, both of them, and listened to the air around them. Concern etched into the lines around her eyes.

"Oh." The fear drained out of her and her soft smile returned. "I know who it is."

CHAPTER TWENTY-ONE

F RANCESCA RAN DOWN THE stairs to the entryway.

"Aunt Frankie, look!" Danny yelled.

"Gia." Francesca swooped her sister up in a hug, holding her close. She pulled away a fraction simply to take her in. "*Tired eyes, dark circles, too skinny as usual.*"

"*I'm alive.*"

"*I was so worried.*"

"She's home." Ava ran up and down the hallway and finally squeezed herself between Francesca and Gia. "Mama always comes back. Look, Danny, she brought our dog."

"What?" Gia said to Ava.

"Hello. Who are you?" Francesca asked. A man stood next to Gia. Or beast, perhaps. He was as tall as Niko, but with enormous muscles, those of a lumberjack. Fitted gray long-sleeve shirt, dark jeans, heavy motorcycle boots, and something strapped to his back. His brown hair was thick on top but shaved up the sides. Gray flecks in his goatee highlighted the sharp planes of his face. And his eyes. Francesca could almost always get the measure of a person from their eyes. And he was...furious.

"You!" Niko surged forward, and grabbed Francesca, setting her next to him, his arm in front of her for protection.

"You're—" The man swept Danny, Ava, and Gia behind him in one grasp of his enormous arms and unsheathed his sword all in the blink of an eye.

"What the hell is happening?" Gia shoved him and stepped back out, arms crossed, glaring at the man.

"Niko's a vampire," Danny said, sneaking his head around the man's enormous frame. "We already know. He saved us. He's friendly." Danny patted the man's back as if the sword he wielded was fake and couldn't slice them all in two.

"He hasn't shown us his teeth yet, though," Ava said, pouting and clinging to the man's trunk of an arm as if he were a swing made exactly for her.

"What...I..." Gia's eyes were huge and confusion tore across her face.

Oh, shit. Francesca linked Niko's hand in her own and gave it a squeeze.

"You knew?" Niko said and she almost laughed because she'd never seen him like this before, shocked and flustered and bristling with anger all at the same time.

She nodded. "I tried to tell you," she whispered, brushing her hand over his cheek to soothe. It eased her worry when he leaned into her touch. She'd fully expected him to pull away.

"How, why didn't you say anything?"

"I tried—"

"What the hell are you doing in the home of this vile creature?" The man demanded. "All of you?"

"You dare," Niko swore, lunging toward him as Francesca reached out her arms to control him. "Get out of my home."

"It's all right," Danny said. "Niko protects us the way you do, Hugh. He saved Aunt Frankie's life, and he brought us to his home to make sure the dark shadow couldn't get us. He has two hounds who aren't as big as you, but they watch over us, and they like to play fetch outside. Wait until you see Niko's land. We like it here."

The man stilled, sheathed his sword, then knelt in front of Danny and ran his hands over the boy as if checking to make sure he was all right.

"This is Hugh," Danny continued and glanced at Francesca. "He, or rather, his other form watches out for us too."

"What the hell is going on?" Gia seethed with anger.

"He's the pretty black dog in my dreams," Ava announced.

"This is the wolf shifter marking your apartment." Niko's thoughts thundered with anger.

"It's all right." Francesca soothed Niko again and assessed the situation as a whole. Her senses were fired up, at the height of their power. The aroma of chocolate cookies drifted from the kitchen. Newly bloomed Evangaline roses in Niko's solarium were bright with scent. Even the threat of a cold front moving in breathed through her. Confusion marred her sister's face and

the children's hearts beat at a normal rate. Aside from Niko and Hugh's blood both boiling in defense, nothing struck her as a threat. *"I have no idea why he put his mark there, Niko. I've never met him before, but you have nothing to be jealous of, or worried about. And he doesn't scare me."*

"You trust too easily." Niko was controlling his fury, but the muscles beneath his shirt vibrated with it. It was a sight to behold, watching him bank all that energy. She couldn't wait to explore that later. But right now, there was a situation to defuse.

"No, I absolutely do not. I trust my instincts, which have never let me down. And they're even more powerful now." She raised her eyebrows and rubbed the spot on her neck where he'd barely pierced his skin. Niko followed the path of her fingers, his eyes growing silver and hooded. *"Trust your own."* He stared into her eyes with the utmost focus, but she could tell his senses took stock of his surroundings, as hers had. Finally, he gave her a soft nod but did not let go of her hand. If anything, he gripped it harder. Until this morning she'd only guessed at his strength. Now she was surrounded by it. It was intoxicating, to say the least.

"You've been spying on my children?" Gia accused Hugh. "How...why...?"

"He wants to keep us safe, Mama," Ava said. Hugh gently ran his hand over the top of her small head.

"I've been watching over you," Hugh began, eyeing Gia with a dark expression. "The three of you, since that first night."

"Without telling me?" Gia's temper was a thing to behold and could blaze out of control quickly. "Just because we...I...we work together doesn't give you the right to invade my home, my children's dreams."

"I didn't invade. And you're not safe." Hugh's voice was a barely controlled boil. "They're not always safe. I can feel it."

"You should have told me." Gia took Ava from his arms.

"Would you have allowed it?" Hugh softened his voice, but the warning, the conviction was still there. "Would you have listened to a thing I said, stubborn woman? I've been trying to tell you for weeks—"

"You're not my keeper. You don't tell me anything." Gia turned away, which, to Francesca's amusement, didn't lessen the sparks zapping between her sister and Hugh one bit.

"Whoa," Francesca interrupted. "Let's take stock. We're all okay. We're happy you're here and we have a lot to tell you." Flames licked between Hugh and Gia as if they were engaged in a very heated battle.

"Very interesting."

"Not interesting at all," Gia tossed the words Francesca's way for everyone to hear.

"We were in an accident." Leave it to Danny to cut to the chase.

Gia softened and got down on the ground, pulling both kids with her. "I know, loves. I'm sorry. Let me look at you."

Danny pulled away and stood in front of Hugh. "There was a dark shadow at the accident. It was awful. I could sense the evil. It tried to hurt us. I yelled and got Aunt Frankie's phone and called an ambulance." Then the boy fell against Hugh's legs. Hugh didn't hesitate a second before lowering and wrapping his arms around Danny.

"So brave," Hugh said gently, calmly, clearing his throat. "You should be proud of yourself."

"I was terrified." His voice was muffled as were his tears.

Gia stared at them with pure anguish on her face.

"Perhaps it would be the right time for some lunch." Marie stood at the end of the hallway.

"Who..." Gia said, anguish turning to confusion and then to recognition. "You're...I recognize you...how? Who are you?"

"Your cousin, dear. I was your mother's first cousin. My name is Marie. And you must be Gia."

"Again, would someone please tell me what in the hell is going on?" Gia said. Her pale skin highlighted the weary circles around her eyes. She was skinnier than usual, withering away. Lunch was a brilliant idea. Sometimes a meal was what was necessary. Nourishment, good flavors, love. A tiny satchel of peace for the moment, a reprieve.

Francesca squeezed her sister's hand. "A lot's happened since you've been gone."

CHAPTER TWENTY-TWO

I T WAS HOURS LATER, after a delicious but tense lunch, after a day playing with the dogs in the sunshine, and pizza for dinner on the back deck, after the kids had gone to bed, before the adults had time to talk about important things.

Gia stalked into Niko's library with Hugh on her heels.

"Could you stop for a minute, woman?"

"I don't need a follower," Gia snapped.

Niko stood in the corner close to Francesca but cloaked in shadows. Francesca was making them all a nightcap with the delicious bourbon Niko had stocked on her vintage cabinet. One more little thing he noticed and did for her, without telling her, without expecting anything in return. She hoped after their breakthrough—she giggled at calling being fucked against his door a breakthrough—that she could acknowledge and thank him for all the ways he cared for her. And she was going to lavish that care right back on him.

"I'm not trying to follow you. I'm trying to have a conversation."

"You can start by apologizing."

"For what, making your son feel safe, protecting you?" Hugh leaned into her sister's space.

Uh-oh.

"For interfering in my life and not telling me!" Gia might have been almost a foot shorter than Hugh, but her anger was massive. She snagged the cocktail out of Francesca's hand and flung herself onto the sofa. Her sister was kind of acting like a child. Infuriating men could do that to you. It was rare for Gia to evade or back down. "You went into their dreams?" So many emotions rolled across her sister's face.

Hugh sighed. It looked as though he visibly tried to calm himself down with deep breaths. "Not exactly. The first time was after the company party. I dropped you off. Something didn't feel right. *I* didn't feel right leaving you." He put his hand on his heart. "I could hear him...Danny...having a nightmare. I knocked but you didn't answer. You were uh, I could hear you in the shower. I couldn't sit by and do nothing. I promise you I would never hurt those kids. I waited outside his window, tried to urge my calm onto him. He found me, in his dreams, somehow. I'm not even sure how it happened. Surprised the hell out of me, honestly."

Gia plunked her glass on the coffee table and gripped her head with her hands "His nightmares are awful."

"So." Niko prowled out of his dark corner towards Hugh.

Uh-oh again. Here came her avenging angel. Francesca knew that tone.

"You entered the dream of a young child, some strange man taking advantage of a boy in pain."

"Never. I went as my—"

"Your beast," Niko snarled.

"Look who's talking, bloodsucker." Hugh faced off with him, hands on his hips, vibrating with anger. "I was just a big friendly dog to Danny, one who listened and walked by his side. Ava showed up later in one of his dreams and acted as if she'd known me her entire life. I know it wasn't the best way to handle it, but I was worried, and I would *never* do anything to harm or scare those kids."

"All right, you two." Francesca pushed them apart. "It's obvious you both care a great deal about those children. Niko quit being a jerk, I know you have friends who are werewolves." She raised her eyebrow at him, remembering Callum at the pub. "And Hugh, Niko has kept us all safe. There's nothing to worry about. Please put aside your...dislike of each other so we can all talk." Hugh and Niko both took a step back, but neither sat down. Francesca curled up on the sofa beside her sister.

"The accident. Start there," Gia said. "Why didn't you call me immediately?"

"Because she was undergoing surgery for a collapsed lung and multiple other injuries including a broken arm," Niko seethed.

"Oh, Frankie." The anger collapsed from her sister's face. "I'm so sorry," Gia said.

"I'm okay now. You know I heal quickly. But I think who-ever, or"—she caught Niko's gaze for a moment— "whatev-er did it, was after the children."

"A demon bent on destruction or something I can't quite put my finger on," Niko said.

"What?" Gia stood. "How do you...what makes you think that? God, it's all my fault."

"No, stop. None of us knows for certain but there was this evil presence at the accident. Niko sensed it. And it seemed like Danny also recognized it." Francesca set her drink down. "Niko also discovered it back at my apartment after the accident, and..." Francesca put two and two together. She turned to Hugh. "Your scent was there as well, —preventing the evil from getting close enough."

"I had a bad feeling," Hugh began. "Couldn't get ahold of Gia. I know who you are, Francesca. I went to your place. I was there when the demon arrived. It couldn't get past my powers. But it got all my hackles up. Something else had me on edge as well. My instincts were correct so I did everything I could to find Gia."

"You were in our dream that night too at that warehouse, weren't you?" Francesca said.

"I blew a hole through the side to get Gia out before they..." Hugh glanced at Gia.

"Before they killed you," Francesca finished, wrapping Gia up in her arms again. "You were almost killed, and he saved you."

"I don't know who saved me. I was unconscious," Gia insisted. Hugh eyed the ceiling as if to give himself patience.

Francesca got up and wrapped her arms around Hugh. Niko stepped forward, but she raised her eyebrow and he stopped. "Thank you for saving my sister, Hugh. I was so scared when I couldn't get to her. Nothing good was happening and she was in pain."

"I don't have a clue who'd want to hurt the children," Gia said. "I mostly target...humans, not...uh...other creatures. And you know how careful I am to let nothing that I do bleed back into our lives. You *know*."

"I do, honey." Francesca sat and took her sister's hand, trying to send some calm her way. "The whole thing is very strange. Whatever it was—"

"A hybrid demon," Hugh said. "If I had to guess. Shapeless or able to change shapes and it left behind a distinct tar-like substance. My sense of smell never fails me, and this one was weird."

"It started tailing us after I took the kids to the bird sanctuary up in the mountains," Francesca said. "I noticed nothing out of the ordinary before that. I certainly didn't detect its scent at my home."

"It can change its shape?" Gia asked.

"Yes," Hugh said. "But it's more complex than that."

"Oh, great, a complicated demon." Gia huffed out a laugh but there was no humor in it.

"Indeed. It was off, something about its makeup. There was such rage present at the accident site," Niko added. "Not to scare you further, but it's important you know what we're dealing with."

"It reminded me of something," Hugh said and paced the room, arms crossed over his massive chest. The man had yet to smile, and Francesca was a bit worried about him. "But it was difficult for me to tell. It was cloaked in layers to distract us, to hide its truth."

"Yes," Niko said. "Shit." He raked his fingers over his face, pure rage filling his expression. "A relative of Asmodeus."

"Fuck," Hugh swore and something silent and menacing passed between the two men.

"What is it?" Francesca asked.

"Francesca." Niko pulled her up and wrapped his arms around her, leaning his head into her neck. It was amazing how well they fit together. She wiggled subtly closer, loving this touchy-feely Niko, but still a bit shocked at this kind of behavior from him, since they'd only come together before her sister arrived. But his body was rigid, full of tension and...and fear. "I don't think the demon was after the children." All warmth in the room evaporated at his tone.

"I...that's a good thing. Right?" She pulled slightly away and faced him because it *was* a good thing, but the temperature in the room was icy with everyone silent and staring at...at her. He kept his arms banded around her as though he needed to protect her from what was to come.

"Asmodeus and his descendants are demons of lust. Your car, your apartment. It was simple coincidence the children were with you when it...when it attacked. I think the demon was after you."

"Oh, shit." She tried to pull away, but Niko wasn't having it. She rested her hands on his chest and faced him. Sickness boiled low in her stomach as everything coalesced into a clear image in her mind. "So, I'm the reason the children were nearly killed." The words hurt to say. Panic filled her chest. "I...I..."

"No." One harsh command and he had her pinned to him again. He rested his head in the crook of her neck, breathing her in, somehow calming her with that simple gesture, that touch of his lips against her fragile skin. "Never your fault."

Her pulse skittered around until it landed beneath his touch. She listened to the cadence of his voice against her body.

"None of this is your fault, or your burden to carry. I've got you." He whispered the last with a featherlight kiss against her neck and she settled fully into him.

"But it's still out there," she whispered back.

"I'll find it."

"How, Niko?"

"I can track it," Hugh insisted.

"No." Francesca whirled around. "I'll not put another person in danger because of me. If it's me it wants, I'll draw it out."

"You mean use you as a lure?" Gia asked.

"No fucking way," Hugh said.

"Over my dead body," Niko ordered at the same time.

Gia rolled her eyes. "You two Neanderthals do not get to order us around. Christ, typical." She stood and paced the room. "When women try to take charge, the men get pissed. What are we supposed to do, stay barefoot in the kitchen baking cookies?"

Francesca let out a choked laugh and her sister sent her a side-eye reprimand and look of confusion.

"I mean, barefoot in the kitchen baking cookies did end well for me right before you arrived."

Gia gaped at her.

"I'm teasing, kind of." She tried to placate her sister. "Of course I don't want to be told what to do while the men do all the grunt work." She faced Niko and Hugh. "Whatever we do, we do together. Don't cut us out and don't for one second think you can order us around."

"This thing is extremely dangerous. It almost killed you once," Niko said, sounding tortured again. "And I...we"—he gestured to Hugh— "have special powers, strength."

"Yes, yes..." Gia rolled her eyes again. "Big strong vampire and werewolf. Go beat your chests somewhere else. Francesca and I also have special strengths, if you will." Gia could barely get the last word out as an enormous yawn overtook her.

"You're wiped out and still healing. You need sleep."

"Don't you dare try to run my life now," she snapped at Hugh.

"Hugh's right, honey. You're exhausted. We all are. It's late and I feel in my bones that we are safe here for now. Let's call it a night and see what the morning brings." Francesca wrapped Gia in another hug, and it was a sign of her sister's true exhaustion that she let her.

"I should...uh...I should go," Hugh said.

"Nonsense. It's late and there's plenty of room, here," Francesca said, giving Niko a glare before he could protest. "I'm sure Marie already got a few extra bedrooms ready for you."

"Francesca," Niko started to protest.

"We're all safer here together with you and Hugh both protecting us."

"Oh, lord, Frankie, way to lay it on thick," Gia said.

"Too thick?" She giggled.

"Goodnight." Gia snuggled into the hug and then slowly walked out of the room. "I'll check with Marie about bedrooms." Francesca didn't miss the tiny glance she sent back in Hugh's direction.

"I'll make sure she makes it to bed safely," Hugh said and disappeared after her sister.

"Oh my gosh." Francesca fanned herself. "Those two."

"What are you doing?" Niko was there, wrapping himself around her from behind.

"Swooning," she said and leaned her head back, so he had access to her neck again. He hummed against her, and all thoughts of Gia and Hugh flew out of her head.

"Swooning, huh? I like your emotions, Francesca, every single one of them. I like seeing them and knowing I'm free to soak them up, taste them." He dipped his tongue out and licked against her neck, up, up to her ear lobe where he nipped at her and whispered sweet things in her ear. "So expressive, so full of joy and light, so fucking full."

"Are you going to make sure I make it to bed safely too, my dark angel."

CHAPTER TWENTY-THREE

"**H**OLD ON," HE COMMANDED in the deep rugged tone of his that stole over her in a dark caress. Before she could blink, Niko swept her up in his arms and whirled them upstairs to his bedroom. She was on her back in his bed with him on top of her, finally. "You're here, with me, exactly where you should be."

"Wow." Her heart raced, exploding in fireworks. "Impressive." The hushed whisper of her words faded at the intensity on his face.

"Tracing." He shook his head and ran his nose along her cheekbone. "It's nothing."

"Ha," she said and captured his lips in a soft kiss. "So *not* nothing."

"Well, to a powerful healer such as yourself, it's not that impressive."

"Wanting to heal has always come naturally to me, but there's so much I don't know." She whispered now, too afraid to admit all her shortcomings aloud. Right now it was only the two of them and she huddled into their space.

Niko paused and studied her. "A healer indeed. But that's only a part of you, isn't it? You can dream walk, and I suspect kitchen witch is also part of your repertoire. Although I don't know how you managed to hone those skills in that poor excuse for a kitchen in your apartment."

"It's all I've had, tiny, outdated kitchens."

"No longer," he said nuzzling into her chest. "May I?" He tugged at the sash around her sweater again and all thoughts of kitchens and and whatever the heck *no longer* meant flew away with the sound of his voice, simultaneously reverent and needy.

"Yes, please." Her reply was breathy and excited. She loved this, being free in front of him.

"This thing toys with me like nothing ever has, soft, seductive, gracing your body, and now that I know what's underneath, a treasure indeed. Christ, Francesca. You're all I can think about, all I've been able to think about for months, agonizingly long months. And the last week, imagining you right here beneath my sheets, without me, has been torture." He paused and seared her with his molten silver eyes, flowing in a coil of desire.

She recognized that look now and blushed under it.

"And speaking of months," he continued. "All this time, you knew what I was?"

"Pretty much, yes," she confirmed and ran her fingers along his cheek and down to his neck. She placed her other hand against his lips, mesmerized by how soft they were, while the rest of him was so, so hard.

"How?"

"Oh goodness are we really going to talk now?"

"Indulge me for a moment." He slipped her sweater open and rested his hand on her belly.

"You're making it awfully hard for me to concentrate, Nikolav." She arched toward his touch as his hand slid up to her breast.

"I'll keep you happy if you tell me. Try, Francesca. I want to know everything."

"Oh." She whimpered as he brought his lips to her breast. She gripped his head to her. "I...I have a sense about people, beings. I wasn't one-hundred-percent certain, but there was something unique...you from the beginning...and..." He toyed with her nipple, sucking and lavishing attention with his tongue. "Niko."

"And?" he said.

How could he follow along so clearly?

"How are you not mad with desire the way I am?"

"You are testing the last shreds of my patience, the scent of you surrounding me, all this naked beautiful skin. Tell me, Francesca, put me out of my misery," he said this as he eased her leggings down, kissing along her body. Her panties disappeared in a whoosh, and she was naked and breathless underneath him. "Tell me." He dragged himself back up, the fabric of his shirt and jeans teasing her sensitive skin.

"The more we worked together...inside here..." She patted his chest. "Was so different, so cold, yet...curious." She paused to watch him stand to tug his shirt off and toss it aside.

"Dead?" He scoffed. He stood away. The separation nearly caused her to cry.

"No." She shook her head and reached for him, begging him silently to come back to her. "Not dead at all, not to me. Your blood, your heart beat a unique way, like it was meant for me."

His lips softened and the dark sparkle in his eyes met hers.

"The closer we got, something clicked into place."

"Mm," he said studying her, and she didn't know what that *mm* meant. She was going to ask when he finally leaned in and spoke against her lips, sending little vibrations through her. "Not just a healer, an intuitive, intelligent being who pays more attention than I realized."

"I'm paying very good attention right now, Niko." She wound her hands down his back, along the curve of his spine, through the waistband of his jeans, and...he was naked underneath. How lovely.

"Say my full name," he commanded. "I like the way it sounds on your lips."

"Nikolav."

Next to disappear were his jeans and before she knew it, he'd settled back into her body, naked. She widened her legs to accommodate him, to welcome him.

"And you're not afraid of me?" he whispered, capturing her gaze again.

Nothing would have her looking away at this moment. *Oh, oh.* He was worried and vulnerable. That was what he really wanted to know.

"You're not the least bit scary."

He scowled and she grinned, hugging him to her.

"Not to me. I've never been afraid of you. I...I..."

"What? What did you see, emptiness?" He scoffed and slipped one hand under her head to cradle her there. The way he touched her, learning every part of her.

"No," she whispered and brushed her hand over his brow and down his cheekbone as if she could rub her feelings into him. He closed his eyes and moaned at her touch, compelling her on into all the dark depths.

"I saw arrogance..."

He huffed out a laugh. "Is that all?"

"And a heaviness, deep thought...intense consideration. And...well after the bus accident, I could feel your anguish across the room. It was..." His eyes opened and pinned her, his dark, shimmery silver gaze all on her. The intensity flowed through her blood, charging every cell. There it was, that link between them, fierce and fragile at the same time. "It felt like a lifetime of sorrow rose in you. So strong it almost knocked me out."

He studied her so intently she wondered if she'd made a mistake saying it. "But still you came to my side?" he asked. Such disbelief in his voice as if he didn't deserve her.

"Always."

He tightened his grip on her head.

"You needed me."

"I should have saved him," he whispered on a strangled cry. Tears swam in his eyes. Such beautiful tears.

"You can't save everyone, darling."

"But I can. It's the only thing I'm meant to do. I should have been able to find every single wound in his little body and I... Fuck! I failed."

She held his head in her hands and forced his gaze to hers. "There were too many patients that night, for any of us. It's a good thing you were there at all. You saved many lives. You worked steadily for hours."

"I excel at healing. It's all I am." Tortured words.

"You are so much more than that," she whispered.

"How can you tell?" A desperate plea. It was worse than she'd imagined, the shattered state of his emotions.

"I see you, Nikolav. All of you. You've been letting me in little by little. And now that I'm in, I see your depths, your intensity, your protectiveness, your caring, your longing, your... You have many losses inside here." She rested her hand on his chest. "But you're not alone anymore."

"I'm not?"

She smiled at him. "Silly man. Do you think I'd give myself to just anyone? A casual fling?"

He laughed and it broke the intense heaviness of the moment.

"No, Francesca, I don't for one moment think you'd suffer any fool." He brushed his thumb along the column of her neck, softly, lovingly.

"You're safe with me too," she whispered. "You can share anything with me." *Please.*

"Anything?" He used that seductive tone, all angst disappeared for now. "Can you see the desire in me too? How I ache for you?" He raised up and dragged his hard length against her heat.

"Niko," she moaned.

"How fascinated I am by you? Your mind." He nuzzled into her belly and kissed her there. She felt every delicious rasp of his skin against hers. He kissed her temple, dragged his lips down to hers. "Your body." He took her mouth and she arched into him. He devoured her, licking out with his tongue, demanding entrance.

She opened for him, and the kiss turned hungry. Each of them battled for control to taste to lick. Heat climbed inside her, and everywhere they touched, shimmers slicked across her skin.

"I want...your...everything." Gripping her along the way, roaming his fingers over her as if he aimed to map the whole of her, he slid lower, placing kisses and whispered words down her belly again. He parted her thighs with such efficiency and strength she'd likely feel his touch there for days. "I'm fucking restless for you, Francesca. A year I've dreamed of this, of you in my arms. Twelve months of torture." Each word whisked against the delicate skin of her inner thighs as he drew his mouth closer to her core. "Look at you, legs spread wide for me, and your pussy, as pink and pretty as the rest of your flushed skin."

She whimpered and arched closer.

"What should I do with you, now that I have you?"

"Niko." She reached out for him. He took her hand and placed a kiss on her palm before he set it back down and lifted her legs so her aching pussy was right there before his devilish mouth.

"Can you feel my desire now, Francesca?" He paused to glance up at her, silver hooded eyes burning deep.

"I can." She practically panted out the words. "Can you feel mine?" She arched into him, lifting her hips in invitation. "Please, Niko."

"No need to beg, Francesca. I'll take care of you." And with one movement, one lick against her folds with his eyes still capturing hers, he blew her world into the stars above.

"Fuck, Nikolav." He licked again, teased the hood of her entrance while his fingers dug into her hips, holding her to him. And then, he devoured her, using his thumbs to caress. "That feels...that feels."

"Mm, you're beautiful." His words played and rippled against her sensitive skin. "I can feel your pulse down here, Francesca. So fucking sexy how you beat for me." She did. The lifeblood of her body was magnetized to him, to his voice. "Do you have any idea what that does to me?"

"What, Niko?"

He didn't answer. Instead, he kissed and licked into her. She didn't know whether to miss the feel of his rough voice humming against her or praise his silence so he could...do other glorious things. The flickers of his tongue were going to be her undoing, driving her higher and higher. She was close to the edge. Finding her clit, he sucked it into his mouth, causing her to whimper and thrust up into him. She shook with the need to come.

"Niko, please," she begged, gripping the sheets of his bed to hold on.

"Give it to me, give me all your pleasure, Francesca." His voice rasped against her core and one more time he swept his lips over her, flicked her clit with his thumb, and sent her crying out her orgasm as she fell over the edge of pleasure, giving it all to him as he'd demanded.

"My goodness, Niko." He knelt up between her legs drawing lines along her thighs. "I'm going to have to add talented to your list of attributes."

"Really?" The smug look on his face told her he was pleased. Pleased that he'd brought her to pleasure.

She beckoned him forward. "There is something phenomenal about being with a man who's arrogant and efficient and talented when it comes to a woman's body."

"Good. I aim to obliterate all other men from your memory." His grumpy tone shouldn't make her smile, but he was adorable all rumpled up.

She chuckled. "What other men?"

"Exactly." He dragged his enormous hard cock through her wetness.

"Oh." She hushed out a breath. "Wow." Ripples of her orgasm still streaked through her and the feel of him, begging for entrance, sent her skin on fire. "I need you, Niko." She caught his gaze and sent all her silent messages to him. *Only you.* "Inside me, please." And when he sheathed himself into her in one swift movement, shattering her into a million sparks with more pleasure and such fullness, her body pulsing around him, she felt as though she'd been made only for him, forever.

"I..." He pulled out and thrust back in again.

"Can't...God..." He watched their connection as he pushed in. "Can't get enough of you. Fuck. You feel..." He ran his hands over her hips and up her belly to her breasts, raking his thumb over her nipples.

"Tell me," she said.

"There aren't words powerful enough."

"Then show me, my angel."

"I'm no angel, Francesca." He powered into her, moving both of them with the strength of his muscles.

"Come here." She was panting now and with each thrust he took her up again. "I want to feel you on me, body to body. He leaned onto her, never breaking their connection. "You undo me." She held him there and offered her neck right where her body cried out for him to mark her, to make her his. It was a sense she had, that she would belong to him, fully, if only he'd sink those mysterious teeth of his into her. Every cell in her tingled as that thought bloomed in her mind.

"Please, Niko. Make me yours," she whispered. Her essence sang with ripples of pleasure from his hard length stretching her, his hand on her breast cupping her, his breath, right there against her neck.

"Fuck, Francesca." He turned his head away and moved his hand to where they were connected. He pushed against her, playing, teasing. "I need you to come for me. I want to feel you come all over my cock."

"Oh, God."

"You want that don't you, to grip me, to lure me in, to capture me and pulse your pretty pussy on my cock. Drag my release from me, beautiful."

The rumble of his words, all his dirty talk, and the way he toyed with her. She had no choice left, no control. The band snapped, and she did what he asked, coming all over him, holding him in tight.

"Francesa," he cried as he powered up into her one last time, his magnificent frame bowed over her, still for a moment until he too lost all control and drove his orgasm into her, shattering her heart into brilliant pieces. "Beautiful witch." He spoke the words against her neck. "Beautiful stunning witch."

If this was how it felt to be high, Francesca wanted to bathe in the sensation. To dance, to spin, to yell her discovery to the stars. She tingled with flushed awareness, sparks shooting here and there.

"My goodness, they had it all wrong," she teased. "Or at least only part of the story."

"I beg your pardon?" Niko stopped the soft caress on her hip and dragged his head up to capture her gaze.

"Vampires," she whispered, "Vampire lore. Gangly, washed out, boyishly light good looks." No, watching him there raised above her, using his arms to hold his weight, all those muscles put to such good, good use, there wasn't one boyish characteristic about him, except for maybe his vulnerability. She laughed at the appalled look on his face.

"Tell me though, darling," she asked once she'd sobered. "Do you bite?" She rubbed her fingers over his kiss-swollen lips.

Harsh lines invaded his expression as though she'd wounded him. "It's not a game, Francesca."

"I never said it was." Serious now, she studied him. Gone was the open, vulnerable loving man from a few moments ago. "You...you almost bit me...before, in the kitchen. Tell me."

"It's complicated." The words dragged from his lips as if without his consent.

No sound in the room, save their breathing. Something heavy and confusing hovered between them. "Niko? You can tell me anything. Please. I want to kno—"

"Shh, gorgeous woman." He gathered her in his arms and lay next to her, with her back to his front. "We have time. Let me have this moment. Let me cement the last hour to memory. It's the most beautiful one I have." Niko held her to him as if any moment she'd disappear.

Oh, Nikolav. She trailed her fingers down his forearm. She wanted to explore his entire body, his mind, the inner workings of his soul. There was so much to learn and yet she wondered suddenly if she'd never gather it all, like he'd never let her.

Chapter Twenty-Four

"**W**HY SO MOPEY TODAY, my love?" Francesca turned at the sound of her sister's voice. She was sitting outside on the beautiful back flagstone patio, breathing in the morning dew. Even with the chill in the air, the day had promise. Blue skies and a freshness that came with all the rain and then the unbelievable growth underneath it all, finally bursting into bloom.

Crocuses were starting to make their way up out of the dirt. Such simple flowers, but they always brought Francesca immense joy when they popped up in spring. So much hope and life after darkness and ruin. The cycle of the seasons, the balance—it awed her and settled her. It grounded her into her being. She didn't feel grounded this morning.

"What?" It was useless to lie to her sister, but she was in no mood to talk.

Gia sat next to her on her lounger, hugging her arm over Francesca's waist. "I mean if I'd had earth-shattering sex last night with a hot vampire who was all kinds of lost for me, the last thing I'd be doing is pouting all by myself as if the end of the world was near. I mean, I think the entire forest heard you two."

Francesca snuck her hand around her sister's shoulders and hugged her. "Ahh, my dramatic love. You're obviously feeling more yourself this morning. No earth-shattering sex for you last night?"

"You're hilarious." Gia shoved her. "And stop trying to change the subject. Why so sad?" Gia looked up at her, all drama gone now.

"It's complicated." What could Francesca say? She didn't understand it fully herself.

"Complicated sex? Or complicated other things?"

Francesca chuckled. "The sex was not complicated at all."

"That good, huh?" Gia pinched her side.

"Owe! I'm going to push you off if you do that again. Quit assaulting me."

"Fine, give me all the luscious details. I may as well live vicariously through you since I'm never having it again."

"Never? What about Hugh? He can't take his eyes off you. By the way, you have so much to tell me."

"Hush, we're talking about you."

Francesca let out her sigh, allowing her confusion to wrap around her. Maybe the only way to make sense of it all was to go through it, not try to ignore it completely. "I've never had sex like that before," she whispered. "He...he..." The blush crept up her cheek as she remembered. "He was amazing, attentive, powerful... The way he played my body. I don't think a man has ever reveled in pleasing me, Gia. I felt lost before him, and I didn't even realize it until he touched me."

"Wow."

"Yeah."

"Your soulmate?" Gia whispered. "The one you've always dreamed of?"

"Mm." Francesca gave a noncommittal answer. The half admission choked her because she wanted to scream, "YES!" But when she'd tried to dig deeper, he'd put distance between them. Then he'd gotten a cloth to clean her, climbed into bed, wrapped himself around her, and soothed her into sleep with sweet, whispered words. Who knew the man could be sweet? And she'd let him, unable or unwilling to shatter the precious moment.

"And he doesn't feel the same?"

"Oh no." Francesca shook her head. "I'm quite certain he feels even more." His words, how he worshipped her body. He'd made her feel extremely beautiful. His deep vulnerability before they'd indulged in each other's bodies, his worry that she feared him.

"Oh, goodness. So what's the problem?"

"He's afraid of something." Admitting it, even in a hushed secret whisper sent an ache through her heart. She wasn't yet ready to tell her sister everything. Saying she wanted a vampire's bite, and he wasn't willing to give it to her sounded all kinds of wacky in her head. Even though she knew she was meant for him and instinctively sensed his bite was part of them being together. She had so much to learn about vampires.

"A vampire afraid of something?"

"Exactly." She huffed.

"What are you going to do?"

"Keep hammering away at all the walls he's built up over the years, centuries."

Gia started to giggle, then curled into a full-body laugh. "Oh, my..." She was wheezing and all Francesca could do was stare at her.

"Hello, weirdo, serious conversation here. Do I need to pinch you back?"

"No, no," Gia said through the last of her giggles. "I just...whew." She took a deep breath. "Can you believe, for all these years we've kept our identities a secret, hiding in plain sight, trying to ignore the existence of other kinds of...supernatural beings? And now in a matter of a few weeks, you're in love with an overbearing, emotionally stunted vampire, I have an extremely grumpy werewolf insinuating himself into my life, and we have a long-lost witch cousin who's thrilled to find us, plus my children are apparently expert dream walkers already."

Francesca giggled with her. "It is a lot. Ridiculous really. And a scary hybrid demon. Can't forget him." They both burst into unhinged laughter. "Good God..." Francesca couldn't stop. "It's not...it's not funny."

"It's not." Her sister snorted out her words.

"What do we do now?" Gia asked after they'd run out of giggles.

"I guess we try to figure out this demon and how we can stop it. Easy-peasy, right?"

Gia sobered. "Criminy. I'll go home and get on my computer, see what I can find out."

Francesca's shoulders slumped. "You're going home and taking my lovelies, aren't you?"

"You're welcome to come with us, but I have a feeling there's something or rather someone keeping you here. I've never known you to hide from a little problem before."

Francesca sat up and dragged Gia with her. "I'm going to pretend it is a little problem. But you're right. You and the kids need your home." She linked arms with her, and they walked toward the house. "Speaking of never backing down from a problem?" she whispered and kissed her sister's head. The man in question sat at the kitchen island making the children grin with something he'd said. "How in the world have you kept him a secret? I want all the details!"

Gia flushed deep red but ignored Francesca's demands, heading through the back patio door to the kitchen. "He insists on seeing us home."

"I can keep you safe," he said, not even bothering to send them a glance. Francesca hid her grin at the scowl on her sister's face as she followed her inside.

"Hughie is coming home with us." Ava cheered.

"Lord help me," Gia grumbled.

"You'll be fine. Indulge me too." Francesca drew her sister into a hug. "Until we find this...until we solve our bigger problem."

"I don't like being outnumbered and ordered around."

"Then give him some chores or something," Francesca teased. "He seems very...helpful." Gia pinched her again and shoved away before Francesca could retaliate.

"Fine, let's go." Gia tugged her bag over her shoulder and took her kids' hands. "Tell Marie I'll be back to visit."

Last night at dinner, Marie had offered to help them learn anything. It was lovely to have another witch, even a vampire and werewolf around. Maybe they could learn more and grow stronger in their powers. Maybe it was time to believe in themselves and cherish what they were, maybe even pass knowledge on to Danny and Ava. Gia was as hungry as Francesca was to understand their powers and ancestry. As scary as it was, they were both desperate for connection.

Francesca gave them hugs, including one for Hugh, and saw them off. Once their car was out of sight, she stood and watched nothing for a moment. But going back inside didn't hold any appeal either. Because Niko was gone. She'd woken up this morning in his bed, all by herself.

Here Francesca was alone again.

CHAPTER TWENTY-FIVE

"**W**HAT DO YOU THINK you're doing here?" Christ, he hadn't seen her since he'd slipped from bed this morning and fled to work. He'd woken up with his body half on hers, his head tucked into her naked neck, his sharp teeth right there...ready to penetrate her delicate skin. He'd nearly taken her without her permission. Escape had been the only option. Biting her had thundered through his mind until he'd reached work. It still lingered hours later. And he was cracking apart at the seams. She was more beautiful than ever, even with that serious look on her face. There were hints of hurt there. Fuck, he'd caused that. But he couldn't pull himself together to act rationally. "And just how did you get here?"

"Excuse me?" Francesca snapped. That sexy eyebrow of hers rose in indignation and he was this close to backing her up into the storage room, licking all that indignation off her expression, and demanding she yield to him. The lush taste of her blood was still on his tongue from that first irresponsible scratch when he'd found her making cookies in his kitchen and lost all sense of control. The fine thread that was left hanging was fraying even now. He was hanging over a cliff. To climb back up and take what he wanted would mean ruin for her. To let go would be his death.

But when she stood close to him like this, all fired up, unafraid, it was hard to think straight, hard to concentrate on what he must do, or rather, not do. Everything around him faded to the background, all sound, all beings, every single scent. Shoved out by her, sweet sexy roses, her spicy blood, there, under the surface, as if it was made for him, as if *she* were made for him.

"I'm working. A half day. You don't have to worry about me." Her angry voice stole into him, lured him closer. He stepped into her space, had to be near her, had to touch her. Gently he placed his hand on her chest. She sucked in a breath, as shocked at the sparks and warmth between them as he was.

"You're not fully healed." He closed his eyes and listened to her heart, the rapid beat of it under his palm, how it leapt for him. "*Fascinating.*"

"What?" she whispered.

"*Your heart, the way it beats for me.*" He did back her into the storage room then, ignoring all reason and sense, instead leaning into the madness. The click of the door closing rang through the room.

"Niko—"

"Don't." He stepped into her space, and drew his hand up to her neck, dragging his thumb along the column of her throat.

He was instantly hard for her. "So pretty," he whispered, bracing himself against the wall with his hand beside her head. Slowly he leaned into her neck, marveling at how, even now, angry at him she tilted to make room for him. He closed his eyes and breathed her in, marveled at her pulse fluttering for him. Lost in her, surrounded by her, he took one delicious lick over her pulse, her moan echoing the path of his tongue. She was so fucking responsive to him.

"Niko," she said, breathless and husky. She gripped his hand that still stroked the column of her neck. Set her other on his chest.

"Yes, touch me. Feel how much I want you."

"Get off!" she hissed and shoved him away. Still half-muddled, he shook his head in an attempt to clear the fog. How rare it was, ever since the curse, for his body to take over thought. Not in hundreds of years had he allowed that to happen. Even in the dark, he could see the anger pulsing through her. Her beautiful green eyes glowed with heat. Her chest rose and fell with her harsh breaths.

"You don't get to treat me this way."

Her words were ice on his desire. He stood up straight and ran his hands through his hair. "You're right. I'm so sorry, Christ."

"Do you even know what you're apologizing for?"

"I...for shoving you into the..." He glanced around. "Jesus, Christ some sort of shoddy storage closet."

"No, Niko." She drew his name out as if he was an extremely slow, annoying child or gnat. "For treating me with such care and...passion, for being so honest. Until you completely closed up. Then leaving without a word, disappearing like a coward, hiding at work rather than talk to me, share with me."

"Like a coward?" Her words pierced him.

"Yes, like a fucking coward."

"You're right," he said. She was, and it seemed less intimate to admit it out loud, as opposed to their quiet connection.

She got in his space, and it was his turn to back up. "You opened up to me. I thought...you trusted me, but you're still holding back. I gave you last night. I didn't push. With as many wounds as you have, I'll be patient. But rather than speak to me this morning, even to say goodbye and tell me where you were going, or, I don't know, talk about things, be a mature adult, you keep running away."

He swallowed through the dry ache in his throat. Things. She wanted to talk about things. Did she have any idea? Standing there before him, a powerful angry goddess. She was right. "We can talk now?"

"No," she insisted. "We cannot. I'm here to work. I'm not having this conversation with you right now, next to the toilet paper and sutures with you not even certain what the issues are." She threw open the door and stepped out.

"You're not ready for work." Niko tossed the words out there, a mistake. He knew it as soon as the words left his mouth.

"You don't have a say in that."

"I'm your doctor," he insisted, digging himself deeper into the hole, unable to stop.

"Not anymore, you're not."

"You're not safe here." One last attempt.

"What in the hell are you talking about? I'm as safe here as I am...as I am at your home." That eased the sharp pain in his chest minutely.

"A feeling...something strange. I can't explain it—"

"Right, sounds like you have that problem in many areas. Forgive me while I don't wait around until you figure it out." She stalked out of the storage room, leaving him feeling like that gnat again, a gnat she'd flicked off with one sweep of her gorgeous hand.

Niko watched her walk away. He tried to gather control of his senses, his instincts, his environment, not just Francesca and her scent of roses, the memory of how soft her skin was. Once again, the sounds and actions around him coalesced. He couldn't explain the feeling he had that something wasn't right at the hospital. It had been bugging him since she'd gotten her cast removed. No, before then, since her accident and at other odd moments.

But the feeling wasn't crystal clear. It lay murky in his chest, not fully formed. He actually couldn't explain it, because he didn't understand it. Unlike the other topic she wanted to explore, which he very well could explain, but didn't want to. *Coward indeed.* Niko slipped out of the infernal closet. When she disappeared around the corner, he did the only sensible thing. He followed her. She was here to work, fine, then he was here to watch over and protect her, no matter what.

Chapter Twenty-Six

"**A**ggravating idiot. How dare he." Francesca swore under her breath as she gently inspected the swelling and bruising along her young patient's foot. Fractured, but Francesca was having a difficult time discerning if it was only in one place. She couldn't see Niko, but she could feel him lurking, not quite in her space, but not fully out of it either.

"All righty then." Lainy invaded, gently taking the patient's foot and nudging Francesca out of the way. "Let's send this one off to X-rays. I'll take her right now." Lainy glared at Francesca and then beamed her smile back at the patient. "Sorry, honey, the doctor wasn't talking to you. Of course she wasn't. You"—Lainy took Francesca's arm—"Come with me."

"What—"

"Nope. Be quiet." Lainy dragged her into the hallway. "I have an idea who you're talking about, but hello! Get your head on straight. You can't speak to patients that way."

"Oh shit. I said all that out loud?"

"Mm-hmm." Lainy's arms were crossed, but her expression held concern. "Go take a break while I deliver this traumatized child to X-rays. I'll find you in a minute. You tell me all about the aggravating devil. I can't wait to hear what's going on."

"Shit, shit, shit." Francesca sighed and slipped down the hall into the breakroom. Unfortunately, in her haste and annoyance this morning she'd forgotten to pack herself a lunch, something that never happened, even when she'd been going through a messy divorce. She loved lunch too much to forget something essential and enjoyable to her day.

Lainy stomped into the room a few moments later. "That one is in the queue at X-ray. Sit down." Francesca obeyed her. "Here."

"What's this?"

"A doughnut, dummy."

"Obviously. I meant did you make these?"

Lainy rolled her eyes. "Of course not. I'm no culinary expert like you. But I'm extremely talented at stopping at my sister's bakery on the way to work and with you out sick, we've all had to pull our weight around here in the delicious snack department.

Francesca sank back onto the old sofa someone had lugged into the break room. It had been here as long as Francesca could remember. The woven fabric had seen better days, but it was comfy. She'd personally had several cat naps on it between long shifts. The simple glazed doughnut, sugary on the outside, fluffy and doughy on the inside, was delicious. She closed her eyes and savored the bite, letting the sugar ease her frustration a bit. "Thank you," she whispered.

"Hits the spot, doesn't it? It's not infused with all your goodness, but a perfect glazed doughnut is at the top of my self-help list any day."

Francesca let out a long sigh. "Are all men this stupid?" she whispered.

Lainy laughed long and loud.

"Shh."

"Oh, no you have to let me enjoy this for a moment. I mean, was that a rhetorical question?"

Francesca gave her a wry smile.

"Listen," Lainy said quietly. "The answer to your question is an emphatic yes, but also, puppy love has knocked that cranky male for one huge loop, honey. He's out there treading water with no idea how to do this correctly."

Francesca raised her eyebrow.

"That stern gaze doesn't work on me, friend. Now use your verbal communication skills and talk to me."

The irony wasn't lost on Francesca that she was super frustrated with Niko for not being able to talk to her while she sat here keeping all her cards close to her chest, even in the presence of her best friend, someone she trusted with...well, literally with her life. Francesca was suddenly uncertain what to say. It was one thing to joke about puppy love, but the word love was not funny to her at all. Her heart leapt at the thought. *Yes, that's what this is. Please let me have it.* She was surprised her desperation wasn't loud enough for Lainy to hear.

Lainy studied her. "You do know he's in love with you, right? I mean, flat-out, no funny business, can't concentrate on anything but you, intends to give you the world, kind of love."

Love. "I...I don't actually know what that's like," Francesca admitted. She wanted it, ached for it, but how stupid really, to not be able to recognize it. She suddenly felt like a small child on the playground with no friends. Alone, always alone and uncertain.

Lainy melted in front of her and squeezed her hand. "Oh, honey."

"He's holding so much back. He's so...he's been so kind and thoughtful—"

"That side of him I would love to see."

Francesca let out a small laugh. "Yes, he is rather arrogant and closed off here, isn't he?"

"Mm, he has his walls up high, that's for sure. He—"

"Oh, shh." Francesca put her hand over Lainy's mouth. This time both women quieted, eyes turned toward the doorway. Dr. Blythe was especially overcologned today.

"Ladies, taking a much-needed break, I suppose."

"Actually..." Lainy stood and dragged Francesca up. "We're finished.

Here." Lainy shoved the box of doughnuts in his direction, putting a barrier between them.

"Oh, none for me. You two should watch what you eat too. Don't want to gain too much more weight, do you?"

It took all of Francesca's willpower, which was extremely compromised at this moment, not to smash him upside the head. As if she hadn't heard versions of that comment her entire life. Christ, could they at least be original in their criticism? Niko was right, this man wasn't her friend. Thirty-five and she was still learning how to recognize healthy relationships.

"Although swimming helps keep you in shape, I suspect."

Huh, had she ever mentioned swimming to him? She couldn't remember. And there he went reminding her about her weight again. Yep, not her friend.

"Okay, time to go." Lainy took the biggest doughnut in the box, a large apple fritter coated in icing, and took an enormous bite out of it.

"I suppose you heard about Dr. Madison?" he asked. "She hasn't reported for her shifts the last two days. They think she might be missing."

"What?" The unease in Francesca's stomach turned sickly at the news and...the odd, thrilled tone in Dr. Blythe's voice. Some people thrived on drama and bad news.

"Missing?" Lainy's voice filled the awkward space. "That's horrible."

"Isn't it," he said and plucked a chocolate bomb doughnut, studied it with that shimmer in his eyes, and then dropped it back in the box.

Francesca raised her eyes at Lainy. "We should get back to work. Enjoy your doughnut, Doctor." She tagged Lainy's hand and drew her out of the room. "Was it just me," she whispered as they rushed away down the corridor, "or did he seem to be enjoying the fact that one of our female doctors might be in serious trouble?"

"That was creepy," Lainy said. "I may never eat another doughnut as long as I live." She shuddered and tossed the rest of her apple fritter in the trash. "But he's right. She hasn't shown up for her last two shifts. I didn't think anything of it at first, because to be honest, it was nice to have the break, but she's never missed a shift."

"No. She might be difficult to get along with, but something feels off."

"I have the same awful feeling."

***

"What's wrong?" Niko's voice was that soft deep rumble she adored. It wrapped around her like a hug. They hadn't said a word to each other since he'd kindly offered her a ride home after her shift. She'd been set to turn him down when she realized again that she no longer had a car. Booth had dropped her off this afternoon, which now felt like a million years ago. It was amazing what worry could do to the day, how it could turn each hour into eons. Confusing, difficult, and extremely exhausting.

"Many things. Perhaps you shouldn't ask unless you're prepared to listen and talk. Give and take, rather than acting like an iceberg. And I'm not only speaking of the physical."

"I'm an iceberg now?"

"Yes, Niko. Something imposing and frozen, with many hidden layers," she snapped.

He was silent for so long hope began to fizz out of her as though she had a tiny pinprick somewhere in her body and was deflating as they drove.

"I'm trying, Francesca. I...I..."

"I know," she said quietly. "You're afraid."

"Perhaps we can start with the less...uh...less fearful things that are bothering you. Please, let me help." She couldn't ignore it when he bared his soul, such open pleas coming from his beautiful lips. Perhaps he was as lost as she was in this world.

"Fine," she huffed. "I'm worried about Dr. Madison. It's not like the ice queen to ditch work with no word. Dr. Blythe acted giddy at the news when he told Lainy and me."

Niko gripped the steering wheel tighter. "I don't want you anywhere near that...that..."

"Trust me. I might be slow to learn, but you're right. He's not my friend."

"What did he do, Francesca?" The temperature in the car plummeted. "I'm going to ruin him. I'm going to have him fired, run out of town, eviscerated."

"Let's just say his comments on my size were not all that original, Niko." Francesca sighed. "I don't want to waste our time on him." Gently she rested her hand on his arm.

Niko seethed beneath her touch. Even with the layer of his coat between them, she could feel his rage. "He will never come near you again. I—"

"Hush. Let's not talk about Blythe anymore."

"You're right." The words seemed dragged from him under extreme torture. "I'm sorry." He sent a glance her way. "You look tired."

"Niko. I swear to the goddesses." Francesca rubbed her eyes.

"You're beautiful to me, no matter what. I meant, well...*are* you tired? It was your first day back. Don't ask me not to worry. I can't give you that. Only a few weeks ago I had your lungs and heart in my hands, sewing you up, pleading with everything I am to not let me make a mistake like I did with that child."

In an instant, he could cut her open emotionally. Francesca closed her eyes and rested her head against the window. She brushed her way down the length of his arm and linked her fingers with his. "That was not your fault, Nikolav, darling. Please, no matter what, I need you to accept that. Promise me." She opened her eyes and sent him her most serious gaze.

"Fine. I promise. If you let me care for you."

If she'd had enough energy, she would have laughed. *Good play, sneaky bastard.*

"Now please tell me how you're feeling."

"I'm exhausted," she said. "Is that what you want to hear? Today was difficult, but not so much because I'm still healing. And I'd tell you if I wasn't feeling okay, as far as my injuries are concerned. Worry makes me tired. I was already angry at your desertion when I left the house this morning, then you and I...well I don't need to explain our last interaction. Add to all of that, I didn't eat breakfast and I forgot my lunch. I never forget my lunch." God, she was pouting. She really must be exhausted.

Niko gave her a soft smile before turning his gaze back to the road. "No, I suppose you don't forget your food, do you?"

They pulled into his driveway, and he'd parked and was around her side before she could open her door. He crowded into her space and took her head in his hands. Why did she love it so much when he did that? Such warm hands touching her, and that commanding look in his gaze that she couldn't pull her eyes away from even if she was ordered to. It had seared itself into her heart, latched on. Connected. That was what she wanted, what she'd always hoped for, this intimate link with another human being. It was the confusion over him connecting and then pulling away that hurt.

"I want to be everything you desire, Francesca. I'm trying to find the words to explain myself to you, my deepest darkest sins. But right now, I need to care for you. I'm aware my recent behavior shows I don't deserve them, but please allow me these moments."

There was such agony in his eyes again. What sins had been committed upon him? Because she didn't think he even realized how much trauma lived in his bones. "Okay," she whispered.

The relief that bled from him was another indication, of what she couldn't know exactly, but her instincts told her he'd also been left before. And at least right now, she didn't want to be another person in his life who abandoned him. Physically or emotionally.

"Why don't you shower, and I'll see what we have to eat." He linked their fingers and led her into the house, giving her a gentle shove up the stairs before he turned and disappeared down the hallway to the kitchen.

All right, she told herself. *Focus on what you can. Shower then eat.* At least he was here with her, trying. She only hoped it would eventually be enough because she knew in her heart that she deserved the world. It remained to be seen whether Niko could be that person for her or not.

CHAPTER TWENTY-SEVEN

TOO STUNNED TO SAY anything, Francesca picked her jaw up off the floor at the sight that greeted her in the kitchen. Freshly showered, wearing comfy clothes, and smelling loads better than the hospital, she finished tucking her hair up into a loose bun. When Niko looked up at her entrance, his eyes blazed. The man could light her up with one burning stare. The power in that did not go unnoticed by her eyes or the rest of her body. A shiver ran across her skin at the memories of what else he could do to her when he was worshiping her. She should probably shore up her defenses to his physical allure, but she was too tired to fight right now. Not to mention the aroma in the kitchen made her deliriously happy. The dogs both lay on their sides close to Niko. Her heart thudded against her chest.

"You cook?"

His hooded eyes followed her as she made her way around the island to where he stood. She thought there might be a scorched path in her wake from the force of his gaze as he dragged it down her body and back up to where she played with a curl that had come loose. Her neck heated with his stare, red blooming across her skin as he pierced her with those silver eyes of his. Was she teasing him? Not purposefully. She wanted him to open up to her, to trust her. "Uh, here." He broke their connection, handed her a glass of red wine, and shifted a plate of delicious cheese and crackers her way. "I do cook."

"Please don't elaborate. I can't handle all your babbling." She did tease then. He was wound so tight. It was fun to poke him, and it eased her own stress. "I didn't think vampires needed to eat," she said, devouring a few bites of food and sipping her wine. "Oh, my this is divine, Niko." She closed her eyes and breathed in the scent of the pinot noir, earthy, a hint of spice, something deep and rich. He was staring at her when she opened her eyes. It took him a few very long seconds to blink himself back, and she welcomed it, his unease, the tiny bit of thread fraying at his edges.

"We don't *need* to." The way he emphasized the word had her leaning closer to him. "Uh...eat, that is."

Desire for him pulsed everywhere, even though she was still upset with him. This pull between them was irrational and heady all at the same time.

"Sit down," he commanded, pointing toward the stools at the kitchen counter. "Please." He softened his tone. "Rest. And you two," he motioned toward the dogs. "go to your places." They scampered up and flopped over to their dog beds where Niko set a treat down for both of them.

Oh, this was quite fun watching him be domestic. She walked back around the island to climb onto one of the comfortable stools. It was easy to get lost in him, distracted by him, but they needed to talk. This was good. She could sip her wine, nibble the goodies, and maybe get him to open up.

"I don't require food to live, but there are a few items I appreciate. I enjoy cooking. I...uh wanted some hobbies." He scoffed at the last word as though it personally wounded him. "I've been alone for seven hundred years."

Was he going to break her heart into a million pieces every time he opened his mouth? Did he have any idea what his story, his truths, did to her?

"That's a very long time, darling." She vowed in that moment, no matter how much he frustrated her, how long it took him to be fully vulnerable with her, she would never leave him. His admission obliterated all her careful knowledge of what she was willing to put up with in a relationship and what she wasn't. He was hers and it was her duty, her joy now to surround him with love and affection, with the bone-deep promise that he could trust her. Hopefully he would eventually. He was such a wounded animal, and she must be extremely patient. There were bound to be setbacks. She had to show him she wouldn't abandon him, no matter what. She was strong enough. It was a matter of convincing him she could handle anything he tossed her way.

A shudder went through him as more tension eased from his body. "I like it when you call me that." He didn't look at her when he spoke, instead concentrating on meticulously and precisely cutting some carrots, faster than she'd ever seen anyone chop vegetables. As if he could do it with his eyes closed. His perfection and precision were such turn-ons.

"I know," she replied simply. "What are you making? It smells wonderful."

"A Thai curry, if that's all right?"

"I love curries. You know, not many people have cooked for me, Niko. Not like this as an act of love. This feels special." Give and take, that was what she'd said. He'd shared something vulnerable, now it was her turn.

He did face her then, with that calculating gleam as if he could see everything inside or wanted to. She didn't know which was more exhilarating. "Not even your sister?"

"Gia is many things, but only eat her cooking if you plan to keel over. To her biggest regret? When she was a simple home-maker..." Francesca paused, trying to remember her sister before all the bad things had happened. "She wasn't great at cooking. She'd tell you herself if she even remembers the way she was back then. She was too busy daydreaming and playing with the children. She was such a dreamer, Niko. I pray she finds that again someday."

"Mm. And your parents?"

Even without saying much, his look was intense, all those thoughts running around his head that she craved access to. "I don't remember my father." She closed her eyes briefly and pictured her mom. "My mother adored cooking. Maybe that's why I love it so much because it makes me feel close to her. It allows me to remember the happy memories as opposed to what happened at the end." She shook off the ghosts. "Perhaps we save that conversation for another time."

He nodded. "I assume your ex didn't cook either." She shouldn't laugh at his ornery tone. She wasn't surprised in the least, after everything that had happened, that he knew she had an ex.

"No, he didn't. And I was too busy cooking for him, trying to please him to see that no matter what I did, no matter who I was, it was never going to be enough. Or rather it was all too much for him." She waved her hand up and down her body.

"He was the fool," Niko swore, and his tone could have peeled paint off an old building. "Worse, he was blind or stupid. Your everything is amazing and gorgeous and intriguing and so fascinating I couldn't keep myself away, Francesca. And I will never stop being intrigued by you, wanting to learn from you, about you."

"You're making me blush." When he talked to her like that, so vehemently, she believed him. What a high that was. He was a drug, luring her up and up, making her soar. But when he disappeared on her or wouldn't communicate, it hurt, made her question the high in the first place. It was a dangerous tightrope she walked. If she was going to be all in, she'd have to shore up her defenses.

"Where did you learn to cook?"

"Many places. I studied cooking in Italy and Poland, and I lived in Chiang Mai for half a century. I worked at a clinic there and spent most of my free time studying Buddhism, trying to find a way to live peacefully."

"I'm fascinated by your mind; how much you know of the world and medicine. I have been since you blew through the doors of the hospital like a hurricane avenging all the world's evil, or idiots perhaps. I knew from the beginning you weren't one to suffer fools either."

"I did arrive with quite a chip on my shoulder. All those years...all those years alone...and...not being able..." For once he seemed unable to find the words.

"I imagine being alone for so long would do that to a person." Francesca took pity and finished the thought for him. "Not to mention how intelligent you are. We all must have seemed like county bumpkins, much less fools to you."

"Never," he said so emphatically with those molten eyes piercing her, as if insisting with the flame that she believe him. "That's just...simply my normal way."

"Resting arrogant face?"

"What?" He looked completely flustered and she chuckled at his confusion. The man might have centuries of learning underneath his belt but today's social cues were not his strong suit.

"Sorry..." She tried to contain her giggles. "It's a saying, or rather...forget it. May I?" She snuck a carrot without waiting for his reply.

"I hope, I hope..." The saucepan simmered between them, curry spices and coconut milk. "That I never treated you so poorly. In fact, I'm sure I did, and I apologize for that, Francesca."

"You never treated me like a fool, Niko. You might have been a bit gruff, but now I'm wondering if that was part of the walls you put up."

"To keep you at arm's length, to protect you," he insisted.

"Or to protect you." The words hovered between them in the intimate, warm, setting of the kitchen. The sizzling of the vegetables exaggerated the silence between them. The way he kept her gaze, the flashes of electricity shooting across the link that connected them.

"You could be correct."

Well, there was some forward progress.

"I find my certainty of all things shaken since we've grown closer," he admitted.

Her smile was instant. "Grown closer is one way to put it," she said. The hot gaze he sent her way nearly had her panting. "You didn't think me a fool when we first met? That's something." A thought struck her then. "Did you know I was a witch at first?" Even while she tried to hide her true nature from the world, she had a sense about other beings. Could others sense her?

"I did." He busied himself with stirring the chicken into the large pot of simmering curry. Then he turned his back on her to wash his hands. So silent, so stoic. Was she going to have to dig every single word out of him? She waited for him to continue, content to watch his mind tick. He set a lid on the saucepan and switched off the burner. "We'll eat later." He topped her glass of wine off and came around the island. Heat radiated off him in a powerful controlled wave.

Danger, her mind warned. *Good danger*, her libido chimed in.

She set her glass down, swiveled on the stool so her back was to the island, and opened her legs to him so he could fit himself right there. He sipped his wine, studying her, and she let him, basking in his gaze, all that silver magic pouring over her like discovery and blatant interest, like sweet, sweet desire. Niko inched closer, set his glass next to hers, and caged her in. She hadn't realized how massive he was more than right now as he hovered, claiming her space for his own. *Take it all*, she wanted to yell.

"What gave it away?" she asked. Francesca ran her hands up his strong arms. His deep masculine scent toyed with her senses. The curry was long forgotten. All she could smell was him.

One side of his mouth tipped up in an almost smile. Good God, when the man smiled, he was even more dangerous. "I can sense things too."

"I bet you can." She tried to keep her voice steady. He made her unsteady, or...molten, as if she could simply shed all her clothes and flow to him, fuse every single part of herself to him. "With all those years of experience knowing who and what you are, all that serious focus you maintain." She dragged her hands up until she could feel the warmth of his neck, stroking it with her fingertips. Niko sucked in a breath and shut his eyes, leaning in even closer. A rumble escaped his lips, an abandoned cat purring at a long-lost touch. Francesca's blood heated at the thought that he felt the same fiery pull between them, choices tossed on the floor exactly how she wanted their clothes to be.

"When I first met you. I didn't think you knew, yourself…" His words trailed off as her light touch turned to massage. "That feels good," he whispered, closing his eyes and bowing towards her.

"Didn't think I knew what?" she whispered. "That I was a witch?"

"Mm-hmm." He nodded, rubbing his head into her hands. A cat indeed. The laugh bubbled out of her. He lowered his head into her completely, right into the crook of her shoulder blade so his breath fluttered against her neck. Infinite sparks shot across her skin. She was buzzing and alive for him.

"I love it when you laugh." His words were a caress against her pulse beating for him. Always beating for him.

"Why did you think that?" Her voice had turned to a whisper. It was all she was capable of. "I am lacking in some witch skills but enlighten me." She did as she always did when his lips were buried against the fragile needy skin of her neck—she tilted her head to the side—allowing room for him. *I'm made for you.* The thought rushed through like a spring breeze kicking things up in its wake, delighted, certain, fresh. She brought her hand up through his hair holding him to her. Heat licked at her skin as her pulse sped into its rapid dance, recognizing him. "Niko?"

"You're not what I expected, what I'm used to...in..." He ran his nose along her neck. "A witch."

"Did you expect me to be all black hat and angry warts?" She giggled and he pressed into her, so much closer. Every hard plane of his vibrated against her. "Or maybe dancing with my coven, naked in the fields at sunrise?" She joked, taunted him, blurring all the lines she'd set for herself not to cross today before they talked, before they communicated with words. Christ, he communicated perfectly like this. It was easy to get lost, to shove all the *should* away.

"No, Francesca." He sounded angry but he leaned in even closer and gripped her hips, tugging her legs around him. When he turned and lifted her, her insides flipped and danced. A man who could carry her. His hands on her butt, her arms wrapped around him, holding him close, and his hard pulsing length nestled right there against her. Not to mention the burning focus of his eyes gone molten all for her. "I only pictured you naked, dancing under me, in bed."

She lifted her head back, arching into him. "Yes, please, Nikolav."

There was no quick tracing. Instead, he took his time, climbing up the stairs with her, each step allowing their bodies to rub against each other. The thrill coursed through her to him.

"Say it again."

This time she brought her head to his, her lips on his. "Yes, please, Nikolav. I want to dance naked under you, and beside you, and on top of you. I want to try out that sensual bathtub with you and dance in the shower with you."

"In my bed while I fuck your sweet pussy with my tongue. Or on your knees while you suck my cock with that luscious mouth of yours." His eyes glazed over with lust, and she shivered in his arms, holding on tighter, settling her core even closer. "You'd like all of that, wouldn't you?"

"Mm, I love it when you talk dirty to me, Niko. Who knew?"

"I guess we have a lot to learn about each other, don't we?" he said, tossing her on her bed and prowling over her all dark and mysterious.

She brushed her hand across his cheek. "Let me learn everything about you." How could she convey what she meant with such simple words? "Don't keep me out."

The tortured look on his face almost had her regretting, but she was confident she could get through to him. "There isn't one thing that could scare me away, Niko. I already told you that." He shook his head, and she pulled him to her. "For now, have me, naked and dancing under you. Give and take. Take all you can. I'm not going anywhere."

"You should." He lifted her sweater up and off in one blink of an eye. Then he traced the edge of her bra and kissed her right there against her breastbone.

"No, Niko. I'm right where I belong. With you."

Chapter Twenty-Eight

H E SHOULD LEAVE, FLEE right now, get as far away as he could, put countries between them. But she wrapped herself around him, her body, her unique essence, her exhilaration for life. She was so fucking wet and vulnerable for him, even, knowing what he was, and it was all he could do not to push his way into her immediately and stake his claim. "Your fucking scent. Your skin pulses with it." *For me.* That was what he recognized and why even countries couldn't keep him from her. She was meant for him. There was no denying it any longer.

He dragged his body down hers, flinging her jeans and panties away for good. *"Yes, that's what I should do, demand you be naked all the time so I can have my way."*

"That sounds a bit reckless and fabulous at the same time." Her hands were on her breasts and over her belly. He flung them away too and held them at her sides.

"Reckless indeed. You here in my bed, reading my thoughts, luring me into you." He let her soft capable hands go and brushed his nose low over her belly, following her scent.

"You're not in me *yet*, my love." Deep seductive laughter rippled through her.

Fucking hell, her words were more potent than her scent, than her lushness laid out before him, arching toward him, an offering from the goddesses themselves. She had to be a gift. How incredible she was, how lovely, how kind, how powerful, how she teased him mercilessly. There was no other explanation.

And he knew he had to tell her the truth. Correction, he'd known he'd have to tell her since the day he met her. He'd avoided this moment, this collision, shoved it away because of fear, like she'd said. She knew him well.

And yet, the most important part, the bare truth, all his sins—she didn't have a clue. He balanced on the precipice now. To pull back, or to leap over. Once he gave her what she asked of him, his deepest darkest secrets, she would hate him, be disgusted. Both of which were nothing really, because there was something far worse she would do too—vanish, never to return. And, even after surviving alone for all these centuries, now that he'd had the tiniest most intimate taste of her beauty, her presence in his bleak life, he couldn't withstand her leaving. This night might be his last.

"Mm, your touch is warm...sparks lighting up my skin, Niko." She was the one lighting him up, his mundane existence. She was magic and he was caught. And she had no idea what she asked of him. Everything? He wanted her to be his everything. Perhaps...she could wipe it all away, his misdeeds, his crimes, all the evil inside him.

He smoothed his palms over her hips, nuzzled his face into her soft glorious skin, kissing along her inner thighs. Lifting her hips up to take what she offered, he stole a look at her face. Eyes closed, lips curved in a smile, skin flushed for him. He'd have to make her as mindless for him as he was for her. They could be lost together. Damn the consequences. *"Mine."* He urged the thought into her right before he stroked his tongue along the soft outer lips of her pussy.

"Yes, Niko." Her words rushed to him, urged him on, as did her body, trying to thrust up into him.

"Patience," he ordered, locking her hips in place. He loved her like this, all undone for him, every ounce of her control gone.

"No, no, no. I don't have any patience, Niko." Shaking her head, she tried to move, but his strength outweighed hers. And he wanted to make this last for her, for both of them. He aimed to take all these memories with him, blanket himself with them when she flew away.

"I'm not flying away, Niko. I promise," she whispered.

His thoughts were bleeding out between them, his control slipping with each taste of her.

"Be good. Do as I say. And I'll reward you. I'll give you everything."

"Ahh," she sighed and opened her eyes to watch him. "Is that how we're going to do it this time?"

A shiver ran through her, and he could read her so well now. He knew it was one of excitement. She liked the idea of obeying him as much as he did. He wondered if she knew exactly what he meant when he said *everything*. Not breaking eye contact, he stroked her pussy again with his tongue, eliciting a gorgeous moan from her.

"See, there you go, beautiful. I like rewarding this body." He brought his mouth to her and feasted. Teasing, licking, toying with her until he found her clit, watching and listening to her writhe beneath him. Every cell in her rushed to her core, all her blood, pulsing from there now, calling to him, answering him, begging to be joined with him. His own blood beat in tandem with hers, a special dance, connected as he'd always longed to be.

"Please, Niko. I can't...I can't take anymore...I..."

"Tell me what I can do for you." He stroked her slowly with his thumb, watching her pussy swell for him. She was so fucking gorgeous.

"I need to come. Can't you feel it? Can't you feel how my body aches for yours?"

He smiled and worked one finger into her, stroking her higher, watching her light up. Another finger slid in perfectly and his cock jumped at the notion that it should be right there.

"Niko...I'm begging...I'm..." He clamped his mouth down on her swollen bud and sucked. The desire to bite her, to mark her roared through his mind. He was on fire for her. He was savage enough gripping her hips to him with such force he knew he'd leave bruises, but when she exploded on his tongue and cried his name, it was worth it. His entire life, all the misery and pain had been worth it.

She was still shuddering and panting when he fisted his cock and rubbed it in her juices. "Niko, yes."

He flipped her over and lifted her hips.

"I need you inside m—"

He didn't let her finish. He thrust in, drowning in the last quivers of her orgasm. as it wrapped around him. *Fucking heaven*. He pushed in deeper, gripped her luscious bottom, and moved.

"Yes. More. It's magical." Her thoughts and feelings curled around them in ribbons of gold and teal, in musical notes. It was magical. It was like nothing he'd experienced before, the two of them connected in this way. She met his thrusts, pushing back as if she wanted him deeper too, so deep they could never be parted. Perfection.

His instincts urged him to lean down, to bite her. Her neck was there, gorgeous soft skin, a few delicate freckles, her pulse trying to lure him in. Even without that sensation of sinking his teeth into that milky skin, he felt her life all around him. He picked up his pace, acting on the frustration to come and to mark her, to fully make her his. But he'd wait, he had to. A little longer, if she didn't run the moment he told her the truth.

"You are brilliant," he said as he fucked her beautiful body. "Look at you, on fire for me."

"Yes, Niko. Only for you." She locked into his thoughts. *"Please take all of me."* Her body shook with the movement.

"You are mine," he demanded as if his tone could force her to agree.

"Yes." She nodded into the pillow and tilted her head to look back at him.

"Only mine." He moved faster, held her hips to him so he could fuck her exactly as he wanted, going deep with each thrust, his body a frenzied madness now as pressure sped down his spine through his cock. "I need you, Francesca. Come around me. Work your magic on me, love." Moving one hand between them he rubbed her clit. "Mine," he growled again.

"Yes, God, Niko." She arched back one last time. Her pussy clamped down on him and she shuddered with her release. Niko buried his cock in her and followed.

Chapter Twenty-Nine

N IKO WAS STILL BURIED deep inside her, still half hard, even after that intense orgasm. His body covered hers. Lost in her scent and her softness, he could stay here forever.

"Why won't you bite me?" Her words were a shaken whisper underneath him.

"What?" Slowly, Niko withdrew and turned her to face him. Her eyes were closed. Something was wrong. She hadn't once been nervous and uncertain around him. Is that what he'd done to her, his queen, this powerful being? Had his indecision caused that? How cruel he'd been when he'd intended the exact opposite?

"You heard me," she said quietly. *Definitely feeling uncertain.* Fuck. He'd heard her, not just the waver in her voice but the actual words.

"You *want* me to?" Gently as if she were a doe skittish under his touch, Niko stroked the soft skin of her neck, choked up at how close he was to her, to having everything, and to potentially losing it all. "This precious skin, this offering. It's like you're asking me to bite you, damn the consequences."

"I am," she whispered, tears in her eyes. "And what consequences, Niko? Tell me. You promised."

Fuck. He sat up cradling her to him. How could he find the words to expose himself? He'd killed so many with his bite. Then...then he'd been prevented from ever biting again, until...

"Nikolav, I'm not afraid of you, of this. I've dreamed *this*, you and me here fully connected as only we can be."

"I've said before it's not a joke." He tossed out the words like a weapon, a starved animal cornered and fighting back.

"I know that too, darling." She soothed with her words and brushed featherlight touches down the taut muscles of his back. Every stroke of her fingers healed another layer of his past. "There's nothing funny about an elemental connection between two mates."

"Two mates? You think..."

"I *know*." There was her confidence, her power surging back into her. "I feel it too." Her eyes were shimmering pools of wisdom.

Trust. Wasn't that what she'd said? And he hadn't trusted someone in a very long time, perhaps longer than he'd been a vampire. Worse. It was himself he didn't trust.

"I don't want to hurt you." He shook his head, trying to hold his own tears back. Unsuccessful, he trudged onward. "I hurt...them." He buried his face in her neck then, seeking solace, hiding in the very place he wanted to find his freedom. "I can't protect you from me." It was time for *the everything* he'd promised her. It went against his self-protection to do so, like a child hiding a sin, knowing there'd be hell to pay once it was admitted.

"You've said that before. Tell me what you mean. All of it. Let it go. You promised. This is it, sharing your deepest wounds and secrets and desires and sins. Not just fantastic out-of-this-world sex."

He smiled at her ability to be brutally honest, even as their world could shatter around them at any moment.

"I'm ashamed." There, he'd admitted it. The truth of it all. It cloaked him as it had for centuries, always reminding him of what he'd done, and worse, what he'd failed to do. But now time was up, and so he began. "I knew you were my mate the very moment I met you. I simply denied it."

"So I wouldn't see your sins? Your trauma? Your pain?"

Perhaps that was the truth of it too. He'd thought to protect her from his physical ability to kill when really he'd never wanted her to know how vile a creature he'd once been, how he still had the potential to be.

"Tell me," she whispered and administered soothing kisses along his brow, softening his resolve, his fears with her touch. "Tell me."

She lured him in, cast her spell. And finally, he broke under it. Shuddering out a sigh, he pulled them down in the bed together, face-to-face, and gave it to her. "I was changed when I was sixteen by a pack of vampires sweeping through our village.

They...they..." He swallowed and got on with it. And, like ripping out the dagger thrust into his leg, the blood came pouring out. "They let me live, turned me into one of them, said I had the potential to be powerful. I could hear them talking and laughing even as my bones broke and reformed."

"Niko."

"Then they massacred my parents, my sisters, and my nieces right in front of me. It happened in seconds. I still felt half human, couldn't make any sense of it, was too weak...too fucking weak to do anything."

He didn't give her a chance to respond. "I went...crazy, went on a rampage. For a long time after my family was murdered, I destroyed lives. I took whatever I wanted, money, houses, people. I spent every moment for almost one hundred years doing horrible things. I tracked down the group that turned me and killed every last one of them. I didn't care. I was uncontrollable, filled only with rage, blood for vision. It was all I could see. Sex and killing were the only things fueling me.

"I kept having a nightmare of my dead sister, Sylvie, her pale blue eyes wide open, and asking why I hadn't protected her as she lay dying. She was five." He was breathing heavily as though he'd fled across continents, been bled dry in reliving it all, in exposing his truest self. Exhaustion seeped into his bones. Exhaustion and turmoil, because now she would leave. The truth was there between them as he'd promised.

"Oh, Nikolav." Francesca's soft voice stole through the pain. "You were a boy. You were in pain, full of grief and anger for what happened to your loved ones."

He wrapped his arms around her tighter, as if he could make her stay. "No." He shook his head. "I was...I am a monster."

"No. Shh, my love. You're not a monster. You don't hurt people anymore."

"They had to curse me to make me stop."

Her hands stilled. "Who?"

"Witches. Very powerful witches. They caught me and cursed me to never kill another human again. They banned me from enjoying comfort or having sex again. Not until..."

"Not until what, Niko?"

"Until I found my mate."

"And you...you continued on, you survived? For centuries? After all that? I...I..." Her voice shook as her tears slipped out. Shimmery beautiful tears.

"I should have been the one to die. Don't cry for me."

Francesca picked up her caressing again, but Niko could feel her brain working, piecing through all that he'd told her, all the rubble and debris, the shell that he was. Her heartbeat changed when she was contemplating serious things. It was powerful, electric, and fearsome.

"After they cursed you, what did they do?"

"Do?" He rested his head on her chest, and let the rhythm of her heart soothe him. She hadn't fled. Magic indeed, a sacred, healing kind.

"Yes, what did they do to help you, show you how to live without your family and your...your nature?"

"They disappeared. It felt like a strange dream in slow motion, the entirety of it all. One moment I was naked in bed with another vampire. The next I was in chains, blinded in a dungeon, kneeling on the hard dirt floor with them whispering their spell around me, too drugged to do anything but listen.

"When I woke, or came out of it, whatever spelled state I'd been in, I was alone, on the street, in the rain. An old man covered me with his coat and got me to the hospital. I could feel the need to drink, and I couldn't do anything to him. Couldn't bite him. Couldn't even speak to swear or yell. All I could do was let people care for me. A few hours later they turned me out to the streets in some borrowed clothing. I was starving, ruined. I'm not sure why or how I survived. Two days later, I dragged myself back and snuck into the hospital. I scavenged, tried to get blood from freshly dead bodies before they wrapped them and sent them to be buried.

"Sometimes at night I'd follow the gravediggers to find blood that way, however meager. Eventually I got a job at the hospital. The same man who saved me was a doctor. He taught me until I became a surgeon. I learned to drink from animals. I could...one can only drink from a dead body for a short period after its death. Once the idea of the morgue was developed and then blood banks, it was easier for me to find blood, especially at hospitals. But that wasn't until the twentieth century." He'd be damned for telling her all these gory details, but his exhaustion

beat everything down, all his inhibitions, his walls, any sem-
blance of what he should and should not be doing.

"They cursed you and left you? Rather than help you deal
with your grief? Witches...my kind did that to you?" Anger and
disbelief vibrated through her voice.

Niko took deep breaths and allowed her touch to bring him
back. She was still here, beneath him, around him. She hadn't
shoved him away. "Why haven't you run screaming from me?"

"I see the truth of it all. My heart breaks for what you endured, even the killing. You were a child, and you were in great
pain and no one helped you. And then, when those...witch-
es found you, they hurt you again and abandoned you. You
survived all of that, despite horrible odds, and kept going for
centuries. And I love who you are now."

"How? How can you see the good in me?" His voice was raw.
He'd spilled his sins.

"Because it's right there in front of me. And because...be-
cause a part of me understands deeply some of what you must
have felt when your family was killed. My mother...she...I didn't
even try to help her, Niko. Gia and I woke to her screaming and
by the time we got to her she was dead. And..."

He kissed the tears leaking from her eyes, both enraged at
what she'd endured and humbled by her compassion.

"Even though I still feel a layer of guilt," she said, mesmerizing
him with the force of her gaze, the love shimmering through.
"I know better now. I was sixteen, just like you. We were kids,
Nikolav, and someone stole everything from us. And all I can

feel now is grateful that we both made it to find each other. And I'm your mate. Your curse is broken."

Niko dragged her closer, his cock aching at her words. He wrapped her tightly, rolled them, and seated himself fully inside her again.

"Nikolav," she said, hushing out his name on a breathless sigh.

"You undo me." He dragged out and thrust back in, keeping their bodies locked together. He was truly never letting her go again. Hiking her leg over his, he thrust, angling himself deeper.

"So deep." She clung to him, whimpering out her pleasure. "You endured and you found me."

"So did you, my beauty." He stroked his fingers over her ass and down her cleft, lower and lower till he found her pussy, found their connection. She was perfect and lush and sexy.

He placed gentle kisses along her neck, even though the last thing he felt was gentle. "Right here, this gorgeous skin is where I'm going to bite you the first time." His kisses turned more demanding, licking and sucking her skin as her body thrummed around him. Fuck, how had he gotten so lucky? She clung to him, her energy lagging.

"Do it, Niko. I'm begging." Her pleas almost tossed his control out the window, but he would do everything he could to make it less painful for her, something he'd never done for a human before.

"Soon, my heart."

"Now," she pleaded again, fluttering around his cock. She was so close, as was he.

"Fuck. You're so tight around me. Don't worry, love." He soothed with his words and his fingers as he rubbed against her clit. "I'll give you what you desire. Have a little more patience."

"Why?" she cried out even as she came around him like the most beautiful butterfly, like joy and passion and love and surprise all wrapped into one.

"Because," he said as he thrust up into her, harder, faster, chasing his own orgasm, "I've only ever taken when I've bitten. For you, I aim to give."

CHAPTER THIRTY

F RANCESCA LAY FLUSHED AND used in the best way, propped up on the pile of pillows Niko had made for her before he'd left. He'd cleaned her with a warm cloth, kissed her senseless, and reassured her he'd be right back. Her heart and body still fluttered with satisfaction. The man toyed and teased and seduced her body, as though he were carving out her true essence, providing a brilliant space for her to shine. She was all boring parts before, or at least those were the parts she showed most of the world. He seduced and manipulated and worked her into something magnificent. No lover had her sparking and flying and somersaulting through the air with such intense feelings, physically and emotionally. They'd bared everything to each other.

Now she was flushed and exhausted and exhilarated and still a bit confused. He hadn't bitten her, and it was the way to truly mark them as each other's. But my goodness, open up he had. The first time she'd met him, her witch's instinct had sensed his inner pain, something so tragic he covered it all up with his arrogance and anger. But she'd had no idea the extent of it all. One trauma after another, and he suffered through each one alone and forever changed with no one to guide him or hug him or love him. An outsider suffering through each trauma by himself. Not so different from herself, except she'd had Gia. He'd been truly alone.

And to think it had been witches who'd harmed him too. She wanted to burn them to the ground. No wonder he'd been wary of her. It only cemented, even more, how important it was for her to care for him now, to show him, prove to him that what he'd just said, everything he said and did from now on, his true self, was safe and protected in her hands, in her heart. She had centuries worth of damage to undo.

Before she could worry too much, he was back, black pajama pants hanging low on his hips, his bare chest sleek and on display for her. He carried a tray full of food and wine. Sitting up, she twisted her hair into a knot on top of her head and tied it up with her soft scarf. "That smells amazing."

As graceful as ever, he slid next to her on the bed, bowl of curry in hand. "I intended to feed you earlier, but I got distracted. Now you need sustenance." He passed her a glass of red wine.

"It's true." She laughed and leaned into him. "You exhausted me."

"Mm." He drew his gaze down her body as if still seeing her naked before him even though she'd wrapped the sheet around her. "You'll need energy for what's to come."

"Really?" She leaned in and kissed him, nipping at his bottom lip. Hinting at what she hoped was to come. He did honestly have the most magnificent lips and tongue and teeth. She wanted his teeth on her. Even now, after the workout they'd had, her blood purred at the thought. They were tied in a way she couldn't explain but understood on a fundamental level.

He gripped her neck and held her to him. "Eat, Francesca," he insisted on a growl, and she nearly giggled at how on edge he was. Every single muscle held in control. She needed to loosen him up, get him to relax, and revel in what they'd shared. She was free and open and finally, finally exactly where she was meant to be. Even with him holding himself so rigid, his fingers warmed her neck. How did he do that, comfort her while still grasping tightly to his reins? When he lifted a spoonful of the red curry and rice to her mouth, the flavors overwhelmed her. The warmth of the spices, the coconut milk, the hints of ginger.

"Niko," she exclaimed after swallowing the first bite. "This is lovely, all these gourmet flavors, but true comfort food at the same time. I...I..." He fed her as they sat in silence. She savored all the delicious flavors as they nourished her. It was all too much. "Wow." Words failed her.

"What's wrong?" He could sense her emotions easily. Setting the bowl aside, he cradled her head.

Catching his gaze, she smiled. "Not a thing. I'm overwhelmed, that's all. I told you no one had ever cooked for me, like this, out of love, and I...it must seem silly, especially to you who doesn't enjoy food, but..."

"It's elemental to you. It's who you are, feeding others, caring for them that way."

"Yes. And here you are…doing it for me… Thank you, Niko."

"I should have done it before now. I took it for granted, how precious a gift it is that you have and give to others." He set her wine beside the bowl and scooped her onto his lap so she straddled him, wrapping his arms around her, locking her into their embrace.

She placed her lips on his, needing the connection and truly unable to say anything else before she burst into tears. Her body didn't get the message. Tears streamed down her face anyway. He smiled against her lips and brushed them away.

"A very intelligent young man told me tears hold special magic. And that if I cared for your tears, you might fill me with love." Her heart melted into a puddle. And then it flipped over again in somersaults as he lifted them both off the bed and carried her to the bathroom.

"Time for a bath."

He didn't even give her time to say she was going to spend every single moment filling him with love. He really was gun-shy.

"Oh really?" she asked, resting her cheek against his. "For me or you?"

"Oh, both of us, love. I've been obsessing over it since that night I burst in on you. Haven't been able to get that image out of my mind. I see it, I see *you,* your slicked naked skin everywhere. Now I get to make my wildest dreams come true."

She gusted out a laugh and flushed with joy. "Your wildest dreams?"

"Don't you know? Haven't I convinced you yet?" He kissed her long and slowly, like they had centuries to learn each other. "I found this dilapidated old house, thought it would suffice for a month or two before I moved on, then I walked into the hospital for work that first day and my world changed. Every second I had I worked on this place with you in mind, the kitchen for you, the solarium to remind me of you even when I couldn't have you, and this, this tub, a thing of sensual beauty, carved in your image."

"Wow, Niko. I'm stunned." More tears slipped from her eyes, tears of joy, of love. He brushed them away, tracing his fingers down her cheeks.

"You'd worked some magic into the bath that night. The water glittered. It had a silvery blue aura to it. The steam, the scents all lured me in to you." His voice drew her gaze up to his even as she wanted to linger over his arms, the strength of his thighs, how his cock stood tall and proud, all for her.

"The way your breasts teased up over the water." He tore the sheet away and brushed his fingertips over the tops of her breasts. She shivered. Desire strummed through her, pulsing deep and low at her core. His eyes blazed a deep silver mystery, looking at her like she was a gift. Being with him, she didn't feel as though she had to diminish any part of herself. It was as though all of her, her height, her weight, her lips and breasts, and full laugh, were to be celebrated. As though her everything was exactly what he craved with a ferociousness. As though she finally belonged somewhere exactly right.

"What did you do?" He moved a step closer, aligning their bodies. He slid his hand behind her and brought them flush, her nipples hard and aching against his chest.

She was wet already and he hadn't even touched her. And oh she wanted him to, could feel how heavy and hard his cock was pressing against her pelvis, caught between them. He scented her neck and as always she opened for him, bending her head away, offering herself to him.

"Francesca?"

"Wh...what?" The way he said her name, the way he mesmerized her body, the feel of his breath on her, that barely controlled hiss of his words. She didn't have a clue what he was talking about anymore.

"To the water. That night." His teeth grazed her earlobe, and she nearly lost her balance, but he held her. He wouldn't let her go, wouldn't let her fall.

"Oh." She whimpered as he stopped nipping at her only to stroke his fingers down her back. "I...I...Niko..." She leaned in and rested her head on his shoulder. He held her confidently with one hand while he stroked the other across her skin, leaving a trail of fire and sparks in its wake. Slowly his caress feathered over her butt until he gripped her there, lifted her, and had them both sinking into the steamy water in seconds. She clung to him. The path of his hands, the way he held her to him, the hot water stunning her skin. It was all so much amazingness in one precious moment.

"Tell me, so I can make the water how you like it," he demanded.

Oh, good lord, he was caring for her again. Her mind was a pool of mindless lust. He did that to her, shoved away all rational thought, until all she could feel was desire and need, raw and elemental, as he'd said. She'd intended to care for him, to ease him into her trust and all this time, since the accident, he'd been caring for her. Tonight, he was front and center doing it. The cooking, the sharing of his deepest secrets, the bath. My God, she was lost for him.

She straddled him as the water flowed around them. Carefully she took one of the small bottles of scented oil and magic she'd created and poured a few drops into the bath. Setting the bottle back, she twirled her fingers through the water, feeling her power surge through her at the intimacy of this moment. Swirls of glittering, iridescent blue coiled around them.

"It's one of many combinations I create." *How had he known that night to come to her?* "This one I made months ago." She ran her hands over his chest and down to his cock, still waiting patiently between them. "After you..." *Oh*, the way he gripped her butt and kneaded her flesh, pulling her into him, causing her seam to rub against his hard, delicious cock, every movement and sensation heightened by the water, by her sensual spell, by the magic they created together. "After you turned me down, that one morning all those months ago, that day when our shifts were finished, and I offered to make you a meal."

"One of my biggest regrets." He rubbed her thigh muscles, sneaking his thumbs into her inner soft skin, so close and then stealing away. He drifted his gaze up and down her body, the silver in his eyes potent. "I was an idiot."

"Really? You looked at me like I was..." His fingers were wicked.

"How did I look at you?" He wasn't looking at her that way now. Now he was all certainty and desire. It spilled out of his eyes and into her.

"Like I was an apple you wanted to eat but were too pissed that you did in fact want to. Or so I imagined."

"Huh. You're right. I was bowled over with...with such intense heated desire. Only centuries of practice or numbness or absolute confusion had me turning away rather than grabbing you and absconding with you immediately. Although now that I have you here," he whispered his words over her skin full of awe and delight, "it's a wonder I had any control, with the drought I'd been in and then...then you." He leaned in slowly and took one aching nipple into his mouth.

"Mm." She hushed. "Absconding, huh?" It was difficult to think and to talk, but she loved it too, communicating while being intimate. It heightened everything to share while he touched her. She rubbed her body up and down and along his. "I came home, and I was extremely frustrated, and I...I made this oil, a bit of rose and jasmine, some sandalwood and sage, a hint of blue cypress, a heady combination. It made me think of you, of us...us..."

"Together?"

He seemed so surprised, and she loved that she could give him a moment of satisfaction, of her desire for him all those months ago. She wrapped her hands around his cock, gripped him, and dragged up, pulling on that sleek rock-hard part of him, eliciting a moan from him so deep and feral it sent her own body vibrating.

"Yes, Niko. You and me, naked, the hot water swirling around us, my magic drawing us closer, luring us on into all these secret promises." She placed his cock at her entrance. "Can you feel me pulsing for you now?"

"And then," he said, watching her hands where they gripped him. "That night I slammed in here like a rutting bull, demanding to know if you were okay, while you lay here and bathed in front of me?"

Yes, she absolutely loved this, this sexy conversation while they lured each other closer to the edge, that delightful, sensual, exotic edge. "Oh, that night, Niko." She arched into him. "I was, well frustrated again, but mad too. At you, for you, for us. I knew we were meant to be together, but I was confused by your cold ability to pull away." Rubbing up against him, she knew he could hear the needy whine in her voice.

"Mm." He tossed her hands aside, gripped his cock, notched it against her opening, and surged into her. "Not confused anymore, are you?"

"Niko." The moan escaped her as he sheathed himself confidently inside her. "No...not at all." She ground down on him, drawing him in deeper, loving this position, feeling him inside her. "How...God, how amazing you feel."

"It's you, Francesca. Christ...the way you grip me." He held them in a way that her knees never touched the tub, all his powerful muscles surging in and wrapping around her, and the most intimate one thrusting up into her. "You here, in this tub that I designed on purpose, big enough for you and me together. I denied it, denied myself, for so *fucking* long. And that night I found you here by yourself, I was this close to tearing the thing down around you, giving you nowhere to hide from me." As he spoke, he dragged her legs around him.

"I wasn't the one hiding." She brushed his hair off his forehead, leaving drops of water trailing in her wake. Rocking against him, she got lost in the sensation of him rubbing inside her and the way the water moved with her, tantalizing her skin, and sending flitters of her magic around them. The steam rose and her scented oil drew them even deeper down the well of desire. The water sluiced over her legs and hips, drifted up and down her back. And he? He was still coiled tightly, but this time she got to feel that wonderful tension inside her and it was a revelation to be filled and stretched with him so hard, all for her. Francesca's body was alive with tingles, with awareness. Her magic was a song, had found its perfect tune, and was singing inside her, surrounding her, surrounding them both.

"I was hiding, damn it." He hissed as she tightened around him and she did it again, loving how close to the edge of sin and darkness she drew him, a darkness that was only theirs. "I wasn't strong enough to face it, any of it. I am now." He gently gripped her neck.

"Now?" She panted, ready for him. It was them now, for always. No more being alone.

"Now," he said deeply, ominously.

Silly man, as if she was ever going to be afraid of him.

"Are you ready?" He traced the skin of her neck with his thumb, his gaze lost there now, his eyes a breathtaking silver. Where he touched her pulsed its answer, a flutter of excitement, her forever offering. The water glowed its silver-blue around them.

"Yes." She rocked into him, held his head, and brought his gaze to hers. "We belong to each other, Nikolav. Our strangeness is beautiful together. I felt you calling to me before we ever met. Inside me was an emptiness until that night you walked into the hospital. And you stole my breath. You have all of me, darling. Make me truly yours." She gave him what he needed then, tilting her head to the side, finally a gift he would now take from.

He cradled her neck like it was precious and he was never letting go. He licked and sucked, his cock growing even harder inside her, their pelvises rubbing gloriously against each other. Shimmering magic swept through her and from her, circling them, gilding the edges of their connection with sparks. She started to shake, her orgasm approaching.

"Hold still, darling." His command was deep and throaty.

She wanted to watch him, wanted to see his eyes when he finally sank his teeth into her, but she couldn't at this angle, so she concentrated instead on sensations, the rippling anticipation, how her insides gloried with the knowledge that he was hers, concentrated on obeying him as best she could with his cock pulsing inside her, stretching her, luring her over the cliff, with his deep masculine scent drifting around her. The feel of his soft skin covering those muscles, held in control for her. And oh would he finally, finally lose control?

With one last lick up her neck, he growled and, in an instant, pierced her skin.

"Niko," she cried out and gripped his biceps. It was only a tiny prick of pain, but it was also definitive, a beginning, a shell ripped off her old life and then, *then*, catapulting her into the new.

And how catastrophically beautiful! The world exploded into gems of color around them, the rich greens of forests and bright orangey red of radiant flames, an iron-deep blue of the deepest oceans, a multitude of snowflakes, and sparkly fireworks exploding through the air. Euphoria sang through her, a stunning orchestra lighting her up. Niko wrapped even tighter around her, to keep her from fleeing—she wanted to yell that she would never leave him—or to simply be as close to her as possible through this spectacular experience.

Spectacular was the word that spiraled through her. Being uniquely connected to another person, *her* person while he filled himself with her blood and her essence. As she'd foreseen, it didn't drain her at all, but somehow, miraculously, magically filled her up to bursting. A rainbow of fireworks continued to burst in the brilliant sparkly air, on her skin, zinging through her blood, surging into her bones. She swooned and arched to get closer to him, to the pinnacle. And as if she were one with the fireworks, the trees, the winter storm and spring breeze, the ocean, fire, and all Mother Nature herself, she leapt into the dance and exploded all around her love.

CHAPTER THIRTY-ONE

U PON FIRST BITE, THE sensations stormed back into
Niko, obliterating the ashes around his soul, flinging the dust and grime and nightmares away as if they
would never leave a trace behind. Blood, exhilaration, and
hope flowed into him. A gleaming world in full color spun
through him.

It changed almost immediately before he had time to
connect to the old familiar. And thank the goddesses because what came next was so much deeper, so much more
powerful, so exquisitely beautiful beyond anything in his
wildest dreams. Soaring through fireworks in a midnight sky
connected to his one true mate.

He drew his body around hers while he sucked and licked and
drank, tasting her, delighting in her, the way she moved, dancing
as one with him, her glorious, sexual moans singing to him. Still
connected, his cock surged with renewed life, pulsing into her,
making her whimper and cling to him. Nothing was exactly as

he'd hoped. It was a new dream, a richer, more fulfilling life as if he hadn't been half-dead for hundreds of years.

And when she tensed and shattered around him, it heightened his senses. It had never been like this. No other time when he'd engaged in sex and biting at the same time. He thought he knew what euphoria was, but *nothing* came close to this spectacle of beauty. And now her blood, her magic, her soul linked with his truly meeting for the first time.

"More." He needed more.

"Take everything, my love. It's so...it's...you."

Even their wordless communication sparked and tingled between them. Its own new language of shooting stars formed with this intimate connection.

"Christ, Francesca, I will never get enough. And yet you keep filling me, giving to me. And your strength is still as powerful as ever as if what I'm doing isn't depleting you in the least. Where on earth did you come from?"

She held his head to her neck. *"I only know in my essence I was made for you."*

"Say my name."

"Nikolav. Darling. Love."

Every emotion he'd thought long dead stirred when she spoke his name. She writhed into him, with each plea clung to him with her legs and arms.

He could see inside her. She was infinitely more than bones and blood. The most beautiful gardens bloomed inside her, luscious green leaves, and deepest pinks of roses. Neon oceans at sunset surged and tumbled into the cobalt blue of the world's beautiful lakes. Star tips glowed. Even the air was fluorescent. Her scent perfumed everything with her truth. Sensations and wonder passed between them. Nothing else in the world mattered but the two of them right here, right now, and the magic life force flowing between them. Another orgasm was within her, and his ego soared at being able to give her pleasure while he drank from her. There was power in that, such magnificent power.

A tear landed on his cheek.

"Francesca." He pulled his mouth from her skin. Giving one last lick to seal the wound, inwardly gloating that she would now wear his mark forever, he caught the next tear that fell. "Gorgeous?"

"I'm good." She laughed and smiled through the tears, more brilliant than she'd been before, glowing with her magic brimming around her as she sat on his lap, her body rising above him. She linked her hands around his neck and, bringing his lips to hers, she kissed him, gently, slowly, exploring her taste on his lips. Sighing into him she came again around him, in one slow flutter after another, breathing out little moans, and it was that that finally took him over the edge. Not loosening his hold one bit, he ground her down on him, spilling his essence into her, grunting out his release.

"I...I...that was...I feel...wow," she said, her words a quiet hush. "I am speechless."

"Mm." Niko stroked her back. He lifted them both out of the tub and dried them off, then whisked them back to bed and settled them under the covers, together in a cozy warmth.

"How do you have any energy left?" she whispered again.

"Why are you whispering?" He grinned at how cute she was, completely spent and rumpled and so fucking gorgeous he'd never tire of studying her. "It's just us. No one can hear you."

"Something so monumental, so...spectacular...it feels intimate. Too precious to share with anything or anyone but you." She draped an arm over him and sighed, her eyes fluttering closed and a soft lazy smile on her face.

Now he could have all her smiles. He could gaze upon them out in the open instead of hiding behind corridors and patient charts and nurse stations. He ran his hands through her red curls, free now not only to steal her smiles but to touch her at will.

His greatest fear, that he would destroy her, hadn't happened. And more, something hot vibrated between them, forever linking them, her blood, yes, her magic, absolutely, but it was more than that, a golden thread had been sewn between them, thin but strong, unbreakable. He was stronger. Power and energy surged in him, but instead of ruination, love erupted inside him. An emotion so intense he reveled in it.

"Were you really afraid you'd hurt me?" Ahh, she wasn't asleep after all.

"I thought you'd drifted off." Niko cupped her cheek.

"Mm." She stretched like a lazy satisfied cat in the sun. "I feel like I could sleep for a year, but also, acutely alive and aware of everything around me. I'm buzzing, Niko."

He stroked his hand down her hip and back up, the possessiveness growing in him again already.

"Was that what you were afraid of?"

"That and..." He rested his hand on her belly, drew it up to cup her breast. *Mine.* "Being my mate, it will...it will make me..." He met her gaze, the gold in her green irises pulsing with energy.

"Yes?"

"Extremely needy is one way to put it."

"In what way?"

"Every way one like me needs a mate. And there can only be one mate for me, forever."

"Do you want me to be yours, Nikolav?" Her voice was soft, but there wasn't one hint of tease in it.

"More than you can know."

"That makes me happy," she whispered, her eyes shimmering with tears.

"Good." He kissed her deeply, thoroughly. "Now I get to spend a lifetime making you happy."

"We aren't leaving this bed." She cupped his cheek as he settled into her.

He laughed and watched the smile bloom across her face. "There are other ways I aim to make you happy as well, my love."

He nipped at her shoulder. His body tightened with wanting her again already.

"Mm, I know." She wrapped her legs around him. "I meant because of what's brewing out there in the world. We have to face it." So serious she'd grown, and she was so fucking beautiful like that too.

"We will," he promised. "Other things first." He hiked her leg up higher, allowing him to slide in slowly, feel the path of her on every inch of him. He would do whatever it took to protect her, to end the demon bent on ruining her, but for now, other things.

CHAPTER THIRTY-TWO

THE EMERGENCY DEPARTMENT LOOKED like the aftermath of a crime scene when Francesca walked in for her first full shift back after her life had been remade into something wondrous. And it was ironic. For weeks, she'd itched impatiently to return to her normal schedule, but now she'd rather stay home in bed all day with Niko, or on the floor, or up against that fabulous wall in the library, or the table in the solarium surrounded by the stars and roses. Or in the tub, all the goddesses in Heaven, that tub.

For the last two weeks, they'd had what Francesca could only call a love affair. A dreamy, sensual time together, learning, laughing, whispering, moaning. Nikolav Sarkozy had even gotten her to beg. He'd been ravenous for her; they'd been ravenous for each other. It appeared him taking her blood didn't harm her at all. Instead, it acted as an aphrodisiac, a strength potion, adrenaline on steroids, health, and love. It was an all-encompassing potion for both of them.

She'd taken only short shifts at the hospital to appease his worry that she was back to work too soon and only on days when he worked too, not wanting to be separated from him. Marie had given her lessons on infusions for her food and herbology. Some of what Marie told her she already knew, but it was different to practice a thing alone without the guidance of a much smarter witch. Francesca was growing and blossoming along with the plants in the garden, bursting with new life, curiosity, and love. Spring was here and nature was alive. When she and Niko were together, they were together, wrapped up in each other. The rest of the world hardly mattered. Even when her sister and the kids visited for Sunday dinners, Niko was by Francesca's side, helping her cook.

And Niko seemed to walk ten feet taller, boasted a regular smile on his face, and had shed the dark cloud around him. Or, she thought as she'd walked beside him that morning to the hospital entrance, holding his hand and sneaking glances, he hadn't shed it. More like his aura had healed and the darkness was now simply a healthy part of his being. The way midnight was to sunrise, both unique, both beautiful, both full of aspects she adored. The darkness was his passion and mystery mixed with his pain and his loneliness. The dawn, his humor and curiosity, his stubbornness and love. But the darkness was his love too, because it was grief and memories as much as it was passion and attention. Love flowed through both of them. It was glorious.

Unfortunately, once they entered the hospital, they stepped into a heavy atmosphere with grim looks and several police officers swarming about. They had to show their identification to enter. And it was quiet. A quiet ED was usually the jinx no doctor wanted. The calm before the storm, or the insidious kind of injury and disease no one knew how to treat, or too much death. Death wasn't always screaming out its arrival. Death could be eerily quiet in its own way. Francesca heightened her awareness. Something awful lurked in the air.

"Oh, Francesca, thank God you're here." Lainy threw herself at Francesca and hugged her tightly. Then she grabbed her arm and tugged her into the ED office. "I was so worried when you didn't answer your phone this morning."

Niko followed. Francesca eyed him over her shoulder. With one look he read her mind. *"What's going on?"*

She'd been lost in her bubble with Niko. "I'm so sorry I worried you, Lainy. What's wrong?"

"They found another body." A shiver rippled through Lainy.

"Dr. Madison?" Francesca asked, fear sitting low in her belly. God, she'd almost forgotten the woman had been missing for two weeks now.

"No...well...we don't know for sure." Lainy's face was pale and gaunt.

"What happened?" Francesca prodded. She rested her hand on Lainy's arm and sent her warmth and comfort through the touch. It was a sense that had always come normally to Francesca, but one she'd been careful to use only in conjunction with her patients, too scared to use her powers in any way that would show she was different. But Lainy was her friend, and she was learning how important it was to be true not only to herself but the ones she loved. Niko and Marie were helping her learn that her powers were a gift, not to be hidden or ashamed of. Lainy sat on the sofa and put her head in her hands. Francesca followed, crowding her friend in.

"It was like the other times beaten, sexually assaulted. Hair ripped out like whoever is doing this was impatient...No that's the wrong words to use. Whoever is doing this is losing their fucking control," Lainy whispered, tears leaked out of her eyes, and she gripped Francesca's hand so tightly she thought her bones might break. "And..."

"What, Lainy?"

"Two more women, nurses, from the hospital, have gone missing."

"From here?" Niko asked.

Lainy nodded. "Not just any nurses."

"What do you mean?" Francesca asked, that same nauseating feeling she'd had in the car crash overtook her.

"ED nurses specifically."

"He's targeting the Emergency Department," Niko said.

"Christ," Francesca swore and gazed through the doorway out into the ED where the cloud of worry hung low, like its own monster. "But why? And why now? Why is he ramping back up all the sudden?"

"I don't know." Niko rested his hand on her shoulder. His touch soothed her the way hers did Lainy and she was grateful for it, for the connections between them. "But we'll figure this out."

"Yes, we will, all of us together." Even while fear surrounded them, a new confidence shimmered through her. She wasn't alone anymore. None of them were. And Francesca was pissed. How dare some monster impose his cruelty on her town, her hospital, her people? "We need my sister."

"What's Gia got to do with this?"

"She's a genius when it comes to information and patterns." The police may be working hard, but they were unable to find whoever was responsible for these crimes the last time they were happening. We need to take a closer look at each victim and all the information associated with each one, not just names and injuries but more specifics as well as their connections to the hospital.

"If you think she can help, get her here," Niko said. "I'll speak to the detectives and alert them of her arrival.

***

"Oh good you brought Hugh," Francesca said as Gia, followed by Hugh, both wearing scowls, stormed into the hospital an hour later.

"Of course he knows the detectives at the door who let him in." Gia glared at Hugh.

If things weren't so serious and scary, Francesca might have laughed at the two of them. Francesca hugged her sister and didn't want to let go. Their specific connection always gave her strength, and right now, she needed all she could get. She would take and give from each person close to her heart until they all felt as powerful as she did. This menacing horror had gone on long enough for the town of Mercy. It was time to stop it. "Where are the kids, honey?"

"At school," Hugh answered before Gia could open her mouth. "They're protected."

Gia huffed and untangled herself from Francesca. "I set up a protection spell around the school. I don't need your help."

"Yes, you do. You're not safe." Hugh stood, arms crossed over his chest as he leaned up against the wall beside her, looking, for anyone not paying close enough attention, as though he were bored out of his mind. But worry and anxiety pulsed through him. His feelings were heavy in the air around them.

Gia rolled her eyes. "I'm as safe as I've ever been."

Hugh glared at her, and Francesca watched, fascinated as an entire silent conversation passed between the two of them.

"I promise, I would never knowingly put my babies in danger," Gia whispered the words as if they were meant only for Hugh. "You know that."

Hugh closed his eyes and pushed off the wall, stepping into Gia's space, all hint of casual boredom gone. He towered above her sister, who had to crane her neck to maintain eye contact with the sexy hottie. They were all but mauling each other here in the hospital hallway. "I know," he gritted out. "But I...I care. And something very dangerous and old is at play here and..." He stopped mid-sentence and glanced around, his dark eyes black as night and...

"Are they glowing?" Francesca silently asked her sister.

"Yes. They uh do that." Gia said. *"When something, when something isn't right...or when...uh—"*

"Don't leave the hospital. Don't go anywhere without me," Hugh ordered and strode down the corridor, leaving them both in the wake of his anger.

Gia's mouth hung open. A million emotions warred across her face, anger, confusion, a few Francesca couldn't recognize.

"Wow," Francesca whispered, linking her arm with Gia's.

"Ugh, the man won't leave me alone," Gia huffed.

"Yes," Francesca nodded. "I think *leave you alone* is the very last thing on the planet he aims to do. It's fascinating."

"It's annoying." Mm-hmm, Francesa thought. But now wasn't the time to dissect her sister's relationship with a hot werewolf. Gia flipped the leather strap of her laptop bag across her chest and took a steadying breath. "Please tell me the coffee here doesn't suck. I need boatloads of caffeine and then you're going to explain everything to me. Start talking."

CHAPTER THIRTY-THREE

"**A**UGUSTUS, WHAT DO YOU know?"

"Took you long enough." The hospital's pathologist towered over his computer typing furiously. His eyes, through his dark glasses, were steaming mad but he held himself in control. He spared Niko a glance before returning his gaze to his task. Niko was a seven-hundred-year-old vampire with so many dead because of him he'd lost count, but even he knew enough to tread carefully. Augustus was seething.

The demon did a double take, stared at Niko, and narrowed his eyes. "You, you..." A smirk put some life in his grave expression. "Wow, you almost look alive. Nikolav the vampire resurrected. Finally get your head out of your ass?"

"I didn't take you as one to use stupid sayings, Augustus. Why start now?"

Augustus huffed out an almost laugh. "Looks good on you."

Niko tried to hold back his smile, but even in the morgue surrounded by death and the latest hideous death to be specific, he couldn't lessen his joy for Francesca. Didn't even want to try. He'd exhausted his stores of anguish and cold-hearted emotions. Now all of her, everything that came with her, all the beauty and light and hope burned him from within. "She does look good on me," he agreed. "I was an idiot for waiting so long."

"Difficult to trust after...well, after your past."

"Indeed." Niko hadn't spoken of his past, but Augustus was centuries older than Niko, and he'd heard the stories, Niko's in particular. Niko only knew snippets of the other man's past but it was possibly—he could see now that he'd found Francesca—even darker than Niko's.

The form on the table brought back the present nightmare. "Is this the victim?"

Some hideous creature was out there torturing women. It was fucking taunting them all with the torture. His anger flared.

"Brace," Augustus warned.

"I've seen horrors." Hell, he'd caused plenty in his past. It stopped his breath for a moment, all that he'd done, all that he'd been, and the realization that he didn't have to punish himself indefinitely for all his sins anymore. Nor did he ever want to return to living that way. His world had changed, and he'd do what he needed to protect his and Francesca's happiness.

"Not like this." Augustus swallowed, clenched and unclenched his hands, and continued, "This is... Might as well see for yourself. Whatever did this is angrier than anything I've come across before."

A what not a who. Augustus' confirmation only intensified Niko's anger.

He stole across the quiet concrete floor as Augustus removed the sheet. "Good Christ!" Niko swore and braced himself. He had to close his eyes at the onslaught of madness. And then, sucking back the wild fury inside him, he forced his eyes back open to the body in front of him.

It wasn't even recognizable as a woman anymore. A body covered in bruises already turning a sickly hue of greenish yellow, a sign they were days old, perhaps even weeks. Broken bones were exposed in her arms. Worse, so much worse, this victim had been mutilated and sewn back together. A Frankenstein experiment, pure torture. There were uneven stitches around the ankles, and feet that didn't appear to be her own sewn onto her. The same thing at her breasts, brutish stitch marks around each one. And something very odd about the shape of the body.

And her skin? Her skin was dotted with brown ink or paint or something, as if the evil being had painted dots all over her. Her dark hair had been ripped out in places. Other locks singed down to her scalp. The marks and scent of burning hair still clung to her body. And burning...skin. Christ, Niko leaned in closer and took in the spots again. They were tiny burns. Along with, along with...a riot of images flooded his brain.

"What is that smell?" He needn't have asked because the answer came before he finished speaking. "Our hybrid demon." His breath seized.

"What the fuck?" Hugh's snarl of outrage drew their attention to the doorway where the beast stood gripping the door jam.

"Holy shit," Augustus exclaimed. "Hugh Webb?

"You know this asshole?" Niko scowled at his friend.

"He And his family are legends in this town," Augustus said.

"That smell." Hugh strode toward them, disgust marring his features. He covered his mouth and nose with his hand.

"Powerful fucker." Augustus studied the mutilated body.

"I recognize that scent," Hugh said.

Me too. Niko's blood grew heated and powerful. "Wait, is this the same—"

"Same perp," Augustus said. "Different game. It's obsessed, out of control this time. With all the ones that came before, it was toying with them, toying with us, one hideous game."

"But now, he's enraged," Niko said.

Augustus nodded. "Something has this demon extremely pissed off. There was a wig on the victim this time. Long curly red hair." The true horror pierced Niko's chest like a dagger, and he sucked in his breath. "And his genitals have been cut off."

"His?" Shock coursed through Niko's body. That's what had been odd about the shape of the body. It was a man, not a woman as they'd all assumed.

"Fuck," Hugh snarled.

Recognition dawned in Niko's mind, and he took off at a run. "Francesca," Niko swore and traced to the floors above. Hugh's stealth had him only seconds behind. The sisters were in the office making coffee. Niko stole the mug from Francesca's hand, slammed it on her desk, and wrapped his arms around her.

"Niko," she soothed in that gorgeous voice of hers, while her hands smoothed over his back. "Darling, what's wrong? I mean, what else is wrong?"

"Fuck, it's here in this hospital." It was coming together in his mind, the whole macabre picture, a hell of a lot slower than it should have. "Something in this hospital is after you, my love."

"What?" Gia's words were a whisper. Hugh stood against her back, his hands on her shoulders.

"The demon," Hugh spoke. He leaves a scent behind. It was the same one at your house, Francesca. It's...he, it left it behind on the latest victim in the morgue."

"It's the same scent I detected at your accident site," Niko said and watched Francesca's face pale. Then, seconds later all the color returned along with her fury.

"You are fucking kidding me?" She swore. His witch was golden and on fire when she stepped into her emotions. Fucking gorgeous, even if it was in this horrible scenario. Unfortunately, she wasn't just pissed. She was hurt. It surged through her, and Niko caught the reverberations of it as he held her. Fuck. He would do anything to protect her from this. They'd both had so much emptiness and despair in their past that they deserved goodness and joy.

"There's more. There are threads of it I've been smelling around Mercy since the night I started working here. I couldn't put a name to what it was. Every time I entered the hospital, I couldn't smell it anymore, but I think that's because it was masking its scent when it changed form."

"Changed form?"

He nodded. "Remember how Hugh said it can change shape? A hybrid demon can shift, especially when it has enough energy, when...when it's been feeding, taking energy from its victims to use for its own purposes."

"And its scent can disappear?"

"Something like that," Hugh said.

"I'm going to rip his insides out through his throat when we find him," Niko swore.

"I'll help," Hugh said. "I've never wanted to shred a monster with my teeth so badly before."

Francesca pulled away and grabbed a Kleenex. Fuck, now she was crying. He couldn't handle her tears like this, not over something this vile. "How did you...what made you think or know that it's, ugh..." She sighed.

"She means explain," Gia said and moved to squeeze Francesca's hand. "What's happened? What's going on?"

"A demon leaves a scent," Hugh began.

"We all leave one, or almost all of us," Niko added. "Unique to each of us."

"Some vampires don't," Hugh scoffed.

"Why haven't we, or why can't we smell this demon?" Francesca asked. She had her arms crossed over her chest, but she hadn't let go of Gia's hand yet, or maybe Gia hadn't let go of her.

"They are often very good at masking their scents," Niko said.

"Even from us," Hugh added.

"Hugh and I smelled it separately at times," Niko said. "And—"

"Wait, I did too," Francesca said. "In my dream walk and somewhere else I can't remember. Why now, or why at the accident scene?"

"I'm guessing when it's enraged or in its demon form it doesn't mask its scent as well," Hugh offered.

Niko studied her. "We haven't talked about it until that night in the library, all of us together. It clicked in the morgue for me. The demon stalking you, Francesca, is the same one hurting these victims, and whoever or whatever it is, is—"

"Is enraged at me," she whispered.

"Right, but we didn't know it was the same monster. And honestly, I can't tell if it's enraged at you or doing this for you," Niko whispered.

"Christ, Francesca. I'm sorry."

"What else?"

"Stop. I know you two are talking to each other," Gia said. "But Hugh and I can't understand you, and we all need to know what the hell is going on."

Niko practically roared and scraped his hands through his hair. "The victim downstairs is the first one I've seen fully naked."

"Sick fucker," Hugh said.

"What?" Francesca pleaded and if he could take this all away from her, he would, in a heartbeat.

"I need to see the case files of every victim," Gia demanded. "From what you're saying he's ramped up his anger or his..."

"Tell me, please," Francesca demanded. "Tell me everything, Niko."

"Something is making him angrier, perhaps that he can't have you, especially after the accident. And now he's taking more victims and making them look like you." Niko spoke and the silence was heavy in the room.

Chapter Thirty-Four

FRANCESCA WAS OUT THE door and running before he could grab her. Fuck! He chased her, catching her as she entered the elevator and pushed the button for the basement. The doors closed behind them as he lifted her off her feet.

"Let me go!" she screamed. "I need to see her."

"No, hush. It's awful. It's the things nightmares are made of."

She went still and hung her head, gripping his arms with her hands. "I know, Niko. I still have to see her. He, *it* almost killed my loves in that car accident, chased us down, terrorized those kids. The roots of a two-hundred-year-old tree dug itself out of the ground and surrounded us to protect us. I can still hear Danny screaming at it to leave us alone."

"Shh. I know, love. But I don't want you to torture yourself."

"Niko," she whispered. "Someone is toying with me. I might be able to help. I might notice something different."

Fuck yes, she would.

"And with Gia's talents, maybe we could narrow it down."

"I don't know if I'll be able to forgive myself if I let you go in that morgue, Francesca. You can't unsee it. He burned the victim's hair off in places, put a red wig on, *branded* the skin with freckles. That's not the worst of it." The crimes were unspeakable.

"Please let me do this," she said. "We need to put a stop to all of it. He's targeting the nurses now. Two more are missing. You heard Lainy. He's ramping up in anger and in frequency."

"There's more. It's not..." he began. "It's not a female."

"What?"

"The victim, this time. It's a man. Made...made to look like a woman, like you."

The doors opened, she shoved out of his arms and ran.

It took every ounce of strength Francesca had not to puke immediately upon entering the morgue. The stench alone had her wrapping her arms around her stomach and lurching backward. Niko handed her a mask. Augustus sighed and stepped aside, taking the sheet with him.

The body lying before her wasn't Dr. Madison, as Francesca had thought, but it was death in its most gruesome. She called upon the oldest, most powerful spirits deep in Mother Earth to help her. Grounding each step, building strength as she went, she made it to the side of the table. Niko was right, a thing of nightmares. Something so cruel and disgusting it tested the bounds of her humanity. Worse than any of the victims so far. Emotions boiled inside her, rage and sickness and despair and compassion and sadness and fear. A bone-deep fear settled inside her. What did this demon want with her? And what additional lengths was it willing to go to destroy her? A shiver ran through her, and Niko was by her side in an instant. "I need...

"What?" Niko asked.

"Space. I need to wash my hands...then gloves, and..." God she needed to keep her own rage inside her. Now was not the time. Now was the time to be methodical, cold, and brave. Yes, this would take a type of bravery she didn't know she possessed. And she must bank everything inside her.

"No, daughter." Her powers whispered to her.

Francesca froze and listened.

"*Denying emotions is not how it works. You must pay very close attention to each feeling. Draw from them, the anger, the grief, the confusion, the love. Especially the love, dear. It's so great and powerful in you that no demon can cross it. That's what you must remember. That's what makes you different."* Francesca shuddered at the instructions and took a deep breath.

"I have all of that here for you, Dr. Banetti."

"Thank you, Dr. Clarke."

"It's Augustus, please. We're friends. Never more than now, I'd like to think."

She wiped away her tears. "Right. Augustus, tell me what you've discovered. I need to see if I can detect anything in the pattern or the injuries that will help me, help us all solve this so we can be done with it. We must save the other victims before it's too late."

"Francesca." Niko stood beside her, vibrating with more emotions than her, if possible.

"Give me time, please, Niko. Allow me to concentrate. I promise I'll come back to you when I'm all finished. Right now, I need to focus."

Niko took her face and pressed his forehead to hers as if their connection were his dying breath. It was a scorching touch, a demand, a reminder that she was his and she should never forget it. How could she?

"I'll be here in an instant. Call for me."

"I know." She answered with the truth. Then he swept away outside. Through the glass windows in the door, she could see Hugh holding her sister to his chest, his large hand wrapped around the back of her head, protecting her from this sight. Good, this was good. Now Francesca could focus.

***

Francesca worked silently and carefully, taking mental notes of everything she saw. There was a different kind of exhaustion that came with inspecting a dead body, especially one cut apart, mutilated, and put back together again as what, a lookalike, a gift to her? Both a manipulation and an offering, twisted though it might be. Her cells rebelled at the horror she witnessed. Each cut and bruise, each broken bone, every odor the demon had left behind along with another stale scent...oh God!

Francesca keeled over and vomited into the trash can. She made it to the sink and washed her mouth out before Niko got to her side. "It's Dr. Blythe." She nodded to the body.

"What?" Niko spun around and took in the body again. "Christ! How could you...I can't...he doesn't look..."

"His cologne. It's there, faint but under all the other macabre layers." She didn't look back at the body. She couldn't. Dr. Blythe may not have been the good friend she'd thought, but no one deserved this, man or woman.

"Let's go back upstairs, Niko, before the others come in. We need to regroup."

He took her hand and led her out of the morgue. The taste of bile stayed in her throat while they explained the new development and got to work organizing all the information they had.

***

"Do we need a break?" Gia asked hours later. Her laptop was open, and she'd programmed in the details all of them could think of. They had each victim's name, address, location kidnapped from, and as far as they could tell, where they'd been found. Oddly or simply enough they'd all been found in the woods close to Crystal Lake, parts of the woods still roped off by crime scene tape. What was special about the lake? Why was he dropping them there? With Gia's help, they added each victim's relationship to the hospital and to Francesca.

"From what I can tell," Gia said. "The first few victims may have been random. Then last spring something changed. There were two women kidnapped from your neighborhood. And then..."

"Then what?" Francesca asked.

"Not only were they all found near the lake, but every time a victim was brought in, you were here on shift."

"Wait," Francesca whispered and stood in a rush. "We're forgetting Kara."

"Kara?" Gia asked and scrolled through the names.

"She's one of his victims, but she's the only survivor so she's not in this stack of files from the morgue."

"She might know something," Niko said. "Will she talk to us?"

"She'll talk to me, as long as Rich is with her. She'd want this all to end."

CHAPTER THIRTY-FIVE

I T WASN'T EASY GETTING Kara to agree to meet with them. Niko and Gia were tasked with finding her and bringing her to the hospital. Whatever the demon wanted, it had to do with Francesca, and possibly, if it saw Francesca and Kara together that could be very dangerous for either or both of them. Additionally, Niko was their best bet in finding Rich and Kara since he knew their unique scents. No one at the hospital knew who Gia was so it would potentially keep the suspicion at bay.

First, they had to locate Rich, who was on duty and currently miles from the hospital helping a drunk man at the park who had somehow shed his clothes and couldn't remember where his home was. Yesterday Niko would have scoffed at the human's stupidity. Today he wished for such simple problems to solve.

I swear, when this is over, I'm taking Francesca on vacation far away. Christ, he hadn't been on a vacation in his life. Wasn't sure he'd know how to vacation. A small smile stole across his expression. Francesca would teach him, no doubt. He fever-ishly anticipated every second of learning.

Niko used his powers of persuasion to convince Rich's EMT partner to take a break for the rest of the day, which left them with the ambulance to pick up Kara. Then, thanks to Gia's suggestion they brought Kara back to the hospital undercover on a gurney and went straight to the basement where Augustus, Hugh, and Francesca were waiting.

"I don't know how I can help, but I'll try," Kara said sit-ting next to Rich, their hands linked. Rich was watching her with the focus of a hawk and the look of a man desperately in love. Another thing Niko might have scoffed at only a few days ago. Now he knew the feeling intimately.

"Kara," Francesca said in that soothing way she had. If Niko hadn't already been entranced, she would have lured him in. She could mesmerize a rock with that voice. "This may be difficult, but I believe in you. I believe you're strong enough and we're all here to help you."

She sat in front of Kara and held her other hand. "You know Niko and you met my sister, Gia. This is our friend Hugh, and this is Dr. Clarke. He's our head pathologist. All of us, including you, have some intimate knowledge of who is hurting these women. Niko mentioned to you that two more women are missing. I don't mean to scare you. But if we pool all the information we have together, we might be able to stop him."

That was the goal, and then Niko would obliterate him so he'd never set foot here again. Even the fiery pits of hell were too good for this abomination.

"Okay," Kara said. "But I...it's...it's hard to talk about."

Francesca nodded. "I know, dear, and you've spoken to me in detail when you could. I have all those notes. Perhaps if you talked about that day, even before you were taken or anything you remember. The environment, scents, sounds. I want you to close your eyes and talk. I'm going to hold your hand in mine, like I've always done when you needed me."

Kara nodded and glanced at Rich. The man swallowed, gripped her hand tighter, and gave her a nod in return.

Good man. He was upset and worried for her, but he was encouraging her nonetheless.

Kara rested her head on Rich's shoulder, closed her eyes, and started talking. "I was leaving the hospital, walking home after having lunch with Rich."

"I shouldn't have let her walk home alone." Rich put his head in his hand. Niko recognized the words of a tortured man.

"It's not your fault," Francesca soothed. "It's not any of our faults. Mercy is our precious town we all love. I walk by myself all the time. We all do. And we will again, without this cloud hanging over us. I promise."

She was a helluva lot more confident than Niko was. Even if they caught the monster, it would be a long damn time before she was out of his sight.

"It was such a pretty day, sunny," Kara said. "I remember all the tulips were blooming down by the courtyard. I had my camera and was taking pictures. And then...that smell I told you about, like sewage. I started walking to the park and the lake to get away from it. It was awful. I stumbled into the woods to...to throw up and then..."

"That's where it found you," Francesca whispered.

Kara nodded. "I don't...I don't know if I can talk about all the things I remember after that."

"I know it's difficult," Francesca said. "Give me one more minute. Is there anything else, any small or even insignificant detail you felt or saw that might help."

They waited for what seemed like hours but was only a few minutes as the anxious silence spread around them.

"The lake," Kara whispered. "He...it...I remember it mentioning Crystal Lake. It made him very angry and...and almost gleeful at the same time ..." Tears streamed down Kara's face. Rich had his eyes shut, but there were tears on his cheeks too. "When he was shaving my head. I don't think he thought I was awake...started talking to me...his voice was so weird. But he started talking like I was...a patient, and he was going to make me all better. 'Fix you right up,' he kept saying in this awful singsongy voice. But...he'd untied me, said my hands were going to be next. That's...that's how I got away. The windstorm saved me. When the power went out and he was in a frenzy, he left, just left me there. And I got out."

"You saved yourself, you wonderful, brave woman. You saved yourself," Francesca said.

Kara nodded and wiped her tears. "I ran, as much as I could. The pain...I ended up behind Mrs. Kauffman's flower shop. She found me."

"That's right, love."

Kara blew her nose and straightened. "He said he couldn't go into the lake. *He* can't go into the lake, but...that makes him angry because 'she', whoever he was talking about loves Crystal Lake."

"He's leaving them for me," Francesca said, her voice a shot in the night. "He's leaving them as an offering."

"Or a trap," Niko said.

"Leaving them close but not in the water," Augustus said. "I don't think a hybrid demon can touch the water."

"A what?" Rich said, elbows to his knees, hands in his hair, a wild angry expression beating out onto them.

"Um," Niko said realizing the complexity of what had just been disclosed. "There are some other things we haven't told you and Kara yet."

"It's not of this world, is it?" Kara interrupted breathlessly. "I thought I was going crazy. I thought it was leftover trauma, but right after it took me, I woke up briefly then too, and whatever had me was bigger than a man. It was dark and, and almost flowy. We flew through the forest. That's what it felt like. It wasn't solid. And the smell, it was the same one that made me sick. I passed out again, but all this time..." She looked at

Francesca. "And I never told you. I didn't tell anyone because I thought I was hallucinating. I thought it was all part of the nightmare, but it was real. All this time I...we assumed it was a man, but it was a monster." She said it with such conviction.

"Yes," Francesca said. "A real nightmare, if you will."

"Frankie?" Gia touched her sister's arm. "There's something else I just realized from each crime's notes. There was sexual assault, but no semen.

"You're right..." Francesca paused. "They never found any DNA."

CHAPTER THIRTY-SIX

"SHIT," FRANCESCA'S MIND SPUN. "I can't believe I never realized it."

"What?" Niko demanded. "What is it?"

"Dr. Madison."

"She's still missing," Augustus said. "No one's been able to find her."

"No," Francesca shook her head. "She...she never had a scent. In her human form. That's why she was unbalanced. And she always hated the lake, hates water. I just assumed it was one more aspect of her I could never understand. She's...it's her. She's the demon."

Her words killed all sound. Everyone stared at her in confusion.

"You're sure?" Gia asked.

"She's right," Augustus said. "Don't know why I never realized it."

"Shit," Hugh said. "A lust demon, but not to take Francesca, to take *from* her."

"I'm going to burn her to the ground, raze her back up so I can do it all over again," Niko swore.

"You can't, darling."

"Don't darling me right now." Niko's eyes were slits of deadly silver. Anger and rage pulsed through his cells. She loved this about him, his power, his energy, but she had to make him see reason, even through this horrible turn of events.

"She's right." Augustus and Hugh spoke at the same time.

"I sure as hell can."

"It can't be killed how you're thinking," Augustus said.

"It can be killed however the fuck I want." Niko seethed but he kept Francesca's gaze.

"I know you're upset. I am too, darling."

"Upset? She...worked alongside us. She insulted you. She hit on me, and I didn't realize. She tried to kill you. How did I not see it?"

"I'm as sick as you are."

"Niko, Christ. It can shift and change shapes and scents. It's more powerful than any of us," Augustus called.

"Nothing is more powerful than I am right now," Niko swore.

"Right, an egotistical vampire. Haven't heard that one before. Listen to me. If I remember correctly, there's only one way to rid the earth of it," Augustus continued.

"Demons? A vampire?" Rich hissed and dragged Kara into his arms.

"It's all right, Kara, Rich. It's not what you think," Gia said. "Or it is, but...Look, I know it's strange that I'm the voice of reason, but we need to explain to our friends about supernatural beings and also, more importantly, figure out how to solve this problem we have." Gia sighed.

"Niko, please," Francesca pleaded. "We need a plan. We don't know where to find her...uh find it."

"I'll find it. I'll watch it suffer."

"Stubborn man."

"This isn't me being stubborn. This is me enraged, Francesca. I should have figured it out earlier. I smelled it every time I came to work. Every single time outside, seeped into the ground."

"I feel the same." She put her hands on his face and brought his forehead to hers. "You said it masks its scent. Which she obviously did at work. We can't worry about the past now. We need to tread carefully because she has two other victims. Please."

"Fine." He took her hand and held her gaze.

"Kara, Rich," Francesca began. "I can assure you, none of us in this room would ever hurt you. We are...we are different, but we've been living among you for centuries and these people here in this room are your friends. I can understand if you go and I'll be forever grateful for the information you shared, but I hope you'll stay and listen."

Kara looked at Rich and a silent conversation passed between them. She rested her cheek on his chest and said, "I'd like to listen."

Rich studied them. "I...I've worked with you, Dr. Banetti and Niko and Dr. Clarke for years and I've never felt uneasy around any of you. I'll do what Kara wants."

"Good," Gia said. "Here's the situation. Vampire, werewolf, witch, witch." She pointed to each of them. "And I don't know what you are, Augustus, sorry."

"No worries. I'm a petara."

"He's a guardian demon," Niko said.

"Well, that's one way to tell them." Francesca rolled her eyes.

"What?" Gia said. "We don't have time to waste, and they can handle it. She was kidnapped by a demon, tortured, and survived to help us figure out who it was and how to end it." Gia nodded toward Kara and sent her a wink. "Badass!"

"So, you're a witch?" Kara asked Francesca with awe.

"We're surrounded by a vampire, werewolf, and demon and you're fascinated by the witch?" Rich mumbled, giving Kara a squeeze.

"Well, yeah," Kara said. "She healed me." Kara face-planted into Rich, who wrapped his arms around her. "In so many ways."

"Yeah, babe." Rich's eyes were still full of shock, but he wasn't running for the hills. Francesca had always liked him.

"So." Kara let go of Rich's chest but stayed tucked in his arms. "Dr. Madison is the...she's the one who took me, took all of them." Her words were quiet, and the hint of fear was back.

Francesca nodded. Once the realization dawned, she could look back and see so many clues. Clues she'd missed or attributed to Dr. Madison being insecure or unbalanced. All this time she'd been...Christ, a demon... Francesca took a deep breath. It was time to end the horror they'd all been living with. "Right, then, time to take down a demon."

"We could lure it toward the water," Gia suggested. "It obviously has a thing for that place."

Francesca nodded. Her sister was right. "And me. Which means we should use me as bait."

"Are you insane?" Niko swore.

"No fucking way!" Hugh yelled.

"Absolutely not," Augustus said eerily calmly.

"How cute," Gia said. "The men trying to control the women again."

"You have no idea what you're dealing with, how powerful this monster is," Augustus warned.

"No offense, because I just met you and I like you, but you have no idea how powerful Francesca is." Gia crossed her arms and faced off with Augustus.

Francesca almost laughed. Her sister was damn confident in Francesca's powers.

"Augustus is right," Niko insisted.

"So is Gia," Francesca said. She took his hand and laced their fingers together. "And right now we need to act fast. You'll all help me. I can't do this alone. But this is what's going to happen. I feel it, Niko. I've always had a special connection to that lake. I swear it's what drew me to this town. There's great power there. With my magic and with all of you, we can do this. We have to try. No more sitting around and waiting. She's..." Dr. Blythe's torture was forefront in Francesca's mind. "She...it's ramping up, Niko. You saw what it did."

"Um, Francesca," Kara interrupted. "I thought of something else." They all turned to face the young woman. "When I escaped. I had two broken ribs, could barely see out of my swollen eyes, and was barefoot. I'd been gone for two days, but I made it back through the woods, back to town. I couldn't have done that if it had been a long distance."

"It's in the woods by the lake," Hugh said. "Now that we know her demon scent, I can track her there."

"What if she's in her human form?" Niko asked. "The one with no scent."

"I'm counting on two things," Hugh said. "One, that if she's ramping up, she's losing her shit and making mistakes. And two, that she might shift between her demon and her doctor to perform..." Hugh cleared his throat. "To, you know, hurt them."

"It's a good idea," Gia said, eyeing Hugh.

"Then we don't need Francesca to lure it out," Niko said.

"It might be too strong for any one of us alone. It's enraged. It can shift forms. Unlike a vampire or werewolf, it can transform into the wind almost, hard to grab. If you will, hard to kill," Augustus said.

"Then it will take all of us," Francesca said. Somehow, she knew in her heart this was the way to go. Her senses were humming. Everything was in tune. She put her hand on Niko's cheek. "Trust me."

The silver in his eyes shifted and grew and sparked. Each shift a whisper, a kiss, a promise on her skin. He didn't answer with words, instead, he took her face in his hands and kissed her with all his power, a claiming kiss of love.

"Hugh, we'll follow you, if that's alright," Francesca said. "It might take all of us, as we've said. I will get its attention and then Niko will trace me to the lake. We'll need to be quick. Niko's strength will wane the longer we're out in the daylight. The demon will know that."

"Let's hope it comes after you," Gia said.

"It will," Niko swore.

"If it doesn't?" Augustus asked. "What's our plan?"

"We don't need another plan. I...my instincts, my connection to nature tells me this is the way. But quickly."

"What can we do to help?" Rich asked, still holding Kara in his arms as if nothing would separate them. "I don't want Kara anywhere near...it..."

"Stay here," Augustus said. "It fears rotting corpses, oddly enough which is probably why it tosses the uh...sorry, for lack of a better word...bodies when she's...when it's finished. This type of demon would never approach a morgue."

"That's a good idea," Francesca said. "When it's all over, we'll find you. Rich, we might need you then to help the nurses when we find them alive." She turned to the rest of them. "And we should go now if we have any hope of finding them alive. I can feel it in my soul. It's time."

CHAPTER THIRTY-SEVEN

T HE DAY WAS BRIGHT before them as they set out, five beings who never belonged, now connected by the necessity to rid their town of a powerful demon. The welcoming blue sky and puffy clouds were an odd backdrop to the task ahead, almost as if the evil that awaited them was fake.

Once Hugh and Niko picked up the scent, it was remarkably easy to find the hidden path on the edge of town toward the rolling hilly side of the lake where the evergreen trees were more crowded and secret places ran deep. It was a powerful scent. Even Francesca could smell it now, soiled rotting garbage and acid-like tar. She'd smelled hints of it before but hadn't ever considered it was a supernatural being.

They were a unique group. Hugh resembled a punk guitar player with his mohawk, black leather jacket, and black jeans. Even his intense scowl was black. The only softness in him was when he stole glances at Gia, the badass herself, also dressed head to toe in black like she was on one of her covert assassin missions.

She had knives hidden all over her body and a scowl to match the werewolf's.

Niko stalked behind Francesca, and she didn't have to see him to feel his rage. Augustus brought up the rear, moving as silently as a cloud through the sky. But Francesca felt each of them, their unique steps in front of and behind her. She took steady breaths and used her time to connect to the ancient powers beneath her in the roots, the soil, the air the water. Every living being was tuned into her. This was her journey, had always been.

"Wait," Hugh whispered and raised a hand. They all stopped. Down a small incline was a cabin, nearly hidden by moss and thick ferns, appearing at first glance as if it were a fairy house sprouting from the woods. Only if one didn't stare too close for too long. A murky, heavy aura clung to it. In an instant, the air began to charge around them as they stood in the center of massive old-growth cedars. The perfect blue sky disappeared. Wind kicked up and angry clouds rolled in, and with it the same sooty fog at her accident. *"Ahh, it uses the fog to its advantage."*

"This is not advantageous, Francesca."

"The fog is simply one more element I'm in tune with. I didn't know it until recently."

"You—"

An ear-deafening blast ripped through the forest. Branches shattered and flew at them. Rocks, plants, and debris shot through the air. The ground rippled beneath their feet. Things happened in slow motion, or so her brain processed. A limb from a tree spiraled into her sister, shoving her off her feet. With a roar of anger, Hugh shifted in the air from man to werewolf in a matter of seconds and launched himself at Gia, wrapping himself around her and rolling down the hill. Augustus slithered low to the ground like a sleek predator, disappearing and returning, howling in outrage that he couldn't get closer.

Something massive but invisible pushed at Francesca. It tossed her up and through the air. It felt like, it felt like fragmented emotions spitting and howling. Disgust and frustration rolled over her. A whorl of anger tried to slam her down, but she was ready. Seconds it took her to steady herself floating above it all, using the air to hold her, guide her. The energy flowing through her was massive. She could feel Augustus trying to shove the demon back.

"My pretty toy!" the murky mass of tangled threads yelled, its voice gathering strength around her as it grew and cackled. "You came! I knew you would eventually. Mine to play with. Mine to destroy," it screamed and shot out a menacing limb to grab her.

"Mine," Niko roared back at the monster. Only a second before the demon's hideous black limb oozing blood reached her, Niko was there, his hand in hers. "Now!" he yelled over the roaring in the forest and traced her away.

The fog attempted to swallow them as it rose and tunneled after them in chase, bellowing out its intent. Rain pelted down, and black featherlike clusters grabbed at them, its speed increasing along with its anger. But none of that mattered to Niko whose pace was instantaneous and confident. It was a thing of beauty for Francesca to see and feel as he dipped them low over the lake.

"Set me down now, love. It's time."

"I can't," he yelled. The thundering anger of the demon reverberated through the forest, rippling the grass toward the park and the water. She could hardly hear Niko through it all.

Francesca kissed him, pouring all her love into that one kiss. *"We belong to each other. Nothing now can separate us."* Ripples of anger reached the lake, snarling and hissing at them, surrounding them. It angled its wrath toward the lake and threw the water up in massive dark streams directly at them. One giant surge punched Niko aside, severing their connection.

"No!" Francesca screamed. The water whirled beneath her as she hovered over it. The demon was there at the edge howling, tossing trees and park benches, and throwing a de-mon-sized fit. Drops of water sprayed around her. "Niko!" She tried to find him through the black mass of tendrils rolling like tornadoes. She couldn't see him, couldn't hear him.

"Niko."

"I'm here." It was weak, but his thoughts were detectable. *"It's powerful...surrounding you. I can't...get to you."*

"No one keeps me from you!" Digging into her magic, her emotions, all the anger and passion and love she possessed, Francesca gathered everything in her heart. The water mother and her daughters sang from within, swirled up through her fingertips, shifting like turquoise waves through her body, giv-

ing her strength, their song a melody she recognized, one full of ancient all-knowing power.

Through the assault of the demon's roars, she raised her hands in goddess song with all her might. A beautiful wall of deep blue water shot up in front of her. Closing her eyes now, Francesca let the power wash through her. She hummed with magic, her connection to nature, to her true self. Digging in deep, Francesca silently called the water to her, its strength, its beauty, its life force. She lifted it higher, and, holding it above her hands, concentrated on locating the demon. So dark and putrid.

How can anything survive this way? Howling screams battered her. It took all her reserves to feel the right moment and when she did she shoved, bellowing out her intention. With one strong push, the water crashed, wave-like toward the demon who howled and reared and splintered into a million pieces, spitting rage and pain. Francesca nearly crumpled at the energy it took to fight such a massive, damaged soul.

In seconds Dr. Madison's form half reemerged, angry, beaten, threads of black tar clinging and hanging from her warped body. The trees vibrated with power, fed it into their roots, through the ground, all the way to the water and up into Francesca. The fog melted away and the world appeared again before her. Niko rose up and raced toward the demon.

"Yes, come to me!" the demon shrieked at him.

Water. It's the water that will end it. The knowledge was in her as if it were her beloved. And cherish it she would. Raging howls threatened to split her eardrums as the black masses covering Madison shifted and dropped to the ground in pieces, reforming into something not fully formed, half human, half demon, dripping black streams of its own wicked magic. A twisted, bloated form of near death.

"Go!" Francesca shouted to Niko, wanting him away from the danger. This wasn't the end, not yet. Suddenly the demon pieces reconnected and slithered around the lake, forming itself into a circle, surrounding her. Howling out its anger, the demon rose up in a massive cone, closing Francesca's sight off from any loved ones or friends or guardians. Even the trees were lost to her vision now.

The sky grew black with fog. There were only glimpses of the forest through the demon's shifting power. Francesca and the water fed off each other, transferring strength, but the hollow, nightmarish threads of anger and madness wrapped around her middle, squeezing tighter and tighter. Her breath stuttered and pain twisted her lungs. It was trying to crush the life out of her with its hold on the wind, whipping it around and around. Its screams punched through her eardrums.

Francesca closed her eyes and thoughts and soul to the horror, to the hold it was gaining on her.

"I will ruin you forever!" The demon's screeches were barely coherent.

Never. My love is too powerful for you. All the love in the world was inside Francesca now, feeding into her heart, strengthening it. She didn't need to see it to possess it, to wield it.

"Give up!" The demon spewed black residue toward her.

Francesca glowed with magic, but she bordered on exhaustion. Her arms were lead; it was difficult to raise them. Each breath took so much effort as though she'd been running for hours without rest. Every second she hovered fractured her strength. She could only hold on so much longer.

Reaching into her reserves, she called to Niko silently. The mated link between them bloomed within. Through the shifting massive fog, Niko was there, holding his hands up toward her, chanting her name.

The water beneath her settled and rippled, and she began to fall toward it. "No," she screamed fearful that the demon was gaining power.

"Yes," her goddesses sang back. *"This is the way. You must take it into the water. You know this. Go now!"*

"Francesca! No!" Niko's voice reached her through it all. His hold on her tightened.

But the voices of her mothers were calling to her, singing her a song she knew to be true in a peaceful goddess melody made of colors, her own brilliant turquoise shining through. Her tears fell as every element guided her. This was her path. Niko's love filled her. It was a part of her now, forever. *"Let me go, darling, I'll be all right. I have your love inside me. It's my, our biggest strength. Let me use it."* She pushed the words to Niko with all the emotion in her heart. Brilliant blue and teal and green sparks shot through the madness and she would never forget the sight and the feeling as long as she lived.

Niko raged out his denial, shaking the earth with his refusal to let her go. "Never!" he bellowed.

Francesca closed her eyes, shutting out the evil that surrounded her, the howling rage, the rotting smell, the pounding chains of despair. She let Niko's love feed into her bones and her magic, twining their powers and journey together. It was now or never, now or death for all of them. Of that she was certain. The choice was hers to make.

Francesca sent one last message of forever love to Niko and then sliced the hold he had on her, setting him free. Ignoring the pain that lanced through her heart, she opened to the goddesses, to their power, to her magic soaring in her, to all the love in her bones and memories. Raising her hands to the sky, she opened her mouth and sang the words the mothers were teaching her. The black wall of evil stopped to listen. Lured closer and closer, it followed the siren song right into Francesca's fingertips, down into her heart, and deeper still to her soul.

The demon's rage began to compete with her song, her guidance, but she was certain this must be done. One more second, she had to hold. Her entire being shook with magic. Love was fierce and brilliant, a shimmering light nearly blinding her. Yes, she thought. This is right. The park and forest became clear as the demon bled into her. Niko roared and tried to push through the mass. She ended her song and dove down into the lake, pulling the demon and all its howling evil with her.

As soon as the demon hit the water, it bellowed out a denial, thrashed, and tried to escape, but Francesca dove deeper, cut to the bottom of the lake, and pulled with her song and her magic and her love. All the power in Mother Earth belonged to her now, and she used it to bury the monster who had been terrorizing her town.

The sound of horror coiled in on itself and pressed against her, down, harder and harder, until she couldn't withstand the pain, but neither could she cry out. All the breath she'd stored in her lungs began to crumple away. Her heart screamed to be set free and her lungs were on fire. Numbness began to take over her body. *It's going to kill me.*

She'd thought she could destroy it. Francesca opened her eyes and glanced up toward the sky, hoping and praying for the sunlight to shine on her one last time, and for any last bit of assistance. She fell to the lake floor watching the glittering rays as they broke through the darkness. Then, with one last earsplitting scream, the demon exploded all around her, sending the lake's water into a million tiny drops of magic into the air, where they hovered for a moment like all the stars sparkling in the sky. Seconds later they fell back to the lake in a shower of glitter. Finally, then, peace.

"Francesca!"

"Niko." Her heart was still beating. Francesca closed her eyes and, under the cool blue water, sought the lifeline to her mate.

"Francesca, come back to me!" It was there, his essence, guiding her, helping her.

She found the strength, pushed off the bottom of the lake, and surged back to the surface. Niko grabbed her out of the water, sat down, and pulled her onto his lap, wrapping his legs and arms around her. Holding her head to him, he rested his forehead against hers and breathed. Francesca held him back, glorying in their connection, gulping in air.

"I almost lost you, damn it!" His hoarse cry rippled along her skin. He fingered the spot on her neck where he'd bitten her. His mark. His beautiful mark. "I never should have bitten you. I never should have taken an ounce of your power, your blood, your magic. You almost died."

"No, shh." She soothed with her voice and her hands, clasping his cheek, and bringing his head up to face her. "Our connection gave me strength. It added to my power. Your love helped me. I wouldn't have been strong enough without it."

"You nearly drowned," he said, his voice on the edge of losing it.

"The water guided me. It was my strength and, as it turns out, the demon's weakness. With the goddesses helping me and your love and my belief in my magic, I destroyed it. I didn't drown. I'm sorry I scared you, darling. I'm okay now. I promise."

"You may have to promise me every day for the rest of our lives. I can't exist without you. You're my heart and soul. I don't have either without you."

"And you're mine." After a few moments of being tucked into his chest, she raised her head and surveyed the park. Trees were smashed to pieces, debris littered the sand and the grass, and park benches were flipped and lay scattered across the land. It honestly looked like a tornado had ripped through the landscape. Near the lake, Dr. Madison's dead body lay folded over a boulder. The lake itself sat still, a mirror of silent beautiful glass before them. And the clouds had returned to normal. Even the sun was shining down on them.

"Oh, the sun, Niko. Are you okay?"

"I'm fine." His voice was hoarse, his grip still tight on her. "Don't worry about me.

We'll find the others and get you warmed up. Then I'm taking you home to our bed and never letting you out again."

"Okay, darling," she said, pouring all her love into him with her words and her touch. It would take him time to believe she hadn't been hurt, and, with a sigh of exhaustion, she smiled, thinking of which fascinating tactics he would use to make her stay in their bed.

CHAPTER THIRTY-EIGHT

C LEANING UP THE MESS would take a while, but the cloud of anxiety was gone and that was everything. Police and crime scene techs swarmed the area in the aftermath, and Francesca was happy to leave the mess to them.

Augustus found both victims alive and freaked out. They'd have to wait out the remnants of whatever drug Dr. Madison had used to subdue them, but otherwise were unharmed, thank the goddesses.

Francesca rode back to the hospital in the first ambulance with one of the victims. Rich, drove the second ambulance and Kara sat in the back with the other victim to offer support. The young woman immediately grasped Kara's hand and didn't let go.

Hugh demanded to ride in the third ambulance with Gia who had been knocked out in the first explosive blast by a tree limb. Francesca suspected a mild concussion, but Gia was awake and spitting angry, feral as a cat, so Francesca knew she'd heal quickly. Niko and Augustus stayed behind to help gather evidence and answer additional questions.

She assured Niko she wouldn't leave the hospital without him. This was after he'd kissed her senseless. She would have agreed to anything in that moment, such was the power of his kiss. She almost giggled. She had a lifetime of those kisses to look forward to now.

At the hospital, even though other doctors were on duty, she personally checked on both victims. Lainy had called their loved ones, and the hospital was full of people overjoyed at having found the two ladies safe, and at hearing the news that Dr. Madison was no longer a threat. Francesca couldn't explain that she'd magicked her to death, exploding her tar-like wrath into a billion pieces, which was fine because the official cause of death was drowning.

"Everything looks good," Lainy said after finally insisting on checking Francesca's vitals. "But you do need a shower. Then some warm soup and lots of rest. I'm glad you're okay...I..." Lainy's tears choked the last words off.

"Me too." Francesca grabbed her friend in a hug. "I need to see my sister first, then shower."

"She's asleep and that big bad hottie hasn't left her side. Shower first, then to your sister. You're shivering and you smell awful."

"Thanks."

"You're welcome. That's what I'm here for." Lainy gave Francesca a gentle shove into the locker room.

"Oh, the kids, Gia's kids, I—" Francesca asked.

"Kara and Rich went with Officer Kim to pick them up. They should be here any minute. Now, shower."

***

When she walked into Gia's room, Hugh was asleep with Ava curled up on his lap, hugging her whale stuffy. Her eyes were closed as well. Danny was lying next to his mom in her hospital bed. They were talking about chess while they watched a video together on Gia's phone.

Her sister noticed her and sighed. "I can't believe I missed everything."

"You mean capturing a demon and drowning it?"

"Yes!"

Only her sister.

"I'm glad you missed it," Danny said. "I don't want you to have nightmares, but I'm not glad you got a concussion. But if you do have nightmares, Hugh will be there to help you. He's really, really good at battling nightmares. He can show you. He said he'd always help us if we ever needed it."

Gia started to roll her eyes, then winced and let out a small laugh. "Serves me right, I guess, huh?"

"Aunt Frankie, how are you?" Danny asked. He didn't move from his mom's side and Francesca understood. He'd already lost one parent and the last few months had been pretty chaotic. She leaned in to hug him and kissed her sister on the cheek.

"I'm good, honey. Everyone's okay."

"I'm glad you got the demon," he whispered. "She frightened me. She smelled wrong."

"Mm-hmm," Francesca said. Damn, her nephew was more perceptive than she'd ever been at that age. She took in her sister's complexion, the clarity in her gaze. *"How long has Hugh been here?"*

"That infuriating man hasn't left my side. I don't think he's ever going to leave." She huffed.

"He saved your life."

"Ugh. I...I don't want to be beholden to anyone."

"I know, love." What her sister was really saying, and what Francesca understood even without the words being sent between them, was that her sister was afraid to lose someone she loved again. A heart could only take so much.

"Where's Niko, Aunt Frankie? I have a new chess video to show him."

"I'm right here." They all looked toward the door where Niko stood, his eyes boring into Francesca. She smiled and held out her hand and he came to her.

"Oh, Niko. We missed you." Ava yawned and snuggled into Hugh, who'd awoken too. Hugh rested his hand on Ava's head. Francesca watched Gia wipe away her tears. This was going to be very interesting to watch play out.

"All done with the police and everything?" Hugh asked.

Niko nodded. "It's over. How are you, Gianna?"

"Better now," she said softly. She hugged Danny to her. "But I don't care what the doctors say, I'm not spending the night in the hospital." Her pout was back.

"You can stay here, or you can go home as long as someone's there to watch you and help you," Francesca said.

"Hugh's coming to stay," Danny said, not taking his eyes off the chess game on his phone. "He said that way we can be in our home..."

"Yes, with our very own routine," Ava added. "He said routine is important. What is routine? Does it have donuts? I really want a donut. And Mama's favorite food in the world is glazed donuts."

"We'll get donuts," Hugh said.

"Can we get a dog too? I've always wanted a dog, a real one, not one just in my dreams." Ava giggled. The kid was going for broke.

"Maybe," Hugh said, and Francesca had to hide her grin looking at the expression on Gia's face, one of petulance mixed with longing. Oh goody, her sister was so screwed.

"Can't you take me?" Gia grasped at straws, sending Francesca a last cry for help.

"I'm taking Francesca home with me," Niko said. "She almost drowned and she was in that cold lake for far too long."

"I didn't know you were hurt." Gia gasped and squeezed Francesca's hand.

"I'm fine. He's exaggerating."

"Men," Gia said with a huff.

"Yes, but I am going to let him take me home like you're going to let Hugh take you all home. Let him help you. He...he..."

"He what?" Gia asked.

Francesca was sure her sister had been knocked out in the forest before Hugh changed to his werewolf self. Francesca had no idea whether or not her sister had seen him that way yet, and that was something between Gia and Hugh. She and Gia still needed to have a talk about her hottie. Her instincts told her Hugh was going to be fabulous for Gia. She agreed with Hugh. Routine was good, and her sister's family needed some easy, happy routine, mixed with a big dose of love. *"Let him help you. You know how he feels about you. If not for you right now, then for the kids' sake. They feel safe with him."*

"Oh, you went there, huh."

"Gia."

"Fine. He is a pretty good cook anyway. Will you sign me out if I agree to go with him?"

"I will."

Gia rested her head back on her pillow and closed her eyes. For the first time in a long time, all the stress and worry emptied out of her sister. *"Okay then. I love you, Frankie."*

"I love you too."

Chapter Thirty-Nine

"**Y**ou know I showered at the hospital," Francesca said as Niko stripped her scrubs from her body in his bathroom at home. Hot water fell from the dual showerheads in Niko's massive shower and for a few moments, it was the only sound between them. Her eyes were closed, and she reveled in the feel of his hands on her, like he was inspecting every inch to make sure for the millionth time that she was okay. His temper still simmered below the surface. And her power still tingled all over her skin. Their mating was going to be a powerful one with all this emotion and magic sparking between them.

"I don't care. I want to see every trace of that horror gone. And besides, I still need a shower after being inside that nightmare shed."

"Thank you," she whispered, sobering at his words.

"For what? I did nothing. I was useless in that madness." He turned and slammed his hands against the wall. "Christ, I almost lost you."

She moved and wrapped herself around him from behind. "You didn't. I'm right here." He grabbed her hands and clasped them against his heart. "Thank you for giving me your love and your trust," she whispered. "I had this amazing power inside of me from you, and it joined with my own magic to finish things. It was incredible."

He turned and grabbed her up in his arms and set her in the shower. Then he stripped off his own clothes. "I saw it and felt it. You were fucking brilliant. A magnificent sea creature at home in the water. But not being able to touch you was gut-wrenching. Now that I've...now that we've..."

"Now that we belong to each other." She soothed with her words.

He stepped into the shower, naked, on edge. He prowled toward her and she leaned up against the shower wall, ready for him. He dragged his powerful hands up and down her body, just as she loved.

"Indeed." His hands were everywhere at once, no longer the search of a worried man, but the intent touch of a lover, kneading and mapping her. First her hips, then down the back of her thighs, and sliding up along her waist to cup her breasts as she arched into him. He kissed her then, nipping and biting at her lips, all hunger and burning lust, warming her with his attention. His thumbs turned her nipples into hard aching points, and he tugged her closer to take one into his mouth as she gripped his head and held him there.

She caressed his back, loving the strength in his muscles, the curve of his shoulder blades, the way his spine dipped. His body was a masterpiece and she had ages now to explore it. She was shivering again, not from cold or worry or fear, but from anticipation.

He walked them both under the spray and took her mouth again in a branding. Then, as if she weighed nothing, he lifted her, set his cock right at her pussy and, not teasing this time, eased into her as he whispered love words against her lips. "I'm never letting you go."

"Good...I'm..." She clenched her legs around him and moved in sync with him. He swelled inside her. It was all so glorious and tight, adding to the magic lit within her and under her skin. "I..." She huffed out her desire. "I'm not letting you go either." Her words were whispers, empowered by his love, by their connection.

"Mine," he vowed, nibbling along her neck until he found the soft spot by her collarbone. This time she was ready when he sank his teeth into her. Grasping him tightly to her, she wove her essence around them. Twirling drops of water from the showerhead through her hands and up over him, she set the spell for love. It came easily to her now that she was filled with it. Love, magic, ever afters. Truth, beauty, trust, brilliance. It was all here, bursting from them, surrounding them, wrapping them up in a bond that could never be broken.

Epilogue

NIKO STALKED THROUGH THE house following Francesca's scent. It was different now that they were mated. Although she still filled his senses with hints of musky roses, he also smelled her magic, the crystal-clear breath of a hidden fresh-water spring. Combined with his aura that had become a part of her, it was a heady combination he craved with a vengeance. It was brilliant, elemental, and grounding.

Early morning pink light stole between the trees in his forest and dappled the lawn with a shimmery glow. The quiet of a promising new day surrounded him. He stopped in the kitchen at the open patio doors leading out to the backyard and smiled. Smiles came easy to him now, what a revelation. There hadn't been any reason for him to smile in centuries, and now it was as if his humanity had never been stolen from him. Francesca stood barefoot, wrapped in her turquoise silk robe, hands lifted toward the sun as it rose over the land. The dogs sat at her feet, caught in her spell the same way he was.

"Morning, darling," she said opening her eyes and gifting him with her joy, a sight more beautiful than he felt worthy of receiving. Good thing he didn't care. He was going to take everything she was willing to give him. "Summer's almost here." Her eyes shone with delight. They'd had months together since the incident at the hospital. Incident. Piddly word for him almost losing her, his heart.

"Mm. Couldn't sleep in could you? Let me wake you with my mouth?" he said.

She blushed at his words. "I knew you'd find me."

He crooked his finger and beckoned her to him.

She threw back her head and laughed but came to him anyway. Neither one of them could withstand the lure of the other for long.

"Happy to be home then, love?"

She wrapped her arms around him and sighed, the sound of a satisfied cat lazing in the sunshine. "Oh, Italy was glorious, wasn't it? Thank you for my trip." She placed a gentle kiss on his lips.

She'd already thanked him a million times in a million different ways for their three-week tour through Italy, but somehow this simple kiss melted him. Perhaps it was the way she looked at him like he was her everything.

"It was so inspiring," she said. "I can't wait to try some of the recipes I got, and to have my own garden and lemon trees just like in Naples."

Hmm he'd certainly been inspired by other things in Naples, their bedroom under the stars, watching her body move through the infinity pool, the outdoor shower, when she'd let him feed her fruit that morning, and how they'd gotten carried away. He kissed her neck, nibbled his way up to her ear, while she arched into him. "Shall I build you a garden then? And how about a pool?"

"I'd love that," she gushed. "But a pool isn't very satisfactory for you, darling, especially in the high sun of summer."

"We'll build an outdoor kitchen with a roof so I can watch you swim while I cook for you. Have your friends and family over for a BBQ?" He buried his head in her neck and chuckled.

"What's so funny?" she asked.

He brought his head up and met her gaze. "I just never had any reason to do something so simple as a BBQ before you came into my life."

"You do know they're your friends and family now too, right?" She cupped his cheek. "And when they all come over later for Sunday dinner you can practice being friendly."

There she was always making sure he felt as though he belonged. Didn't she know her love gave him that sensation every day? "I love you, my stunning, brilliant witch. I love every new day with you, every laugh, every hug, every kiss you give me. I love every new discovery with you by my side. I can't wait to see what's to come."

She melted into him. "I love you too, my soulmate, my heart, my angel."

A whole new lifetime together stretched out in front of them. And for the first time in ages, Niko was looking forward to the next hundred years.

ALSO BY SARA OHLIN

The Graciella Series

Handling the Rancher

Seducing the Dragonfly

Flirting with Forever

Rescue Me Series

Salvaging Love

Igniting Love

Promising Love

Embracing Love

My Graciella Series

Hearts in Bloom

Harvest Moon Kisses

Winter Wonderland Love

ABOUT SARA

Sara Ohlin lives on Whidbey Island with her husband and two kids. Her essays can be found at *Anderbo.com*, *Feminine Collective*, *The Manifest Station*, *Panorama: The Journal of Travel, Place, & Nature*, and in anthologies such as *Are We Feeling Better Yet? Women Speak about Healthcare in America*. She is the author of ten romance novels with Totally Bound Publishing. In the summer she ignores everyone to work in her garden and dream up new recipes. She once met a person who didn't read books and wasn't that into food and it nearly broke her heart.

Visit Sara Ohlin Online

www.saraohlin.com

Acknowledgements

This is the first time I've had the opportunity to write acknowledgments and I'm so excited!

Thank you to my lovely editor, Rebecca who has such a great eye for detail. And to all the writers and publishing gurus who have helped me over the years.

To the readers and lovers of the romance genre, I adore you. Thank you for reading my books. I hope I provide you with a bit of joy and escape.

To my beautiful friends and family who support me and cheer me on, especially my sister, Megan, who should get paid a publicist's fee, my amazing writing partner-in-crime and sounding board, Sara, my brilliant friend, Shannin, who inspires me with her artistic talent every day (P.S. this cover is for you!) My first Andrea friend who is the most amazing doctor and stunning human being, I miss you! My Maine (also main) friend Elizabeth knows how much I adore journals and pretty pens, and my Langley Kitchen coffee date and beautiful friend, Andrea, who could talk about gardening all day with me. My gazillions of cousins and their love for amazing food and family, I miss you and love you all.

My mom gave me a love for reading and for story and I keep her in my heart with every book I write. She was one of a kind. My dad also gave me a love for story. How could I not write? It's in my bones.

Greg, I wouldn't be writing if it weren't for your unconditional love and support, for your technical expertise, and for your ability to put up with my swearing! I love you! Also to Lily and Jasper, I'm so glad you love books and art.

This is my first attempt at self-publishing. All mistakes are my own. I'm still and always will be learning. Cheers!

NEWSLETTER

Would you like advanced notification about upcoming releases and sales? Access to exclusive content and fun recipes? Sign up for my newsletter to keep up to date with the latest from Sara Ohlin.

www.saraohlin.com/newsletter/